D-CON

By: Jerry Avery

First print 2019 June

This is a book of fiction. Any references or similarities to actual events, real people, or real locations are intended to give the novel a sense of reality. Any similarity to other names, characters, places and incidents are entirely coincidental.

ISBN: 9798473880878

Cover Design: Crystell Publications

Book Productions: Crystell Publications
You're The Publisher, We're Your Legs

We Help You Self Publish Your Book
(405) 414-3991

www.crystellpublications

DEDICATION

This FIRST novel is dedicated to my grandma Maggie (R.I.P.) (I am so sorry that I never made it back to see & sit with you.) You're forever in my heart & on my mind.

ACKNOWLEDGMENTS

Special Thanks goes to my mother Brenda, aka Momma B. Thank you for everything! To my twin daughters, Chamoni and Imoni, thanks for giving me the reason to change my ways. To my other screwettes; Ty, Siya, Riecie, Nee-Nee, Niyah, De'Niya, and Kitty. To my favorite uncle, Buddy! (finally got it together). To my second mom/aunt Whimp, thanks for everything as well. Maybe I'll finally get that letter now that you're retired.

To the homie Rodriguez Woodard AKA "Lil Screw", get at me cuz, we need to chop it up. To the true general Chris Heaggins AKA "Taz", you are a mirror image of me, now it's time to really get our piece of the pie. To all the homies in the kitchen keepin' it A-1, much love & respect. To Big Ace, Duece, Hollywood, Milky, Warlocc, Lacey, G-Ball, G-Ray, Big Buddah, B-Wise, Hoover Big John, Rado, Big Cuz, Benard Graham AKA "B", and to all the homies resting eternally, your memory is still here through me.

To all the gangstas across the world, stay true to what you believe in. To the entire Black race, ***wake up!*** You see what they're trying to do to us out here! If I forgot to mention you this time, don't trip, I gotcha next time.

Special Thanks lastly goes to the dumbass who locked me up on some bogus shit! I wouldn't have written this novel had I not been in the S.H.U. for nothing. To my fake ass "friends", "family", "homies"; to the realest bitches I know that's not meant in a good way. I would never address a real woman by anything else other than as a lady) I would put y'all on blast, but your names don't deserve to be in my book. Y'all know who you are, thanks for showing me your true colors. I'm glad I learned who you really were before I really blew up!

To Mimi and Tanya, thanks for all the love & support over the years.

Chapter 1

"Clevon Johnson! Clevon Johnson! Report to the lieutenant's office immediately!" was announced over the prison's P.A. system.

"Oooh, somebody better tie one shoe, 'cause they ass 'bout to be tied up in the other shu. Special Housing Unit: The hole in the federal prison system, Popbelly, the compound jester, screamed from the sideline.

Now wasn't the time for being comical. Every week, for the past 4 years, weather permitting, Clevon Johnson aka "C.J."; William Andrews aka "Dub-1"; Jerome Myers aka "Romeo"; and Marcus Lacy aka "Shoelace" (Lace for short) played 2-on-2 basketball for 100 books of stamps per man. The duos changed periodically, but usually C.J. and Dub were partners.

Just as Popbelly stood upright, still enjoying his zany comment, C.J. threw the basketball with all his might, catching Popbelly dead in the nose. He didn't wait on a response, nor reaction. C.J. simply walked over to the bench, grabbed his shirt, and headed for the recreation gate.

While the onlookers continued to laugh at Popbelly lying on the ground pinching his nose as if that would keep the blood from pouring out, Lace screamed, “Hell naw! Nigga you gotta finish the game! Sheeit, we up! And since the homie quit, we wi—”

“Hell naw! Cuz ain’t quit! You heard’em call’em to the Lt.’s office.” Dub intervened.

“Sheeit they been callin’ his ass all day to the mailroom, and he ain’t went, so what the fuck?!” Romeo said coming to his partners defense.

“You know Cuz waitin’ on his appeal to come back. That’s probably what this shit about. He’ll be back.”

“What they callin’ him to the Lt.’s fo’ then?” Lace questioned.

With a scowl on his face, Dub asked, “What’cha sayin’ Loc? I know you ain’t questionin’ the homies ‘G’.”

Seeing things were about to get out of hand, Lace changed his whole demeanor.

“It wasn’t no shit like that. We all done seen each other’s paperwork, so I know the homie ain’t hot. I was just sayin’ it could be anything. Remember when they called me up there when my pops died a couple years ago? That’s all I’m sayin’.”

Dub didn’t like Lace’s explanation, but he let it ride. His thoughts trailed off and followed his homie up the sidewalk.

During their weekly battles, a newcomer would assume that the two teams were sworn enemies, however in all actuality, they were thick as thieves and tighter than a fat bitch in spandex.

*** *** *** ***

Before C.J. could sit on the lieutenant’s bench, his counselor burst out of the office. Counselor Ames, a real *Uncle Tom*, shit on the tongue, slave style NIGGER, ran up on C.J. and started pointing his finger in his face, then screamed,

"Do you know I should throw your pathetic ass in the shu right now?! Give me one reason why I shouldn't lock your ass up!"

The only reason Ames had put a *'S'* on his chest was he saw the blinds opened before he ran out.

"First of all, I ain't done shit. Secondly, you value your family's lives too much to cross me. Yeah, I've seen your pretty ass wife, and your sweet lil innocent daughter in that picture on your desk. Believe it or not, I got homies that would love to get a piece of both of 'em. Play wit it if you want to!" C.J. warned sardonically.

Ames had read up on C.J. in the state of Colorado's' archives. The mere thought of some of C.J.'s gruesome acts sent chills mixed with electric currents throughout his entire body.

''Look Johnson, I ain't no chump! If something were to happen to my family, I'd hunt you down like a mad dog and gut'cha myself!"

"For everybody's sake, let's hope it don't come down to that!" C.J. shot back, half-stroking Ames ego.

"Just get in there!" Ames replied, half nudging C.J. into the office.

When C.J. passed him Ames swallowed hard. He was thinking about how playing hard could've gotten his family slaughtered. *Man, them crackas ain't even get off they asses to assist me. I'm 'bout to quit kissin' they asses, this shit just ain't worth it*, Ames reasoned.

As soon as C.J. walked through the door, the *House Nigger* came back to life. Some people just can't help it.

"What'cha want me to do with 'im Lou?"

Lieutenant Wellington, a F.B.O.P. vet hated ‘men like Ames, but admired men like C.J. *A real man* is how the Lieutenant summed up C.J.’s demeanor. Lieutenant Wellington turned to face Ames with a disgusted scowl and said,

“Ames, you’s a fuckin’ counsela. So you can’t do shit but get the hell on up outta he’ah! Gone now, you dismissed.”

Ames turned on his heels in defeat, and in his last attempt to save his manhood and wounded ego, he turned and screw faced C.J.

“Ames, that won’t be tolerated ‘round he’ah, so I ‘vise you to get on down that theya compound.”

Not wanting to make matters worse, C.J. suppressed his laughter until Ames was completely out of the office. After a brief chuckle, Lt. Wellington said, “Come on Johnson, they want ‘cha ova at the mailroom.”

CHAPTER 2

At the mailroom, Ms. Revis handed the Lt. a thick manila envelope to inspect for contraband while C.J. signed for it. C.J. knew what it was before the Lt. handed it to him. *My appeal!* Barely breathing, C.J. reached into the envelope. Before he got it halfway out, C.J.'s heart fell into the pit of his stomach. Once he saw the big *D* Denied C.J.'s heart dropped even further, while a lone tear escaped his left eye. He'd been counting on a reversal due to his 2255. C.J. needed to get home.

C.J.'s two daughters were bouncing around from relative to relative, staying with anyone that would let them stay due to their mother being a *China Doll.* C.J. had left Cheryl with a little over $2 million. In the 14 years that he'd been gone; the money, along with his fleet of exotic cars, and jewelry, had all vanished. Luckily, C.J. still had a stash at his *Honeycomb Hideout* out in Limon, Colorado.

Being the first to get out, out of his prison comrades, C.J. wanted to have everything set up for their releases. Irritated, C.J.

rolled up his package of rejection, and continued wringing it all the way back to the recreation yard to finish his game.

"I tol' yo' ass that the homie was comin' back!" Dub announced to his opposition.

Reading C.J.'s facial expression, he knew he'd better mediate the situation.

"Look here, cuz ain't lookin' left, so if he don't want to finish, I'll hit both ya'll fools off on the five minute move tonight...but it's on him."

Both Romeo and Lace knew how C.J. played when he was in his feelings about something.

"All day. But if Cuz—"

"Didn't I say I'd cover it, petty ass nigga!" Dub screamed cutting Lace off.

When Lace nodded, Dub added. "All left then. Shut the fuck up!"

Romeo pulled Lace to the side and whispered, "Ain't no need in havin' both these fool's actin' up out here."

Again, Lace only nodded his head in agreeance.

C.J. walked over to the bench and threw his appeal down, then threw his shirt on top of it.

"That bad Cuz?" Dub asked walking over to his comrade.

"I'm gonna holla at ya'll fools later. Let's serve these chumps and get some party money up for tonight. Y'alls ball." C.J. said as he went to check the ball. Dub went to guard Romeo.

Lace tried to lob the ball over C.J.'s head to Romeo, who outweighed Dub by 25 pounds.. C.J. tipped the ball and pulled it down. Dub quickly ran around Romeo and caught the bounce pass while C.J. broke for the basket.

Dub lobbed an alley, and C.J. slammed it down with a

vengeance.

"9-10 nigga!" C.J. boasted.

Romeo gave Lace a menacing look and stated, "I got C.J."

It was no different this time. After the check, C.J. hit Romeo with a hard jab step, then pulled up with a N.B.A. three pointers.

"10-10!" C.J. said to no one in particular. This brought on Lace and Romeo trying to double team C.J., which gave him the chance to hit Dub with a famous Magic Johnson, no-look pass that Dub scored an easy layup off of.

"Point motherfuckas!" Dub hollered, beating on his chest in gorilla fashion.

After checking the ball to Lace, Lace bounced the ball back to Dub, and backed up to help with C.J. Dub threw the ball high, knowing C.J. could out jump both of their opponents. Instead of bringing the ball down, C.J. tipped the ball back to Dub for a wide opened jumper. Dub anticipated Lace blocking the shot from the side, causing him to adjust his shot and shoot an air ball. Romeo caught it, and layed it up before C.J. could react.

Damn Dub, what the fuck? C.J. thought.

As if being telepathic, Dub apologized, "My bust Cuz. I'll get it back."

"Check nigga!" Romeo said rolling the ball to Dub in a taunting fashion. Even though he was one that was easily provoked, Dub kept his cool. He rolled the ball back with his foot and smiled his famous sinister smile. Before Romeo could pick the ball up, *"Yard recall!"* was announced.

"Fuck that shit, it's game point!" Romeo declared.

"Yeah, both ways!" C.J. shot back.

Unfazed by C.J.'s retort, Romeo passed the ball in hoping to catch his opponents off guard. To Romeo's surprise, C.J. read the whole move. By the time the ball hit Lace's hands, C.J. was coming down in a swiping motion. The ball hit Lace's foot and rolled towards the sideline.

Quick on his feet, Romeo sprinted after the ball and saved it by flipping it over his shoulder, back towards Lace. Dub intercepted the pass like Champ Bailey would've in his prime. He then threw it over his shoulder, in a lob fashion, knowing C.J. could (*and would*) go up and get it.

Lace, hating to lose, fouled the shit out of C.J. as he released the ball on a short jumper.

"Your ball if it don't fall." Lace said as they all stood and watched the ball continuously spin around the rim. Time seemed to stand still until the ball fell softly through the net.

"Damn!" was the only thing Lace could say.

Tower 4 opened, "Lower court, take it in now!" the gung-ho C/O demanded. Ignoring the C/O, Dub ran and jumped into C.J.'s arms.

"Hell yeah! I tol' you I'd get that shit back!"

"That's what's crackin' Loc." C.J. said in a nonchalant tone.

Feeling comical, Dub hollered, "Yo Lace!"

"What nigga?"

"They must'a gave you that name 'cause y—"

"Yo, ya'll check this out." C.J. said ending Dub's standup routine. After putting his shirt on, C.J. passed his appeal around. A solemn look fell on all of their faces, as the trio said, *"Damn!"* simultaneously.

"Damn is left!" C.J. barked, then continued. "We all in this motherfucka, done all this fuckin' time, and these bus-"

C.J. stopped midsentence when he saw Richard Jones, the recreation specialist, approaching them with rapid speed.

Richard Jones, an inactive Crip, was also the quartets mentor. He'd earned their respect as a Big Homie who'd really built a legacy in the mean streets of Little Rock, Arkansas. He walked right up on the gangbangers, and immediately began making a spectacle of himself.

Pointing his finger in all of their faces, he screamed, "Didn't ya'll hear Office Haggins tell ya'll to clear the court?"

" Yea—"

"Don't say shit while I'm talkin'!" Jones screamed cutting Romeo off. "As a matter-of fact, after count ya'll bring ya'lls asses to my office!"

"You got that." C.J. confirmed.

As they headed to the rec gate, and out of earshot of the tower, Jones said, "Ya'll Locs make sure ya'll come see me on the five-minute move. Hurry up, a playa got some trim waitin' at the pad."

" All day, O.G.!" they said in unison. Although they hated being chastised, they respected Jones' *'G"*.

"Everybody ce ready on the move." C.J. said as they headed to their respected housing units. "We'll go holla at the big homie, then we'll go down to the *Boom Boom Room'*. I got some heavy shit to drop on ya'll." C.J.'s words trailed off as he stared out into the treeline.

"We're about to change the world homies." was the last thing C.J. mumbled before he threw up a 'C' with his left hand. Dub, Romeo, and Lace all knew their comrade, and if changing the world was on C.J.'s mind, then the world was in for a rude awakening.

CHAPTER 3

"Five-minute move for Alpha unit, Bravo 1 and 3!" was announced over the P.A. system. Romeo put 20 papers (prison sized joints), of Kush in his sock, and put 50 books of stamps in each shoe before running to the front door so he wouldn't miss the move.

Dub, coming out of A-4, caught up with Romeo at the main metal detector as the move closed.

"What'cha think Cuz got on his mind?" Romeo asked Dub as they slow walked to the rec yard.

"I don't know, but whatever it is, it's got to ce some serious shit!"

"I hope he ain't trippin'! All of us get out soon an—"

"Nigga quit cryin'! Sometimes you make me question your 'G"!" Dub said turning to face Romeo.

"Win, lose, or draw, you come at me like that again, I'm gonna have to see you!"

"Then quit cryin' all the damn time!"

Cuz must think East Coast niggas are soft, or ain't got no heart.

Who the fuck he think he is? G-Ray or Poo. Sheeit! Them the only Acacia niggas I ever heard of!' Romeo thought as he glared at Dub, contemplating whether to swing on his homie or not.

He tested my Gangsta— Romeo's thoughts were interrupted when he heard the next move announced.

***   ***   ***   ***

Lace exited B-2 just as C.J. walked out of C-1.

"Where' ya headed in su'cha rush?" Ms. Ingles, the C-1 officer asked in her heavy Texas accent. Although they'd fucked on several occasions before, for some reason today Shaneka Ingles was extremely horny.

"Not trying to miss the move." C.J. said in a hushed tone. "When I get cack, my pussycat cetter ce purrin'!" C.J. knew when he talked in Crip dialect, Ms. Ingles' panties instantly became soaking wet.

When they first met, their egos caused them to clash. By C.J. being an Aries, and Shaneka being a Taurus, things seemed to be doomed from the beginning. Most men were intimidated by Shaneka's physical presence. She knew it and used it to her full advantage. Standing 5'7 with a 40DD-26-44 frame, compacted into her 160lbs. of *sexxxy*, Shaneka always got her way. Her deep mahogany hue, never having a hair out of place, and nails always immaculately done, Shaneka could make the average man leap to his death for a promised shot of her in the next lifetime. With C.J., it was her exotic scent that kept him in a frenzy. Although he'd never admit it, she was the straw that broke the camel's back.

One evening C.J. had come in from playing basketball and ran into Shaneka shaking his cell down.

"What the hell are you doin' in my cell?" C.J. asked her in an irritated tone as he walked into the cell.

"Niggah, ya can't come in her' while I'm in her'!"

"Well then get out! I got to hit this water cefore the C.E.T. awards come on." C.J. said while taking his shirt off, then reached around Shaneka to grab his shower bag out of his locker.

"Firs' of awl, it's B.E.T. An' uhm no—"

Shaneka's voice was caught in her throat as she stood up and was face to chest with C.J.

C.J. had worked on his body throughout his entire bid. Having great genetics helped as well. Standing 6'3 on a chiseled 225lb. frame, C.J. gave his amigo Jorge plenty of canvas to blast his gang affiliation. *Crip 'Til I Die!* was spelled out in bold Old English letters across his broad chest.

Unaware of her actions, Shaneka traced the letters of the word Crip with her perfectly manicured pinky nail.

"So you a Crip, Huh? Ma bros. ah Hoovas!"

"Well I'm 87 Kitchen Crip!" C.J. boasted, half smiling as he savored the sensation of a woman's touch.

"Kitchen, huh?" Shaneka asked, still mesmerized by the specimen before her.

"Yeah. 87 Kitchen, now slide that big ass outta my way so I can get my shit."

" Get it then!" Shaneka challenged.

Accepting the challenge, C.J. reached around her with both hands, one grabbing the shower bag, the other grabbing a handful of Texas beef.

"Ya cain-"

" I can and I will! Just let me wash my ass first."

" Make sho' ya wash that big ol' thang ther'." Shaneka said

pointing down and grabbing C.J.'s dick that had his shorts tented.

Without saying another word, he adjusted his manhood and headed for the shower. Shaneka left the cell 5 minutes later, carrying an armload of prison issued t-shirts. She'd use them as a bargaining tool.

On her way to the office Shaneka kept cussing to herself; half pretending to be upset, but the other part of the charade was genuine, because she couldn't believe that she hadn't stopped having an orgasm since she grabbed C.J.'s dick. That was the day she officially became his.

C.J. 's thoughts returned back to the matter at hand when he saw Lace coming up the sidewalk.

It's do or die C.J. mumbled to himself. *If they ain't wit' it, I'm gonna kill them too. Ain't no turnin' back!*

C.J. greeted Lace with the universal Crip shake as they walked through the metal detector, heading to the rec yard.

Romeo and Dub were waiting at the rec office door for their comrades, so they could all go in at one time. Reading C.J.'s mind, "I already locked the table down, Cuz." Romeo informed. C.J. was relieved that one of them had taken the initiative to go reserve a table in the *'Boom Boom Room'.*

"That's what's crackin'. Let's see what the big homie wants, then we'll go handle our business." C.J. said as he led the way into Jones' office.

Mr. Jones was in 'Mack Mode' when they came through the office door. He gestured for them to give him a minute, and to be quiet while he kicked his old school game.

"Yeah, ya dig where Big Daddy's' comin' from? Oh yeah...Right, right...Sheeit you about to make a playa bust one now!"

Jones waved a scolding finger at the gangbangers when they started snickering. He thought they were laughing with him, enjoying being schooled by an older cat, but instead they were really laughing at his wannabe pimp ass. C.J., Dub, Romeo, and Lace all covered their mouths, laughing into their palms.

Hitting the speaker button, Jones continued.

"Now tell a playa again what's shakin'."

"Why you got me on speaker phone? Who you try'na impress?" the sultry voice on the other end of the phone asked.

" Dig it bitch—"

" Hol' on, I know you ain't just call me no bitch!"

" Bitch, never interrupt a boss playas' pimpin!" Jones shot back. "Now as I was sayin' *bee-yotch*, when I put this anaconda in that big ol' fat ass of yours, the whole worlds gonna hear you, so what the fuck?"

"You ain't never lied Big Daddy," the woman on the other end cooed, stroking Jones' ego. *Sheeit, a bitch gotta eat. He pays good fo' the pussy, so I gotta make him feel like a king. Sheeit, a bitch got bills too, and that nose Candy ain't cheap.* She reasoned.

"Bitch, I know you hear me!"

Jones snapped when he wasn't getting any feedback from his mackin'.

"Yeah daddy...I hea—"

"What the fuck I say then?"

The broad sat dumbfounded, because she hadn't heard a word he'd said in the last minute of their conversation.

"That's what the fuck I thought! Don't worry, when I get done wit' yo' ass tonight, you gonna learn to listen."

"Yes Daddy."

"Look, I'm 'bout to slide out, but I'll be ready to *slide in* shortly, ya dig?"

Irritated by his lame game, the girl simply said, "See you soon daddy. Don't keep this pussy waitin' too long."

Smiling, Jones clicked her off and sat quietly for a few seconds, trying to read each of their body language and eyes before he spoke.

"Look man, ya'll know good and damn well that I gotta come down on ya'll harder than any other car here 'cause ya'll some of mine. Everybody upfront knows my history, and ya'll know this shit too, so what the fuck was ya'll thinkin'? Yeah... that's right, ya'll wasn't!"

"With all due resp—"

"Naw, let me finish Cuz." Jones said interrupting C.J.'s chance to justify their actions. He knew he had their undivided attention when he addressed them as 'Cuz'.

"What was so important that ya'll couldn't stop ballin'? I know it ain't those funky ass stamps ya'll be playin' fo'. Oh yeah, I know all about ya'lls lil grudge matches ya'll have every week."

Shaking his head in annoyance, Jones turned towards his computer and pulled up their accounts on TRULINCS. Seeing what each of them had in their accounts, caused Jones' eyes to damn near pop out of their sockets. Big Homie love turned into a scolding stepparent's disciplinary tone, which was really hatred in disguise.

"All of ya'll got over a hundred thou' on your books, an' yall—" Jones stopped before his bitterness could show.

No one said a word for nearly 2 minutes. After regaining his composure, Jones spoke in a low, but hushed tone.

"I'm gonna take ya'lls rec for a week." Before any of them could speak, Jones waved them off and said, "They wanted to lock ya'lls asses up, but I told them that I'd bestow a far harsher punishment than puttin' ya'll in the shu. So no rec for a week is ya'lls punishment. Now you can have the floor."

C.J. spoke up.

"Big homie, with all due respect, I just got shot down on my appeal, and on some real 'G' shit, and I think I speak for all of us…" C.J. paused and looked at his comrades for their consent to be included. After seeing no protest, he continued. "Taking away our rec will only cause havoc on the compound. This is our only form of release that doesn't involve somebody gettin' fucked up real bad or dyin', so we need our rec!''

"Dig it, I'ma tell those S.I.S. fools that I counseled ya'll; and ya'll gonna do some extra duty for Ms. Meshaw this weekend. Now get the hell outta here so I can go tear that trim up!'' Jones said throwing up a 'C' with his right hand and bumped it against his chest.

"Hey Johnson!" Jones called to C.J. before he could walk out of the office.

"Yeah?"

"You a soldier Cuz, so don't let those white folk's decision cause you to stay in here for the rest of your life! Focus on those daughters of yours. They need they daddy. Ya hear?" C.J. nodded, so Jones continued.

"You're at the end Loc, don't fuck it up! Now gone down to the pavilion, I mean *'Boom Boom Room'* and smoke some of that cheap shit ya'll be down there smokin! Or get some of that rock gut hooch ya'll' drink. Anything you gotta do to keep your sanity, *do it*. Then go down there and break Ms. Ingles off wit' a lil sumthin' sumthin'!"

Before C.J. could respond, Jones slapped his chest with both hands, and gave C.J. a *I know everything* look, but said, "I'm a real O.G., Cuz. I thought you knew!" then ushered C.J. out of the office.

*** *** *** ***

When C.J., Dub, Romeo, and Lace got to the *Boom Boom Room,* it was empty for the most part. Whenever they had country breakfast for the evening meal, it took a while to get the evening hustle and bustle going.

Romeo sat down at the table that he'd put his gym bag on earlier and produced the hundred books of stamps that he owed C.J. Lace then followed suit. He dug his out of his *Knocker* boxer briefs and tried to hand the stamps to Dub.

"Nigga, you better unwrap them shits!" Dub demanded.

Realizing that was a fucked-up gesture, Lace simply took the top sandwich bag off and handed the stamps to Dub.

"Good lookin' homie." Dub said as he arrogantly fanned through the stamps as if they were $100-bills.

Dub sat down between Romeo and Lace. C.J. remained standing. Romeo pulled out eight papers from his sock, then took four '1.5' rolling papers out of his wallet. He gave each of them two papers, and a rolling paper.

C.J. sat down long enough to twist up his joint, then stood again. A *'Border Brother'* approached the quartet.

"I got that lightnin' homes." the brother said as he took his gym bag off his shoulder.

Dub being a stone cold drunk asked, "It ain't that watered-down shit, is it?"

"Naw homes, only one pull on this batch." Hector replied,

referring to the number of times they'd stung the wine.

"It better be, or I'mma run yo' ass back to the border, *brother.*"

Hector didn't find Dub's comment to be amusing, so he quipped back, "What'cha gonna run me with, your spear?"

Dub halfway chuckled. While his homies laughed, Dub yelled, "Fuck you Hector! How much you got?"

"Six water bottles. I'll let you get all six for thirty books and four papers."

"Gimme four papers Cuz." C.J. told Romeo while he counted out 38 books. C.J. gave Hector 30 and handed Romeo the other 8.

"Cuz, I can't char—"

"Don't trip, this is just how real G's do it. Homie love." C.J. said cutting Romeo off.

Hector counted the stamps, then wrapped them in the same shirt that he'd had the wine in previously and stuffed it back in the bag. When Hector walked off, Dumptruck from Florida came over to the Crips table.

"You got some mo' green?"

"I got 8 papers left. Get 'em now or never, 'cause we 'bout to party." Romeo answered.

"I'll give ya 6 cigarettes and 10 books. You know, yo' ass gonna wanna smoke af'ta yo' ass gets drunk."

"Give it up." Romeo said. Although he wanted the cigarettes, and even if he didn't, he would've gotten them anyway on the strength of supporting someone's hustle that wasn't hot. (A SNITCH). After they exchanged merchandise, Dumptruck gave all the Crips some dap, and walked back over to the dice table.

Curious, Lace asked C.J., "So what's crackin'?"

"I'm gonna holla at ya'll in 7 minutes. Let's knock this shit out first, cefore one of those busta ass cops walk down here."

They all grabbed a bottle of 'lightnin' and twisted the tops. "This is to whatever the homie got to tell us." Dub said, eager to get his drink on.

"This is to Crippin'!" Lace added.

"This is to a good time with the homies." Romeo said raising his bottle.

"Homies, this is to changin' the future!" C.J. said looking around before he raised his bottle. They all toasted simultaneously and said, "To the head!" and shot-gunned the strongest wine that's made behind prison walls.

Next, they fired up their joints and smoked in silence. Romeo rolled two of the cigarettes, lit it, then passed them around while they drank the last two bottles of lightnin'.

Feeling quite tight and confident of his plan, C.J. addressed the other occupants of the *Boom Boom Room*. "Dig it, I need to holla at my homies for a minute, and I'd 'preciate it if you'd give me that with no interruptions. Cool?"

"You got that Crip!" was said while others raised their hands acknowledging the request. Some just simply nodded their heads in agreeance.

C.J. felt the intoxicants mixing and his emotions were riding high. *'It's now or never'* he said to himself. "Dig it Locs, as ya'll know they shot my ass down today, so I'm gonna ce here wif ya'll a while longer. Here's what this shit about. All of us are geographically separated but are united by the *'C'* and are together for a common cause." C.J. studied their body language for a few seconds, then continued.

"All of us have been down multiple times and have over a decade under our belts on this one. And why? We in here behind some weak motherfuckas who couldn't do they time for some punk ass crimes! Look at us now! Keepin' it *real,*" C.J. emphasized real by making quotation marks in the air with his fingers.

"We've lost so many years of our lives, money, family, homies...", C.J. paused as he recollected on the demise of all his homies from the set, as well as the entire Crip world. After a few seconds, he shook his head and said, *"Damn!"*

With his emotions at an all-time high, C.J. continued. "Our kids are either grown or damn near. It's time to make these motherfuckas pay fo' everything they've taken from us! Hell, we live for the Big Payback anyway. We are gangbangers, so it ain't shit for us to twist a motherfuckas cap back! I've been thinkin' long and hard on this. What's a man without a purpose? Not a damn thang! We've spent all these years clappin' on rival sets, other gangs, and not understanding who the real enemy is. It's the fuckin' government and these bitch ass niggas that sell their souls to them. A lot, no...*all* this shits 'bout to change! We have to clean up our houses first, then we can start everywhere else. What I need to know left fuckin' now is who's down, and who ain't.

All three held their left hands out, forming a *'C'* with their fingers in the center of the table. C.J. smiled and made his *'C'*, then pounded the other three as a sign of solidarity.

Lace had bewilderment written all over his face, and vague feelings running through his mind. He asked the question, "So what, we gon' start killin' these fools 'round here? Sheeit, we do that, we ain't never gettin' out. I me—"

"What part ain't you understand, fool? Ain't none of these fools directly affect our lives that's here! Yeah, these motherfuckas way of life is fucked up, but they ain't hit us. They'll get theirs too. Eventually, if they would've sent anybody here that snitched on us, they would've been dead! These are goldfish Cuz. We got sharks to slaughter in that big ass ocean they call the *'Free World'*. Ain't shit free, Loc! So what, you ain't down?"

"Yeah Cuz, all day I'm wit it! I just thought…never mind. Hell yeah I'm down!"

C.J. walked up behind Lace and placed his hands on his comrade's shoulders. *Don't let it be you. Please don't let it be you!* C.J. said to himself, then addressed the trio.

"Now that the foundations been poured, we'll build the structure once we've all touched down. This won't ce brought up again 'til we all touch down on the other side. Then, and only then, will this world ever breathe properly again!"

C.J. purposely omitted many details. *Never overexpose your hand*, he thought. C.J. knew Dub was down beyond a shadow of a doubt. Romeo had heart and loyalty. Lace...well, he'd better hope he was too!

The quartet enjoyed the rest of the evening; smoking cigarettes and mingling around the gambling tables talking shit.

Hustleman, whose name was self-explanatory, sold everything from loose candy, to bottles of Muslim praying oil. He didn't indulge in tobacco, narcotics, or alcohol, but by keeping a steady supply of everything else, he stayed in the ranks with all the major hustlers on the compound.

Realizing that the yard was about to close, Hustleman approached the Crips table.

"I got some of that Ed Hardy fo' yo' skin, an' the mints fo' yo' breath. Get it now, fo' ain't none left," he chimed, sitting his bag down on the table, then spreading its contents out as if he were preparing for a flea market or swap meet.

"How much?" Dub asked grabbing a bag of Starlight mints, and a bottle of Ed Hardy oil.

"Fo' ya'll cats, gimme a book." Dub handed him two, realizing that they had to make it through three check points, and they all reeked of alcohol.

Hustleman, a true player to the game said, "Naw, tonight's on me." and handed Dub both books back.

"Tell ya what, real recognize real, so holla at me tomorrow. I got somethin' nice for ya."

Hustleman knew the Crips always played more than fair, so he added, "I said that's on me...but the hustle can't stop and won't stop." Hustleman knew using a Crip motto would bring smiles to their hardened faces.

" See me tomorrow then." Romeo told him as he and his comrades started eating mints and rubbing Ed Hardy all over their clothes.

" Outside recreation is closed. Clear the rec yard gentlemen." Was announced over the P.A. system. Everybody started filing out of the *Boom Boom Room*. The quartet headed for the rec metal detector. After making it past both metal detectors, they all dapped up, and headed down their respected sidewalks feeling good, lost in their own thoughts. One more checkpoint to go; their unit officers.

*** *** *** ***

Seeing the roadblock at the end of the C-unit sidewalk, C.J. made eye contact with Ms. Ingles and rubbed the top of his head indicating that he wasn't right.

That was their signal for her to stop and search him so whichever other officer was out there couldn't and wouldn't search C.J. No officer ever wanted it to seem as if she couldn't do her job.

"You!" Ms. Ingles said pointing at C.J.

C.J. walked over to her and asked, "What's up?"

"Turn around'," Ms. Ingles said turning C.J. herself and roughly patted him down in front of her coworker. After she searched him, Shaneka added, "Ya shouldn't wear so much damn cologne! 'Specially when it stanks."

"Is that why you smell like that?" C.J. shot back.

"Oh no ya did—"

Officer Gun cut her off by saying," Ingles, you jumped out there, so you gotta eat that one."

C.J. shot in the unit, wet a half a roll of toilet paper, then headed back outside the unit just as the move had ended. A few stragglers were still coming down the sidewalk, so C.J. leaned against the fence between C-1 and the C-3 stairwell. When the last man rounded the corner, he threw his head up, acknowledging C.J.'s presence. C.J. pretended to wipe his brow with the wad of tissue. Once the man disappeared into C-1, Ms. Ingles rounded the corner and damn near jumped out of her skin.

"Niggah, ya scur'd the shit outta me!" She said clutching her hand over her heart as if she were having a heart attack.

C.J. grabbed Shaneka and pulled her into him, then kissed her roughly for what seemed like an eternity, but it was only a few seconds. C.J. broke the kiss and patted Ms. Ingles on the ass and said, "You know what to do, so hurry yo' sexy ass up!"

At that moment, a pussy couldn't have gotten any wetter. Shaneka's pussy started to palpitate, causing her to walk more seductively than usual.

After she went into the unit, Shaneka locked the door behind her and headed straight for the corridor between C-1 and C-2.

"Aaa...Ms. Ingles, I need some envelopes please." Saleem, one of the fakest Muslims alive asked.

"Ya still do! Ya gotta wait 'til Ah get back!" Shaneka responded in an irritated tone. She hated wasting her precious time on Saleem's fake ass.

She stopped at the staff restroom for a few minutes before going into C-2

"Hey Gun, did'ja see ma otha err'rang anywhere? 'Ah los' one somewhere," she said in a pouty tone.

"No, but I'll gladly help you to look for it." Gun answered in a flirtatious manner.

Shaneka needed him to open his front door, so she could creep back over to C-1 from the front. Once outside, she couldn't chance him moving in C.J.'s direction, so she went into action.

"Ah ain't los' no err' rang, Gun. Ah jus' needed ya ta come out her' fo' a minute." She said pulling her missing earring out of her pocket to justify her intentions. Before he could respond, she continued. "Gun, I know ya married an' all, but I thank ya one sexy ass man. If ya evah thank about leavin' yo' wife, I need some of that!", Shaneka said pointing at his now hardening dick.

" You know I'm flattered, but I don't cheat on my wife. Now if—"

" Just fa'get it!" Shaneka said trying to sound disappointed. "Well, let me go so I don't make an even bigga fool of ma'self. I knew I should'na told ya how I felt."

As Gun reached to console her, Ms. Ingles pulled back and said, "No, I'm alright...let me go so I can make ma rounds. See ya at count time." while walking back to her post.

When she rounded the corner of the C-3 stairwell, C.J. pulled her in. This time he kissed her hard, but passionately. Shaneka knew that he was drunk, and almost pulled away, but declined to do so when she saw the camera covered with tissue.

Shaneka reached in her pocket and pulled out her panties that she'd just taken off in the restroom. Breaking the kiss, she pushed the crotch into C.J.'s mouth.

"I want'cha ta taste me while I taste you." Ms. Ingles said while grabbing C.J.'s dick and beginning to stroke him to his fullest potential.

C.J. sucked Ms. Ingles' panties like a newborn would with its first titty in its mouth. Seeing the hunger and lust in his eyes, Shaneka hurriedly undid her pants and pushed them down to her ankles. She squatted down, held onto C.J.'s thighs for leverage, and took as much of *her* 10-inches in her mouth as she could. Shaneka had perfected the art of giving head. No hands, down slow, and back up with the suction power of a Hoover vacuum cleaner.

C.J.'s mind was in a whirlwind. Shaneka didn't know of any of the events that had taken place earlier, but she sucked *her* dick like she was trying to make everything better.

Usually C.J. would grab the back of her head, but tonight her essence had him far too gone to think rationally. Instead, he started a Jamaican styled wind and caught a rhythm that matched hers. Shaneka's panties muffled C.J.'s squeals, but she knew and felt that he was on the verge of cumming, so she stopped. Shaneka swiveled around on her toes and put her hands on the bottom step. She straightened her legs and revealed the meatiest pussy in the world. *Fuck a camel toe, Shaneka Ingles had an elephant's hoof!*

Lost in ecstasy, C.J. took a step forward and fingered *his* pussy.

"Com' on niggah and gimme ma dick!" Ms. Ingles demanded.

C.J. grabbed her right ass cheek, fully exposing her opening. Leaning over, he licked from *his* pussy up to the asshole in one swift motion.

"Ummmm!" Shaneka purred.

Standing up, C.J. grabbed *her* slobber drenched dick and pushed it as far into *his* pussy as he could.

"Ahhhh sheeit nig-gah! Fuck yer pu..pussyyyy!" Shaneka screamed.

C.J. put the crotch of her panties back in his mouth and continued to suck the flavor out of them while he fucked *his* pussy.

The moment was so intense that Shaneka was pushing off the bottom step, meeting C.J.'s every stroke. As he drove all 10-inches into her, Ms. Ingles began squirting her juices all over the bottom half of C.J.'s shirt. After 2 minutes of severe punishment, Shaneka screamed through clenched teeth, "Ahhh shit! Her' she cummmms!'' and exploded all over *her* dick. She shook violently for 7 minutes, as orgasm after orgasm overcame her ability to think rationally. When the wave of orgasms subsided, the front of C.J.'s shirt resembled melted marshmallows.

Satisfied that she was satisfied, C.J. continued to pump vigorously until the same sensation overcame his body. Feeling *her* dick swell inside her womb, she knew he was about to cum. On a backstroke, she pulled forward, and turned around. In the same motion, Shaneka started sucking her honey off of *her* dick, sending euphoric sensations throughout the both of them.

This time, C.J. grabbed the back of Ms. Ingles' head and fucked her mouth with a vengeance. Their eyes locked in a hypnotic trance. He bit down on her panties and hissed like a snake while she hungrily awaited him to spew his venom.

"Uggh!", she gagged as he sent thousands of never to be born seeds down her throat. Although she was choking, Shaneka didn't miss a stroke. For good measures she fondled his balls and pulled at the base of *her* dick to make sure that he was completely empty.

C.J. pulled Ms. Ingles to her feet and pulled her pants up to her knees. He reached in her pocket and pulled out a small pack of baby wipes. First, C.J. wiped her forehead, then between her legs. In return, Shaneka wiped *her* dick and C.J.'s legs which were saturated with her juices. She attempted to wipe her lips, but C.J. intervened by pressing his lips against hers. No tongue action, none was needed. This was pure bliss.

"We gotta tighten up babe." She said holding her hand out.

"Yeah we do." C.J. said sucking the crotch of her panties one more time before handing them back to her.

"Yard recall. Yard recall!" was announced over the P.A. system. "Perfect timin' huh?"

"Everything with you is perfect, Mrs. Johnson."

"Niggah don't start that teasin' shit!"

"On the turf, you will wear my name. Now get in there and handle your fan club. Have them motherfuckas out the way by the time I get out the shower!" he warned.

"Don't take all night neitha, niggah!" Ms. Ingles said unlocking the front door.

Just then C.J. realized that he hadn't uncovered the camera yet. He ran and stood to the side so he could snatch the tissue down without being detected.

"That's what I love about cho' ass. You always on point."

"Not always. I'm in here ain't I? I'll see you in 7 minutes."

Shaneka gave C.J. a *nigga you better not be lying* look.

Reading her facial expression, C.J. assured, "Seriously, we got to chop it up on some real shit. OK?"

"All day babe, but—"

"Yeah, you got a great butt, but hold that thought. I'll see you in

7 minutes."

All of a sudden, incoming traffic flooded the sidewalk. Some going up to C-3, the rest into C-1. C.J. followed the last man into his unit.

CHAPTER 4

After taking his shower and getting groomed up, C.J. called his ol' head up to his cell.

"Wanna twist one?"

Gerod Evans, was a 52-year-old armored truck robbery/murderer, who used to pull heists with C.J.'s father Cleon. In the Wells Fargo heist of '79, Cleon along with four Wells Fargo guards met their demise.

When the DPD (Denver Police Department) surrounded Gerod, he had one of two choices; either join his friend Cleon or give up. Geron chose to accompany his best friend to hell, but fate held the trump card. He came out from behind the Wells Fargo truck firing his .38 cal. A S.W.A.T. sharpshooter shot Gerod in his shooting hand, causing him to drop his pistol. Gerod was apprehended and later sentenced to 4 consecutive life sentences, plus a day. He received the one day for the death of his best friend as a slap in the face and yet another sweet victory for the state of Colorado.

"Yeah, young bloo— I mean son. Man roll, damn! Yeah twist it up. Man, you just like yo' daddy. I swear you are."

C.J. could hear the pride in Gerod's voice every time he mentioned his father, but the pain was recognizable too. It was always written on his face, but his eyes told it all.

"Twist it up then!" C.J. said trying to put some cheer back into his father figure's soul.

"Lil nigga, you know I can't roll shit with this damn hand!" Gerod said holding up the hand he was shot in.

"Well gimme some papers ol' man." C.J. said while throwing a fake jab at his true mentor.

They smoked three joints, revitalizing C.J.'s high. It was now 9:10pm. *Damn, I ain't got but 30 minutes to kick it with Shaneka* C.J. thought.

Gerod saw C.J. constantly glancing at his alarm clock and said, "Ol' girl ah be really pissed if you don't holla at her before she leaves."

C.J. looked at Gerod bewildered.

"It's an O.G.'s intuition Baby Boy." Gerod said smiling like a proud father as C.J. headed out of the cell, down to the office.

Reaching the bottom of the stairs, C.J. saw Saleem's fake ass at the office door. *Damn faggot!* C.J. said to himself as he walked up behind Saleem. When Shaneka saw C.J., her whole face lit up.

Bout time I get a smile outta her. Saleem thought.

"Excuse me Ms. Ingles. When you get a chance, I need to holla at you. It'll only take a minute."

Disappointed that it was C.J.'s presence that made her smile, Saleem turned around to acknowledge C.J.

"What's up slim?"

"What I tell you about that *slim* shit? Ain't shit here slim,

Cuz!" C.J. boomed.

"My bad ock."

"I ain't cha ock neither! It's C.J.! C to the motha fuckin' J, Cuz!"

Not standing a chance of winning an argument (or fight) Saleem said, "Ya'll have a good night black people." then walked off.

"What took ya so long niggah? I thought I was gon' have'ta come up there afta' yo' ass!"

"So what's crackin'?" C.J. asked.

Shaneka handed C.J. a pad of paper and a stack of envelopes. "In the 7th envelope I wrote down what I needed ta tell you since you took all long and shit."

C.J. shifted through the envelopes, but Shaneka protested. "Naw, wait 'til ya get to ya cell. Afta' ya read mine, sit down an' use that papa ta get back at me in 7 minutes. Now gon' and handle yo biz before it's time ta lock down."

When C.J. turned to leave, "You betta not be goin' ta call none of yo nasty lil ho's neitha!" Shaneka said half smiling, but dead serious.

"Don't play me like no Buster, Mrs. Johnson!" C.J. said knowing that comment would sooth her soul. To add comfort, he turned back and said, "I love you."

"Wha…", her response fell on deaf ears because C.J. kept on walking.

"Secure compound, secure compound! Officer needs assistance in Charlie 3!" came roaring through the P.A. system.

Shaneka started to run out of the unit to assist her fellow officer, but instead screamed, "Lockdown! Startin' at 117. If ya get locked out I'm givin' ya a shot!"

"Bitch, fuck you!" one inmate screamed.

"Yeah, lock yo' lips around this big black dick, ho!", another one bellowed.

Other extremities were shouted as inmates and convicts raced to get hot water and change the T.V. channels. C.J. went and got two more papers from Gerod, then went to his cell.

Shaneka Ingles came up the stairs and announced, "Top range, startin at 201!" as she locked C.J.'s cell door, she mouthed, *Tomorrow!*

C.J. hurried and opened the envelope, knowing that she had to come back within his view when she got to cell 232. After taking a deep breath, he pulled the lone sheet of paper out that read, 'I'm pregnant.'

When Shaneka got to cell 232, C.J. gestured for her to look at him, but instead she kept walking and reiterated *Tomorrow!*

After smoking his joint, C.J. sat at his desk and reflected on all the how's, when's, and where's. *No matter, I now have the missing piece of the puzzle. I know my queen won't allow this king to get mated.* Picking up his pen, C.J. began to write.

My dearest Shaneka Johnson,

What more can I say other than wow! I celieve in keepin' it 100% Gangsta, so here it is.

We've never verbally committed to one another, but the life you're carrying inside your womb has sealed our union. The first time I had a chance to ce inside you, I knew that's where I celonged! That's home I told myself. You've allowed a 'G' to feel a freedom I never knew existed, through your ways and actions. You heard me left earlier, ***I love you!*** *And yes, I'm going to marry you, so does that answer all of your questions? You know what's craccin' with our lil Gangsta or Gangstress.*

Left now, I need you to move up the ladder. I need you in a higher position than ceing a C/O. You have several degrees, so put them to a greater use. They have an opening with S.I.S. left now. (yeah, I've done my homework.) Get that experience so you can go work for the F.B.I. or C.I.A. I need you there so we can get to where we need to ce. I'll never leave you in the blind nor cehind, but left now, the less you know, the better off we'll all ce. Trust in me like you trust in God and you'll see that neither one of us would ever hurt you. After these next few days, we won't see each other as much. You know how to do things. Make sure I get plenty of pictures of my seed; ***Our creation!*** *I have a lil pad out in Limon, Colorado. I need you to take a vacation. Use your own money to fly out there. Do you trust me? The address is 1959 Sharryl Mill Rd. Once you get there, go to the back porch, and twist the porch light to the left. (Yeah, everything is left baby!) There you'll find the key to the front door. Go, and this will enhance our trust level. I got a little over a half a mill under the garden tub. Take half for you and our new life. I'll need the other half to put my plan into motion. So there it is. Leave this weekend. Send me a postcard when you get there. Cefore you go, put in for the S.I.S. job, and tell them you want to start when the quarter changes. R U Down, or not? I know you are, I just had to give you the option to ce your own woman and answer it yourself. That's another reason why I* *love you so much!*

2 Real 4 Real,

C.J.

Also,

Your husband, Best friend & Confidant.

***

As she finished his letter, some 70+ miles away, Shaneka laid on her bed clutching her C.J. Teddy bear and a pillow between her legs. She whispered, *"I love you too!"* as both ears began to fill with her tears.

CHAPTER 5

The following morning Shaneka fired up a blunt and sipped on a glass of Cabernet Sauvignon. She reminisced about her latest rendezvous with C.J.. The mere thought of C.J. sent her fingers straight into her panties. While stroking her clit, Shaneka put the blunt in the ashtray and poured the rest of the wine into her panties.

"Ssssss!", she gasped as the cold sensation sent her into her first orgasm of the day. Shaneka picked the blunt back up and took a deep pull as her fingers moved seductively over her clit while R. Kelly crooned about going half on a baby. Holding her head back, enjoying both feelings. Shaneka curled three fingers and pushed them as far into C.J.'s pussy as she could. She pulled them out slowly, then rammed them back in repeatedly until she brought herself to her second orgasm of the day.

The disc changed, and Bob Marley sang *No Woman, No Cry.* However, all Shaneka heard was, *'No C.J., I Cry!'* Taking the last pull off the blunt, Shaneka dropped the roach in the ashtray and continued fantasizing with her eyes opened. All of a sudden, a hologram of C.J. appeared.

"Damn, that's some good shit!" she said as if she were actually talking to someone. Shaneka looked at the roach in the ashtray and made a mental note to thank her brother for the 'Chronic'.

Standing naked, C.J. told Shaneka to keep going as he began to stroke *her* dick. Shaneka, being hypnotized by C.J.'s image, continued to dig in *his* pussy like the big oil pumps due to the ground in Texas. The only difference was that Shaneka's eruption would be white.

As she felt a Category 5 building in the depths of *his* pussy and knowing that her floodgates wouldn't be able to withstand the force of the forthcoming Tsunami, Shaneka screamed "Oo Sheeit! Ahhhh Fuck!" Her screams turned into a deep growl as her fingers moved like pistons in a 454 big block! What Shaneka didn't know was that her dam had already burst.

Her fingers continued to move with rapid speed. The sound mimicked that of a child sloshing around in water puddles wearing galoshes. Shaneka finally convulsed herself into a deep sleep. When she woke back up. it felt as if if she'd pissed in the bed. Shaneka pulled her cum soaked panties off, and then put them in a small Ziplock baggie before she went to take a shower.

Having plenty of time to get ready for work, Shaneka decided to take a little catnap. She drifted off rubbing her stomach and smiled about the future she so desperately wanted, needed, and most definitely deserved.

*** *** *** ***

F.C.I. Edgefield

Later that same afternoon, Romeo played a cat from D.C., 1-on-1, for 20 books of stamps. He was up one game already, but down by a point in the second one.

"Check Slim!" D.C. said, throwing the ball to Romeo with excessive force. Romeo threw it back with the same amount of force, and ran up on D.C.

"Yo Slim, you gotta gimme some room." D.C. said swinging the ball above his head.

"I ain't gotta give you shit!" Romeo said as he stripped the ball, then turned around and made an easy layup.

"Foul Moe!" D.C. cried out.

"Bullshit! Tie game nigga!"

"You fouled the shit outta me Moe!"

"You crazy as a shit house rat. My ball!"

"U ain't respectin' calls, I ain't respectin' no bets, Slim." D.C. said, knowing that he didn't have any money, plus he had about 10 homies on the sideline watching.

A reputable group of Bloods were on the opposite end of the court playing 3-on-3. Hearing the commotion, Pig (the Bloods shot-caller) stopped playing and walked to the half-court line. The other five followed.

"What's poppin', homie?" Pig asked scanning the scene.

One D.C. onlooker came on the court and asked.

"What'cha mean what's poppin', Slim?"

"Just what I said, Fool!" Pig said to the second D.C. dude.

While the Bloods held a stare down with the D.C. crew, Romeo slipped over to his shirt and grabbed his heat (shank). In one swift motion, Romeo stabbed his opponent in the neck.

Schluk!

Blood squirted everywhere as Romeo continued to plunge his

blade into the screaming, bloody man.

Schluk! Slash! Sphhhlt!

Everyone looked on in horror as the once humbled *'G'* turned into a vicious psychopathic killer. Before any more action could take place, Towers 3 & 4 opened and demanded everybody to get on the ground.

Romeo, lost in his own rage, continued to plunge his knife into the now semi-conscious man, until he heard, "Get down now!", followed by the retort of a 12-gauge.

Boom-Yahl!

The shots sent Romeo's mind back to the mean streets of *Smalls Berry*, (better known as Salisbury, N.C.) Although gangbangin' didn't exist in Salisbury until a Crip named Screw came from Colorado and put it down back in 1990, the streets of Salisbury were unforgiving.

Snapping out of his trance, Romeo laid down beside his victim as officers came running down to the basketball court with Richard Jones (Crip O.G.) leading the way.

"Great demonstration homie!" Pig said smiling from some 20 feet away.

"Yeah." was all Romeo had to say. He was now thinking to himself; *I hope this bitch nigga don't die!*

*** *** *** ***

Shaneka arrived at work earlier than usual, but not early enough to draw any suspicion. Her heart needed to know how C.J. really felt.

Her heart sank after learning that the compound was on an institution lockdown. *Damn!* Shaneka muttered under her breath, as she approached the staff briefing room.

Warden Rice, aka *Mr. Gotta*, was in the middle of one of his long drawn out speeches when Shaneka opened the door.

"Ahh, Ms. Ingles, I'm glad you're here. Please have a seat." Cpt. Rodgers said getting up and offering her his seat, next to the warden.

"Your post is C-1, correct, Ms. Ingles?" Warden Rice asked.

"Yes sir!"

"Well the Crips shot caller, ummm…yes a Clevon Johnson aka C.J. is housed in that unit, correct?" the warden asked after scanning a file in front of him.

"Yes." Shaneka answered as her heart began to race a million miles a minute. She came back in tune as the warden was finishing his statement.

"…And so by you having that post, I figured that maybe you could find out what's going on between the Crips and the D.C. inmates. We need to know if it was a hit or a personal beef. There were also some Bloods at the altercation. We're just trying to put the missing pieces of the puzzle in their proper places. So far, no one is talkin'."

"Well, I don't know what I can do that ya'll can't."

"Ms. Ingles don't take this out of context, but you're easy on the eye. Quite frankly, that's how we get most of these guys to talk. Send an attractive woman at them, and they'll tell you about every crime they've ever committed, witnessed, or heard of. You get what I'm saying, don't you?"

After Shaneka acknowledged that she understood, the warden continued. "Plus, he's the head orderly. I'm allowing each number one orderly to assist the unit officers during trash pickup tonight. This'll be the perfect time to see what you can dig up!"

Pissed by the insinuation that C.J. would snitch made

Shaneka's blood boil. However, Shaneka knew that she couldn't wear her emotions on her sleeve, so she simply said, "If ya thank it'll work, I'll try my best."

"You see that….", the warden said to the other occupants of the room. "That's what I call a team player." he finished, pointing in Shaneka's direction.

Most of the staff didn't like Shaneka Ingles, especially the men because she wouldn't give them the time of day. The women hated Shaneka out of jealousy. The salty conversations they had, along with the bitter stares she received, always caused Shaneka to smile to herself. *Hate on motherfuckas!*

Getting up to leave, the warden stopped Shaneka at the door and asked, "Can you work a double? We got a lot of bang outs. You'd keep your same post. That is if you want the overtime?"

"I'll do it!" Shaneka confirmed.

CHAPTER 6

At 3:30, Shaneka walked into C-1 and immediately made eye contact with C.J. who was standing at his cell door, peeping through its narrow window. C.J. closed his thumb around his index finger and raised the last three digits. The sign was he and Shaneka's symbol for *'I love you'*. Shaneka made the same gesture while pretending to wipe the sweat from her brow.

After relieving Officer Holmes, Shaneka locked the front door then made her rounds checking each cell to make sure that they were locked.

She breezed through the bottom range, then headed up the stairs, starting at 232. Shaneka checked the cells in a numeric order so she'd finish at C.J.'s door. She put her *Texy Sexy* walk on, knowing how much it enticed C.J.

"Shake it, don't break it!" one cat caller shouted.

"Throw it in the bushes! I'll go get it!" another one screamed. Numerous other calls were made, but Shaneka didn't even stop to check for the perpetrators. She knew that several perverts would be standing (or laying) with their dicks out.

When Shaneka made it around to cell 201, she stopped and raised her left leg, then placed her foot on the bottom rail and leaned forward. Shaneka didn't bother to look back; she knew C.J. didn't have a cellie. They were about to have telepathic sex. *Damn, I might have'ta give that niggah these draws too!* Shaneka thought as her pussy started palpitating, reliving yesterday, and this morning.

When C.J. was about to cum, he tapped on the door. Shaneka turned around in time to see his face contort. She knew he was cumming by the way his bottom lip quivered.

"Johnson!" Shaneka said trying to stop her mind from cumming as well as turn off the faucet off between her legs. "You'll be helpin' ta clean up afta' chow, alright?"

C.J. just smiled and showed Shaneka the envelope that contained her letter of response.

Not knowing that what the envelope contained was the foundation to a very serious movement, Shaneka smiled a happy, but nervous smile. C.J. took his hand and rubbed from his chin up to his forehead, indicating that everything was all good. If things weren't, he would've done the opposite.

Officer Gun came through the upper corridor loaded down in cheap ass cologne.

Shaneka straightened up and hollered, "Count time! Count time! Startin' at 232!"

After they'd counted both sides and turned it in, Shaneka went and got the mail bag. She always read C.J.'s mail from other females. Never in her 28 years of living has Shaneka ever been envious or jealous of another woman. Nor did she ever think that she'd fall in love with a convict. Shaneka loved a *real* gangstas' swag, but real gangstas don't get caught. *Or do they?* she questioned herself. All of Shaneka's doubts went out the window after her and C.J.'s first encounter. In her eyes, C.J. was the definition of a true *'G'*.

Shaneka took her cum drenched panties from this morning's episode and placed them in a F.B.O.P. manila envelope. She then scribbled a phony return address on it along with C.J.'s name and number too. Today, C.J. only had letters from his oldest daughter Nesha, a Black Enterprise, XXL, and a Straight Stuntin' magazine.

I know he's gon' be a great father to our baby. Shaneka told herself.

Not wanting anyone to see the phony package, Shaneka purposely left the upper ranges mail in the office and proceeded to pass out on the bottom.

Every inmate that had mail asked Shaneka basically the same questions.

"When we comin' off lockdown?"

"Did dude die?"

"What happened?"

Shaneka's response to every question was, "I don't know. I jus' got here." The only thing on Shaneka's mind was her letter, so she hurried to finish the bottom. Her soul craved to know what C.J. had to say.

Gathering the upper ranges mail, Shaneka shot to C.J.'s cell first. Unlocking the trap, she thumbed through the mail and said, "Johnson, ya got a few pieces of mail today."

C.J. walked over to the trap. While retrieving his mail he tried to hand her the letter. Knowing all eyes were on them, C.J. declared loud enough for every boy to hear him. "This ain't mine! This is Cedric Johnsons shit, in B-4!"

C.J. then handed Shaneka the envelope. Initially, Shaneka wanted to protest and tell C.J. to bring it out when he comes out to clean. However, C.J.'s persistence, along with her own curiosity, made Shaneka grab the envelope then turn it upside down.

"Read it now!" C.J. mouthed as Shaneka closed the trap.

C.J. ripped open the manila envelope and smiled. He opened the Ziplock baggie and inhaled Shaneka's aroma.

Damn! Fresh pussy! C.J. said as he laid back on his bunk and tasted her essence.

If Shaneka wasn't conscious of where she was, she would've sprinted back to the office. Instead, she passed out the remainder of the mail in a trance, ignoring all the same questions she previously half-answered.

Once back in the office, Shaneka took a deep breath, exhaled, then opened her letter.

A Ronald McDonald smile escaped her face after seeing the salutation.

Shaneka read, re-read, and then re-read *some more* of her letter to make sure that she had a complete grasp on its contents. A few things remained vague, but her mind, body, and soul told Shaneka to go with the flow and trust her man. *Mrs. Johnson, ya all in now!* she said imitating a poker player pushing all of his chips to the center of the table.

The dinner bags came a little over an hour later. While passing out the meals, Gerod Evans asked Shaneka to pass C.J. an envelope. Knowing Gerod was a father figure to C.J., she gladly accepted it.

Getting to C.J.'s cell, Shaneka said, "Be ready when I start pickin' up the trash." then handed him a bag, and the envelope from Gerod.

C.J. knew who the envelope came from and what it contained. Tearing off a piece of toilet paper wrapper, C.J. took the two papers of *Purple Haze* and rolled a joint. He was a little puzzled because Shaneka made no indication about how she felt about the letter, or if she even read it in the first place. He'd soon find out what was up.

After smoking his joint, C.J. sprayed his cell down with Kenneth Coles' latest fragrance and waited on Shaneka to come get him.

Officer Gun came over from C-2. *What the fuck does this fool want?* C.J. mumbled from his cell door.

Not wanting to be in an isolated area with Gun, Shaneka came out of the office and sat down at the control desk. This allowed C.J. to see how she handled herself around other men. She'd set the stage.

Leaning on the desk, Gun whispered, "I'm leaving Shirley, Baby."

"Oh ma gawd. Are ya serious?" Shaneka whispered back.

" Yep! Just as soon as she signs the papers, I'll be a free agent. So you want to put your bid in now or what?"

"Listen Gun, we'll talk anotha time 'bout this. Right now, the warden got me on some detective shit so that's where my mind is."

"What's up?"

"You remember that inmate wearin' all that ca'lone yesterday? Well he's some shot calla fo' one of them gangs, and the warden wants me to find out some shit."

"What?"

"I can't discuss that. Sorry."

"Well if you need me for anything, you know where I'm at." Gun said slapping the desk with both hands, winked, then walked back towards C-2.

"Damn that shit stanks!" Shaneka said, finally breathing through her nose again. Instinct caused her to turn around. She and C.J. locked eyes. "Are ya ready?" Shaneka asked breaking their stare. His glassy eyes would've hypnotized her if she didn't.

When she opened the cell door, Shaneka handed C.J. a roll of trash bags, and immediately started giving out orders.

"You gotta clean ma office, sweep an' mop both activity rooms, the laundry room, and take the trash out. They want this place ta get cleaned, an' it's gon' get cleaned while I'm on post!"

C.J. only nodded. He knew Shaneka was only putting on a show for the haters.

They gathered the trash in silence. All the other orderlies asked if they were coming out as well.

"Naw, the warden specified only head orderlies." Shaneka answered as she collected the trash and threw it in the bag that C.J. was carrying. After a bag was full, C.J. would tie it and throw it towards the front door.

Once all the trash was collected, C.J. carried all the bags out to the big bin in front of the unit.

Next, he swept the top range and stopped to holler at Gerod for a few minutes. As C.J. and his mentor talked, Shaneka received a phone call. The look on Shaneka's face was unreadable, but C.J. knew that the conversation was serious. The warden had called to check on her progress.

"He's still cleanin' up right now, so I haven't got the chance ta holla at him yet....OK yeah, I'll call jus' as soon as I know somethin'...Yeah, got you...OK Bye." Shaneka said hanging up the phone then gestured for C.J. to come down to the desk.

Shaneka pointed to both activity rooms and the laundry room, then through clenched teeth she stated, "We gotta talk now! We're gonna push the garbage bin up to the metal detector. Let's go!"

Once outside, Shaneka opened "Look, the warden wanted me ta ask or find out if that was a hit today. I know it wasn't, but I had ta ask."

"What's crackin' with that D.C. cat? Did he die or what?" C.J. asked.

"Naw, he jus' got outta surgery. They say he should make it." Shaneka answered.

"Damn, Cuz just snapped!"

"But what for? Ya'll beefin' wit' D.C.?"

"Naw, that's some personal shit I guess."

"So what'cha want me to tell' em?"

"Tell them to have S.I.S. to call me and the D.C. shot calla out tomorrow."

"Ya mean Davidson?" she inquired.

"Yeah, Marco. He's sensible. We can get this shit straight tomorrow. Enough about that, what's crackin' with the letter?"

"Need you ask yo wife a silly ass question like that?", Shaneka said all starry eyed.

"Geah! Now dig this. Tell them fools that this was your idea so they'll feel that you're in touch with the yard. You'll ce top candidate for the job."

"You got err'thang all figured out, don't ya?"

"Just our future Mrs. Johnson. Just our future."

C.J. cleaned both activity rooms, then the laundry room. He knew that he and Shaneka were being watched on both sets of cameras; video and human. He didn't allow his little head to outthink his bigger one.

Unknown to C.J., Shaneka wanted some dick in the worst way.

After a few enticing gestures and knowing that this would probably be their last fuck until he got out, C.J. succumbed to the temptation and gave Shaneka 2 hard minutes of Crip dick; her favorite kind.

To lighten the mood. C.J. said. "Maybe I'll put another one in you to keep our other one company."

"Ya wish." Shaneka said as she strained to push all of his cum out of her into her hand. She pursed her lips and sucked it down in one loud slurp. That drove C.J. into a frenzy, but enough was enough. He had to allow his bigger head to take back over.

C.J. leaned down and kissed Shaneka's stomach, then rubbed it and said, "Lil homie (or homegirl) Mommy and daddy are so happy to have you in there. Cut just wait 'til you get out here. Yeah, we gonna spoil the shit outta you!" It was an emotional moment for the couple. After regaining their composure, they wiped each other down, straightened their clothes, and went their separate ways. Shaneka went back to the office, C.J. went back to his janitorial duties.

At 8:00pm, Shaneka had C.J. start removing things from the office. He wiped the entire office down with some Clorox wipes. He also used an excessive amount of water while mopping to ensure some extra time with his future wife.

9:30 came like a thief in the night. Shaneka broke the silence. "I'm workin' a double so I'll be her' in the mornin'. I'll make sure I holla at faggot ass Sanchez 'bout the job. Betta yet, I'll holla at the warden."

C.J. smiled at how sharp witted she was. "That's what I'm talkin' about! A real thinker!"

"I won't see ya no mo' 'til next week, so gimme some suga."

"You got that." C.J. said and walked into the activity room adjacent to the office.

" Jus' so ya know I swi— "

C.J. didn't give Shaneka a chance to finish her statement before his tongue was Crip Walkin' in her mouth. The moment was so intense that the 1-minute tongue wrestling match seemed to last for hours. Finally, their senses caught up to them and they broke their kiss.

C.J. pulled the thong out of his pocket that was given to him during mail call.

"Refresh these and give' em cack at creakfast." he said knowing his verbiage would entice her to oblige.

"Boy ya tryna drain a sistah ain't cha?" Shaneka said as she grabbed her panties and stuffed them in her back pocket. She knew damn well that she wanted to do what C.J. asked of her just as much as he wanted her to. She smiled, realizing that the night wouldn't be as boring after all.

The next morning as promised, Shaneka delivered. After breakfast, staff started pouring in for interviews. Shaneka personally escorted C.J. to the Lt.'s office. Marco was being escorted up the A-unit sidewalk simultaneously.

Captain Rodgers agreed with Shaneka's suggestion of a meeting with the two shot callers. Although the D.C. car outnumbered the Crips almost 30:1, all the other Black gangs would assist the Crips in a war against the D.C. regiment, and vice versa.

L.T. Eric Sanchez, a pure faggot, had C.J. and Marco sitting in his office while he consulted with Shaneka.

"What's crackin' Marco?", C.J. said breaking the silence "You tell me Moe."

"From what I hear, yo' boy tried to play my homie outta some bread."

"Oh yeah? Well I heard a lil more than that Slim."

"Like what?" C.J. asked, now half-heated.

"I heard your man wasn't respectin' calls, Slim. So Moe felt some kinda way about it."

"Well it was head up, so what's crackin'?"

"It's your call Slim."

After a few seconds of silence and pondering what would really take place if the two sides collided, Marco reasoned, "Yo Slim, I'll holla at my car and let em' know that this ain't gon' be no war. Romeo shouldn't have played Slim. Everybody knows he ain't got no money."

"Well if shits dead, let's let these fools know so they can open the yard and we can clear the air. I'll take full responsibility for mine. You do the same."

"I got mine, Slim."

"Cool. Check it, your homie pulled through surgery."

After hearing about the gruesome demonstration that Romeo had put down on his homie, Marco thought for sure that Ricky would die. Satisfied that this information would help soothe things over with his car, Marco nodded and said, "Thanks for the info, Slim."

At the conclusion of their conversation, Lt. Sanchez walked in with Capt. Rodgers on his heels.

" Alright gentlemenz-", Sanchez said with a lispy tongue, "We have a situation he—"

"We talked, and there ain't gonna be any retaliation." Marco stated.

"Ummm hmmm. So what we hav —"

This time C.J. cut Sanchez off.

"We don't have nothin'! We straightened this out like *real men* do." C.J. said emphasizing "real men".

"Ummm hmmm. We de —"

"Capt.—"C.J. said once again cutting Sanchez off.

"Ms. Ingles said some real shit. She said if I really was a grown man, then I'd be able to work this out with Davidson here in a diplomatic fashion. We already resolved it amongst us, we need to now go let our cars know that this shit is dead. Havin' us on lockdown ain't gonna do nothin' but add fuel to the unknown and have 'Inmate.com' off the hook. I speak for my car."

"And I speak for mine." Marco added.

"Alright then. We'll escort ya'll back to your units. But…if anything, and I mean *anything* transpires, we're coming for ya'll two first!"

''Ummm hmmm.'' Lt. Sanchez emphasized Capt.'s statement.

Captain Rodgers looked at Sanchez with disgust and hatred, then said, "Ya'll got that?"

"Yes sir!" C.J. and Marco responded in unison.

"We're going to stop the interviews. At mainline, I expect the two of you to come to me so the compound will see how the two of you are conducting yourselves as —"

"Gentlemenz!" Sanchez interrupted trying to finish the Capt.'s statement. However, this only infuriated Captain Rodgers, so much so that it caused him to snap.

"Who the hell do you think you're cuttin' off?!" he asked standing akimbo to Lt. Sanchez.

"Ummm—" Sanchez squealed.

"Shut the hell up Sanchez! I've had it up to here…" Capt. Rodgers gestured holding his hand at eye level. "With your mouth and attitude! That bitch ain't here no mo' for you to run cryin' to, so I suggest you learn to stay in your place!"

"Ye…yes s-sir." Sanchez weakly replied with tears starting to fall.

I'm gonna put paperz on hiz asssz. He picked the wrong bitch to fuck with this time Sanchez thought to himself.

CHAPTER 7

Shaneka made reservations for a 9:00pm flight from Atlanta to Denver. Since she paid for it online with her VISA Shaneka also received a free rental from Enterprise.

Needing rest for the trip, Shaneka slept until 3:00 that afternoon. After a brief catnap, she got up and showered. Shaneka chose a cream-colored Armani skirt suit, with mahogany 3-inch heels. Not wanting to stand out, Shaneka decided to go with a set of small diamond studded earrings and her *I'm taken* wedding set. Next, Shaneka packed some clothes for comfort. She'd only be gone for a few days, *so why overdo it?* she reasoned.

After packing, Shaneka loaded up her Lexus 430SC and headed to Atlanta. Her flight landed a little after 9:00pm Mountain time. After claiming her luggage and picking up the keys from the Enterprise desk, Shaneka exited the Denver's International Airport

After setting up the navigation system, Shaneka realized that Limon was about an hour drive. Since she'd taken a nap, and slept the entire flight, she decided to make the drive instead of getting a room.

Shaneka pulled up to C.J.'s hideout an hour and twenty-five minutes later. She could tell it hadn't been occupied since C.J.'s departure close to 15 years ago.

Being a quick thinker, Shaneka's sharp wit had her stop at Albertsons for some snacks and candles.

The entire interior of the double wide trailer was covered in cobwebs.

''Oh hell ta the nawl! I ain't stayin' in her!" Shaneka said out loud, although she was the only one in the dwelling. "I'll just get a room for the night."

Getting back on I-70, Shaneka found a nice little motel not too far from C.J.'s residence. Seeing that it was clean, she smiled, took a shower, and dozed off shortly after midnight.

The next morning, Shaneka went and put a deposit down with the local electric company. They informed her that the lights would be on by 3pm that afternoon.

Shaneka's next stop was Wal-Mart for some cleaning supplies. She dropped the supplies off at the trailer, then headed back to Denver. Mesmerized by its size, Shaneka shopped at the 16th St. Mall until just after 5pm.

Having spent all of her traveling money, a slight doubt ran through her mind. *I hope that niggah really got that money in there.* Immediately, a wave of guilt hit Shaneka like a mack truck. "Yo daddy wouldn't send me on no bullshit mission, would he?" Shaneka asked her unborn child as she rubbed her belly. As confirmation, she could've sworn that she felt a punch or a kick, as if saying, *Don't ever doubt my daddy!* The Joker from Batman couldn't have smiled a bigger smile.

Snapping back to reality, Shaneka realized that she didn't get the water turned on. As she was about to back down the driveway, she saw a well about 100 yards away. *I hope it ain't dry* Shaneka said as she got out the car. She'd find out in a couple minutes.

Going into the kitchen, Shaneka turned the knobs on the sink. *Presto!* She had water. It ran brown for a couple minutes, then it became clear. "Now I can clean this mothafucka up!"

Shaneka dressed in boy shorts and a wife-beater, then went and took inventory of all the tasks at hand. Curiosity grabbed her when she walked into the master bedrooms bathroom.

She stared down at the tub for what seemed like an eternity. Taking a deep breath, she grabbed the rim of the tub, and snatched upward. The entire shell came up revealing more money than she'd ever seen. Death couldn't remove the smile on her face. She danced and shook her ass as she sang, "I'm into mon-ey!" Shaneka pulled all the money out of the hole, then carried it into the bedroom.

The bedspread and sheets needed to be washed, so she put them in the washing machine, and washed them several times. After vacuuming one side of the floor, she moved the money to the fresh side, then vacuumed the rest of the room.

Shaneka counted money until her eyes started to burn and saw double. *$458,000 so far. Damn, I still got a big pile ova there.* Shaneka knew it was closer to a mill than the half C.J. told her about. *I'll finish this afternoon.*

After putting the sheets back on the bed, Shaneka laid down, and let the crickets chirp her to sleep.

The following morning, Shaneka realized that she didn't have time to waste. Her plane was scheduled to leave at 9:00pm, and she still had a lot of cleaning to do. Also, she needed to get C.J.'s postcard. *I'mma stay 'til Tuesday. I gotta handle shit fo' my man!*

Shaneka rescheduled her flight which would now leave at 8:37pm Tuesday night. After thoroughly cleaning the entire crib, Shaneka finished counting the money. $861,810 was the total. *Damn niggah! These dead crackas got a bitch's panties wetta than a mothafucka!* she said referring to the dead white men on the money.

Picking up a post card at the local 7-11, she wrote,

I can give you 861 excuses, but 810 would be bullshit! I'm redecorating so my excuses will dwindle, but not too much!

Love,

Your Wifey,

Mrs. S. Johnson.

Shaneka mailed the postcard, then went furniture shopping. After being assured that it would be delivered the following day, she paid for the purchase with her Visa.

Her vacation time had come to and gone. Before leaving, for some reason unknown, Shaneka stopped and checked the mailbox. A lone letter sat inside, addressed to Mrs. S. Johnson. Shaneka's heart stopped briefly when she saw the numbers 861,810, followed by a simple, *Love Your Future, C.J...*

That niggah knew how much it was all along. He betta be glad I'm a real loyal bitch! Shaneka thought to herself.

Shaneka was back in her own condo at 2am EST Wednesday morning. Tired from jetlag, she flopped down on her sofa, and fell into a deep slumber.

CHAPTER 8

Shaneka arrived at F.C.I. Edgefield at 1:00pm, 3 hours before her shift was to start. The warden was exiting the staff lounge and drinking a cup of coffee when she decided that this was her chance. Shaneka raised her arm above her head and began waving it to gain his attention.

The warden took notice as Shaneka began to sashay her *Video Chick* body in his direction. *"Damn I'd love to hit that!"* he said to himself. Shaneka knew that the warden lusted over her and decided to take full advantage of his weakness.

"Yes Ms. Ingles?" he asked when she was within an arm's reach.

"I need to speak with you in private. Is somebody in ther'?" Shaneka asked pointing at the staff's lounge.

"Umm…actually no."

Shaneka opened the door but stood still long enough for the warden to *accidently* bump into her ass.

"Umm...excuse me Ms. Ingles. Weren't we goin' in here to

discuss something?"

"Yes, Mr. Rice. Ummm, why is you on hard?" Shaneka asked pointing down to the warden's now tented slacks.

"By all means Ms. Ingles. I'm sorry, I-I…I thought…well you know...I thought—"

"You thought I was some kinda jump-off or somethin'? Is that what you was thinkin'?"

"No! I'd nev—"

"Listen Mr. Rice, mistakes happen, right?"

The warden nodded in agreement.

"I can overlook you touchin' my ass and not filin' sexual harassment charges. Plus, yo wife would hate to hear how her husband flirts with all us women at the job, and Lord Knows where else you be at."

"What is it that you want Ms. Ingles, more money?"

"No silly, jus' some help gettin' that S.I.S. job."

"That's all?"

"Well that, an after a yer you can recommend me for a job in the Bureau."

"This is the bureau Ms. Ingles."

"No, I need a job as an agent, and yer credentials will help. A sista is tryna' move up in this world without having to sleep her way up to the top."

"Ms. Ingles consider this conversation as never taking place. You'll be assigned to S.I.S. over the gangs, and then you'll get your recommendation one year from today. I'm promoting you for defusing a situation that could've gotten ugly. My word is my bond. Is yours?"

Shaneka extended her hand and said, "Mine is too!" They shook hands, and the deal was sealed. Warden Rice walked away thinking, *Dumb ass bitch! I would've kicked out big. I need to chill before Martha gets half my shit.*

Shaneka went back to her car to put up her tape recorder. "Fuck that chump!" she said to herself. "If his bitch ass reneges, I got the lil hooka on tape!"

***　　***　　***　　***

After count, Shaneka passed out the mail. A wave of disappointment hit her when the post card wasn't in there. She turned the bag upside down and shook it feverishly. "Damn Ms. I, you act like you waitin' on some mail too!" Saleem joked while getting a few laughs.

"Yeah, ain't nothin' else in that bag Ms. I. Most of us got what we was expecting yesterday." C.J. announced. Hearing the hidden message, a rush of relief passed over her as she looked into C.J.'s hypnotic eyes.

The 5-minute move was announced for C-unit, B-2, and B-4. C.J. waited until the last man exited the unit before he spoke to his woman. "I got it yesterday. Did you get yours?"

Shaneka nodded, and said, "Yeah, I got it. And I passed ya' lil test with flyin' colors."

"Yeah, just as long as what you flyin' is true! I'll see you in 7 minutes."

"Come in at 6. Naw, come in at 7, so you can do some extra duty."

"It's our last night, so I'll ce in at 6. I gotta make sure my wife leaves with a smile on her face." Although Shaneka broke into a big smile, her other lips were ever happier.

***   ***   ***   ***

C.J., Dub, and Lace smoked a couple papers, then C.J. announced that he had a few things to take care of back in the unit. When the move was announced, C.J. hit his homies up and rushed to catch the move.

"What's crackin' Cuz?" Dub asked Lace.

"It's whatever with me homie. Shit, we can go up if you want."

"That's what's crackin'."

Before they got to the metal detector, Lace said "Cuz act like his mind is runnin' a million miles a minute. I guess the sayin' is true: *Crippin' ain't easy*."

Once they made it through the metal detector, Dub hit Lace up and said, "It is when you know what you're doin'! Stay up homie." They both headed to their units. Dub turned left to go into B-1. Lace to the right into B-2.

CHAPTER 9

C.J. checked his E-mails, answered them, then called his daughters. Not able to reach them, he decided to wait until right before lockdown to try again. That thought was easily erased, tonight he was on a mission.

C.J. went to the office door and stared at his future wife.

"What'cha lookin' at?" she asked coyly.

"The sexiest woman alive."

"Is that right?"

"Damn left, it's left! Dig it Mrs. J..., it's our last night toge—"

"Listen, how much do ya trust Mr. Evans?"

"As much as I trust myself."

"Wow!"

"Yeah. That much."

"Well in that case, will he—"

"You know he will, as much as I do." C.J. responded, clearly understanding where the conversation was going.

"Go let em' know that I need em' to help me carry a few

thangs up to those interviewin' rooms."

"Got'cha Mrs. J." C.J. said as he sped off to put the bug in Gerod's ear. Gerod immediately agreed to assist his Godson. He put his headphones on top of the neatly folded blanket that sat in his chair.

C.J. crept up to the upper ranges corridor. Shaneka came up next, followed by Gerod with two duffle bags over his shoulders, and carrying a box.

Saleem saw this as an opportunity to get some alone time with Shaneka. "A Pop! You need some help with that?"

"I need you to get the fuck outta my face, chump, gump, or whatever ya'll call ya'll selves these days! We called ya'll homos, queers, or faggots, so the answer to yo' question is, fuck no!"

Trying to salvage face, Saleem glared at Gerod and said, "If I didn't respect my elders, or my religion, I'd get outta char—"

In a blinding flash, Gerod had Saleem pinned in the shower, with a knife pressed against Saleems throat.

Shaneka calmly said, "Mr. Evans, please reconsider."

"No disrespect Ma'am, but this faggot don't know who the fuck he's fuckin' with!"

Turning his attention back to Saleem, Gerod said, "Now get on yo knees faggot an' suck this old dick!"

Tears started to stream down Saleem's face as he started to lower himself to his knees. Once he was on his knees, Gerod leaned over and said,

"Look at'cha now faggot! I don't get down like that. Now here's how you gonna play it. You gonna go to yo' cell and stay there for the rest of the night. If you mention that this young lady ain't help yo' pitiful ass, I'll expose you to your whole community, then personally kill you myself. Ya understand?"

Saleem nodded, then Gerod slapped the shit out of him with his half dead hand.

"Now apologize to the young lady and get the fuck in yo' cell!"

"I-I'm so-"

"Jus' gone to ya cell Morgan." Shaneka said through gritted teeth. Saleem wiped his face with his shirt and trotted off to his cell.

"Thanks Mr. Evans." Shaneka said sincerely.

"No problem lil lady. It was bound to happen sooner or later. I'm just glad that it was me instead of our boy." he said motioning his head in C.J.'s direction, then added, "He wouldn't have made it home if he would've done it."

The mere thought of C.J. not coming home made her soul freeze. Before turning to go open the door, Gerod made her freeze in her tracks. "Is it his?"

"I beg yo par—"

"The baby." Gerod said cutting Shaneka off. "Ya smell pregnant, and ya look it too!" Gerod's suspicion was confirmed when Shaneka looked at C.J. as if she would melt.

C.J. looked at his Godfather quizzically. A lot of boys grew up idolizing fake pimps and gangsters, but C.J knew that the man who stood before him was a true original. Original Gangster at its finest.

No one noticed the trio disappear through the upper corridor, except Saleem who stood at his cell door with hot tears streaming down his face. No one noticed him neither. The Lakers were down by 17, and Kobe couldn't buy a basket.

CHAPTER 10

Gerod dropped the duffle bags and box in the far corner of the unfinished interviewing room. "Ya'll play nice now, ya hear?" Gerod told the couple with a big grin on his face, as he backed back out into the corridor.

"So this is it." C.J. said pulling Shaneka into his body.

"Fa now. Oh yeah, I got'cha lights cut on and I bought some new furniture. I opened a bank account out ther' with $8,000. The furniture came to a lil' under $20,000, but I put that on my Visa. I brought $9,000 with me. I'll drive back out ther' next month an' bring back enough to hold me an' the baby ova til ya get out. Baby, ya—"

C.J. cut Shaneka off by covering her mouth with his.

"Please me whil' I please you." Shaneka said after breaking the kiss.

"Say what?"

"I want to taste *my* dick whil' you taste *yo'* pussy."

"'69 was a good year, huh?"

"Ain't that the year Crippin' started?"

Turned on by her knowledge of his history, C.J. began unbuttoning her uniform while she tugged at his pants. They were naked in record time.

C.J. laid on the floor. Shaneka straddled his face and leaned forward, taking the head of *her* dick in her mouth. Shaneka sucked viciously to make sure that *her* dick could hold no more blood, then began slow neckin' while keeping her gag reflexes tight. Not to be outdone, C.J. licked Shaneka's clit, then sucked on it as if his life depended on it.

C.J. reached up and tried to insert a finger, but Shaneka reached back and grabbed his wrist, stopping the erotic moment.

"Catch' chit Bay- Beee!", Shaneka screamed as she pushed out two quarter rolls of *'Sour Diesel'*.

"That should hold ya' for a minute. Now make me cum niggah!" Shaneka demanded.

They both returned to their previous mission.

Realizing that he had some Halls cough drops in his pocket, C.J. drug his pants over to where he could reach them. Shaneka was so caught up sucking, slobbering, slow neckin', and moaning that she didn't notice his movement.

Shaneka jerked when something hotter than a regular tongue hit her clit. Before she could pull away, C.J. clamped his arms around her thighs and locked her in. The only thing that Shaneka could do to keep from screaming was to stuff her mouth full of dick. Her tonsils vibrating on *her* dick, caused C.J. to squirm.

Once he knew that her clit was completely mentholated, C.J. pulled back and blew cold air on it, which caused Shaneka to make a false start out of the starting blocks.

Having his tongue coated in menthol, C.J. drove his tongue

deep into *his* pussy, then in *his* ass, and repeated this rhythm until they both exploded in each other's mouths. Neither could move as they both swallowed more cum than they ever imagined their stomachs could hold.

Knowing time wasn't on their side, the couple quickly dressed. C.J. knocked on the door twice. Gerod knocked back once indicating that the coast was clear.

C.J. and Gerod walked back into the dorm first. All they could hear were screams, hoots, and hollering, while inmates danced in celebration. Kobe had scored 32 straight points for the Lakers. With less than a minute left in the 4th quarter, L.A. was up by four.

The duo stopped by Gerod's cell.

"Boy, I know yo' mouth ain't right, but let's burn somethin'!" Gerod said pointing at the dried pussy juice in the corner of C.J.'s mouth.

C.J. looked in the mirror, then made a wide sweep with his tongue in a circular motion and smiled.

"Better yet, you smoke your own an' I'll smoke mine, lil nasty fucka!" Gerod said half joking.

C.J. tried to hand Gerod one of the quarter rolls.

"Now playa, if you want me to have some, then you open it and give it to me. Dig it son, never let another man anywhere near your pussy. You hear me nigga! Man, a nigga will lie, cross you out, or even kill you over *your* pussy if he gets a whiff of it! Guard yo' bitch like you do yo' life! I'm an O.G. to you, true. Hell, I'm your father nigga! No matter how much you trust me, never leave her alone with me. You know why?"

"Cause you'd fuck her?"

"No nigga. Cause once you do it once, it becomes habitual. The next nigga you think you can trust will try his hand, so why put yourself in an unneeded position."

C.J. nodded as he handed Gerod a joint that he didn't lick. After firing up the joint Gerod asked C.J., "You run your car, right?"

Again, C.J. only nodded.

"Well that makes you the king. What's the most dominating piece on the chess board?"

"Your bitch!" C.J. answered before lighting his joint off of Gerod's.

"Damn right! Now what happens to a king when his most trusted piece gets taken?" Before C.J. could answer Gerod blurted out, "Mayhem! You see, you'd start making rash decisions that could cost you the game of life. I see realness in her eyes, don't fuck up a great thing boy!"

They finished their joints in silence. As Gerod tried to knock some weed out of the quarter roll with a pen, C.J. grabbed his wrist and said, "That's all you, O.G. this is mine." showing Gerod the second roll, then licking it.

"Nasty motha fucka! You's a nasty, nasty nigga." Gerod said with a smile.

Shaneka appeared at the door and told C.J. to meet her at the office, then look at Gerod and said, "Umm, Mr. Evans. I kno—"

"Just take good care of my son. That's all I ask of you."

"Yes sir! By the way, Ms. Fosta said she wouldn't min' breakin' ya off wit a lil sumthin' sumthin'."

"You talkin' 'bout *Basketball Booty Judy*, Ms. Foster?"

"Yes sir."

"Now why would she tell you somethin' like that?" Gerod asked, tryin to keep his heart from jumping out of his chest.

"Well ya see, ma daddy was from around her. Ma momma is from H-Town. I've been livin' down ther' since I was 5. When ma daddy got sick, I moved out her' to take care of Im. To make this story short, Ms. Foster is ma daddy's sister. Tomorrow, call Ms. Fosta Moody Booty. She'll know I done told ya'. If ya' want, I can get ya' a job up ther' in psychology. She'd like that."

Gerod couldn't contain his excitement any longer. "Yeah. I'd like that too. Hook it up!"

"Have a good night, dad. Go see ya girl tomorrow, unless ya scur'd of pus—"

"Girl, I put the *'p'* in pussy! Now gon' and go holla at your man before we have to lock down."

Shaneka waved goodbye, then strutted down the catwalk. *Yep, they definitely are family* Gerod thought as he stared at Shaneka's ass swaying from side to side.

Damn!

***		***		***		***

"I didn't get ta tell ya horny ass how shit went down today." Shaneka told C.J. exactly how the earlier events with the warden transpired. Shaneka never ceased to amaze C.J. with her craftiness.

They talked until it was time for lockdown. C.J. stayed out to sweep the floor and take the trash out. Once outside, Shaneka stared up at C.J. as if saying *Goodbye!*

C.J., knowing his woman, assured, "Naw Mrs. Johnson, don't ce lookin' like that. This is just the conclusion to the first chapter. The next chapter is when "*we*" really cegin." They embraced and kissed away the first chapter of their lives.

CHAPTER 11

3 years later (2011): The movement begins

C.J., Dub, and Lace went to pick Romeo up from the Salvation Army (dubbed as a federal halfway house) in a stretched Hummer. Eight provocatively clad women accompanied them.

When Romeo saw the Hummer, he *Crip-walked* towards it and stopped. The driver, Creecha (creature), a former Navy Seal, (who earned his moniker by his physical features) and prison comrade, got out and greeted his friend.

"Damn nigga! Who you workin' for wit all that ice on?" Romeo asked looking from Creecha's iced out chain, to his Dickies, Chucks, and wife beater.

"Welcome home nigga!" Creecha said reaching out to embrace his friend with a homie hug. Just then the back window came down and the prettiest face Romeo had seen within the past 13.5 years, asked, "Can I get a hug too?"

Instantly Romeo's manhood stood at full attention.

"I'll give yo' fine ass more than a hug!" Romeo stated, while grabbing his crotch at the same time.

In a trance, Romeo gravitated towards the back of the Hummer. As he got closer, the lady stepped out the truck to give Romeo a full view of what he'd soon be getting. Having looked at so many Straight Stuntin' magazines, Romeo guessed that she was about 5'2' without heels; with a 42DD-24-42 frame. Whoever this broad was, *Romeo wanted it all!*

"I'll take care of that, Baby." she said removing Romeo's hand from his dick, then began caressing it with her own hand. "Shit nigga, you got enough dick fo' all of us!"

"All of who?" Romeo asked curiously. Hearing that, the other 7 women stepped out.

Damn, these might be the Now and Later ladies. All these damn flavors Romeo said to himself, as he admired eight of Gods greatest gifts to the world.

C.J., Dub, and Lace, crept out the back door on the opposite side. They put their hoods on and drew their water guns. "What's poppin', son?" C.J. asked in his best New York accent.

"Turn around and we'll wet ya head, kid!" Lace added, trying to show his acting abilities.

Romeo looked at the women, then Creecha, searching their eyes and body language for a motive. Standing strong, he asked Creecha, "It's like that, huh Cuz?" still trying to figure out who he had beef with out of New York.

"I get paid for what I do! Man…fuck this fool. Wet his ass up!" Creecha barked.

The women faked scream as the trio proceeded to wet Romeo up with their *Super Soakers*. The first burst hit Romeo in the neck, causing him to drop and grab the back of his neck, checking for a wound.

The entire crew burst out into hysterical laughter. "Welcome home, Cuz!" they all screamed in unison, as the trio continued to spray Romeo until he was completely soaked.

"Let's get the fuck up outta here!" Creecha insisted while ushering the women back into the Hummer. The quartet hopped in behind them. Creecha jumped in behind the wheel and drove off into the afternoon heat.

***   ***   ***   ***

"Man, it's good to see ya'll fools again!" Romeo said to his homies while staring at the women.

"Yeah, it's all love here, Loc!" Lace shot back. Dub looked at C.J., and C.J. nodded.

"Dig it Cuz, we got a master suite at the Holiday Inn. We're gonna squat there while you go holla at your family." Dub said to his comrade.

C.J. added, "Let 'em know we're throwin' you a party for the entire weekend. But tonight's your night."

"Sheeit. It ain't no fun if the homies can't have none." Romeo said in his best Nate Dogg voice. They all Crip whistled their approval on that.

Creecha dropped Romeo off at his mother's house on Martin Luther King Jr. Blvd. Out of instinct, he turned and walked down to the Big V barbershop, that sat between the store and the projects.

So much had changed. When Romeo left the "Free World", MLK was Boundary St. A white man owned the store then, now some African cat stood behind the bulletproof glass. *I guess Ro-Klan, (the nickname for Rowan County) is finally steppin' it's game up* Romeo thought.

All of a sudden, a carbon copy of himself stepped out of the store and caused Romeo to stand still with his mouth open. Bald headed, blue Dickies, blue Chuck Taylors, a wife beater, and a blue Crip rag hanging out of his back-left pocket, RoRo was spittin' some teenage game to a gorgeous redbone.

"Laura!" Romeo spat.

"Ro…Romeo, is that you?" she asked in a nervous tone. At the sound of his father's name, RoRo said, "Pop?"

"Yeah, I'm finally home."

RoRo abandoned his gangsta persona and ran over and hugged his father. Stepping back, RoRo said, "Damn Pops, what's crackin'?"

Romeo gave Laura a hug, and said that it was nice seeing her again, then turned his attention back to his son.

"What'cha mean, it was nice seeing me? Nigga, I've been waitin'—"

"Look bitch! Don't play ya self. I ain't mad at yo triflin' ass, I just ain't fuckin' with you!"

"Baby, shit got hard out here. I was gonna write, and come see you, but—"

"But that bitch ass nigga you left the courtroom with wouldn't let y—"

Romeo stopped mid-way through his sentence then said, "Speakin' of the bitch ass nigga!" he continued when he saw Alonzo coming out the barbershop.

Looking at his car and not seeing Laura, he turned to his left and saw her all up in Romeo's face. "Laura!" Alonzo barked.

"What the fuck are you doin'?" he questioned, reaching for his pistol.

Romeo clutched where RoRo had previously been standing and became frantic not knowing his son's whereabouts.

On some fake ass gangsta shit, Alonzo walked up and bitch slapped Laura, grabbed her by the arm, and pushed her towards his Q-45.

Still feeling himself, he stepped closer to Romeo. "Yeah nigga, what was all that tough guy shit you was poppin' while you were caged up?" Alonzo kept yacking, but Romeo's mind was only concerned with his son's whereabouts. *Where'd that lil nigga go?*

The thought was abandoned when Romeo saw RoRo emerge from behind the dumpster holding what looked like a .44 magnum Super Redhawk. RoRo crept up behind Alonzo, then swung the barrel around and caught him on the bridge of the nose.

Alonzo dropped his 9mm and grabbed his nose, while squealing like a pig. "Pop, go to Big Mommas house, I'll holla at'cha later on."

"RoRo, chill Cuz."

"Naw Pop, you just got home. This here is my turf. Big Screw said to hold this shit down, and that's exactly what I'm gonna do!" RoRo boasted, then added, "You earned yours out here. Let me earn mine!" he demanded.

"Ce smart Cuz. Too many witnesses out here."

RoRo looked around, and for the first-time paid attention to all the onlookers.

"You right O.G." RoRo stated, then Crip whistled. Out of nowhere, ten lil Tiny Locs came running up to RoRo.

Alonzo stood, shaking when he saw the pernicious look in their eyes.

"Put that bitch in the trunk and take him to the spot. I'll see ya'll in one minute." RoRo instructed.

"One homie."

"One."

The Tiny Locs threw Alonzo in the trunk of his own car as he pled and begged for mercy. They snatched Laura out of the passenger's seat and threw her in the trunk with Alonzo. Four of them got in and drove off. *Just another day in the Kitchen.*

RoRo looked around again at the wondering but knowing eyes wouldn't dare stare back into his. Everyone knew what would happen to them, or their family, or someone close to them if any word got out about what had just transpired, and the information had come out of their mouths.

In RoRo's 17 years of life he had earned a reputation that preceded his father's.

Romeo had heard stories about RoRo through Big Buff, a notorious stickup kid who he befriended at Morganton Highrise, a youth prison in the foothills of North Carolina. Originally from Liberty City, Miami, Florida, Big Buff ran from Florida after stealin' 100 kilos of grade-A heroin and killing a Baby Zoe Pound member that was on security detail that night.

Since then, Big Buff's mother, grandmother, and baby sister had machetes shoved into their vaginas and were ripped all the way up to their breast plates. This was 20 years ago. After a few more moves to ensure his daughter's future would be secure, Big Buff was going to go back to Miami and kill as many Zoe's as he could before they killed him.

From what Big Buff had told Romeo, RoRo was more dangerous than him and Buff combined. RoRo only had love for his grandmother, Big Momma, his father, Big Screw, and the rest of his set. He loved few and respected even less.

"Come on O.G., let's go get some grub." RoRo said in such a calm manner that all Romeo could do was shake his head, then followed his son back to Big Mommas house.

CHAPTER 12

Sitting on his mother's front porch, Romeo sat and listened as RoRo give him the rundown about the set. All Romeo could do was smile and nod his head. Looking at his son, Romeo felt as though he'd just been reborn. He now would live through his son.

"Pop!"

"Yeah?"

"Ya listenin'?"

"Yeah lil nigga, how can I not? It's like hearing my own thoughts, son."

Not one to show too much emotion, RoRo stood up and turned around. With his back to Romeo, he lifted his shirt. Romeo leaned forward so he could read the tattooed inscription.

Tru Definition Øf A 'G', that's what my Pøps is 2 me.', then the poem read:

Many cats cømplain when their Pøps ain't N their life. Yeah Pøps cein' gøne has caused me strife.
Cut I'm cut from a different cløth, with a much sharper knife.

Physically he mayce gøne, cut mentally, and spiritually he's always here.
That's why I'm never afraid, and I døn't understand fear.
He's my herø, and I'm his seed.
Crippin' my want. He's my need.
Can't støp. Wøn't støp.
That's høw we Crip. Just ask my Pøp!

Romeo pulled his son's shirt down and said, "That's tight." RoRo turned and walked off the porch when *Colors* ringtone chimed. Romeo looked on, amazed at how far technology had advanced. He pulled out the cellphone that C.J. had given him and marveled at all of its features of which he had no clue about as to how to even turn it on.

"Yo Pop!" RoRo screamed from the side of the house. Romeo got up and walked to the corner of the porch.

"They're, there! You tryin' to go handle this now or what?"

Romeo shook his head no.

Confused, RoRo asked, "Do you want the homies to put that work in?"

Again, Romeo shook his head no.

"Let me hit ya'll cack in a minute." RoRo said while giving his father a questioning look.

Seeing the vague look in his son's eyes, Romeo began to school him, "Dig it Ro, too many motherfuckas saw what went down, so now ain't the time. Where you got them fools at anyway?"

"Out on Old Concord Road. You know, left past the fairgrounds." RoRo answered.

"Keep the bitch there. Have one of the Loc's to ride back through here with Alonzo driving. Tell 'em to ride in the back outta sight, with the steel to that fool's neck. You dig what I'm sayin'?"

"No."

"You want him to ce seen drivin' his own shit after what happened earlier. These fools last seen the lil homies throw his bitch ass in the trunk, so when they see him drivin' his own shit, niggas will abandon the thought of the homies jackin' his ass. Plus, it'll keep the heat off the Kitchen."

Nodding, RoRo said, "I'm feelin' that." He called his left-hand man back and gave him the instructions.

"What time does your G-ma get home?"

"Midnight. Why, what's craccin'?"

"Son, tonight you gonna celebrate with your ol' man. We'll surprise Big Momma in the morning."

"Where we celebratin'?"

"Once I figure out how to use this damn phone, you'll see."

"O.K.! That's the new I-Phone. Give it here."

RoRo tried to explain all the features of the phone, but Romeo was beyond lost. "See if you can find some numbers in it." he asked his son.

After scrolling through several screens, RoRo found the saved numbers, and showed Romeo how to scan through them.

"Yeah, call that one." he said, pointing to C.J.'s name.

"Geah?"

"Come scoop me." They both hung up without saying another word.

Creecha pulled up 20 minutes later. "Now that's what's craccin'!" RoRo said gawking at the stretched Hummer.

"Let's move!" Romeo said to his mesmerized son. They climbed in the back, and Creecha screeched off.

“This is my son RoRo, Creecha. RoRo, this is my nigga Creecha from the other side of the fence.” They both acknowledged each other’s presence with a head nod.

“Hey homie, them bitches been puttin’ on a show. We were just waitin’ on yo’ ass fo’ the grand finale.” Creecha said with a big smile on his ugly mug while looking in the rear-view mirror.

CHAPTER 13

C.J., Dub, and Lace were so caught up in the female orgy that they didn't even notice the other trio entering the suite. RoRo couldn't believe his eyes or luck. All eight women were lying in the middle of the floor, connected mouth to pussy. The sweet aroma of female excretions overrode the euphoria scent that was being passed around.

Dub was first to notice the trio. *That's gotta be that niggas son.* he thought as he looked back and forth between father and son. Smiling, Dub joked, "Damn Cuz, you needed help with the pussy. I see you brought your twin wit'cha."

C.J., Dub, and Lace all greeted the Crip clad teenager with the universal Crip shake. It threw RoRo off because he'd never seen it done before.

Reading his son's body language, Romeo spoke up. "Lil Cuz, that's how we shake in the feds ce cause all Crips are one car...I mean all together."

Not knowing or caring, RoRo began set trippin'. "You mean you kick it wit Cheese toast niggas and Nappy heads?"

Happy that none of his comrades were East Coast or Neighborhood Crips, Romeo put the nail in the coffin. “Yeah, and the Damus are our allies in their too.”

“What!”

“Dig it Ro, we’ll chop it up ‘bout all this later. For now, let’s get this party crackin’.”

“Yeah, O.K.’’ RoRo said not satisfied with how the conversation was going. *Yeah, it’s Pops first day home, so I’mma chill. But this conversation is far from over.*

The women were the bonding agent that sealed the father & son union. Dub, C.J., Creecha, and Lace went into the adjoined room to allow the father and son to really enjoy their selves. They’d already had theirs.

***   ***   ***   ***

The following morning, C.J. rented a Chevy Malibu to take Romeo to see his P.O. They first went shopping at Concord Mills mall. Although Romeo preferred a more simpler dress code, C.J. still spent close to $15,000 on his homies attire, as he’d done for the rest of his comrades.

“Cuz, as soon as my check comes—”

C.J. waved him off.

“This ain’t shit Cuz. Dig it, I’m takin’ you by to holla at’cha mom cefore I take you to see your P.O. Then we’re goin’ to get you some licenses. After that, I got some real shit to show you.” C.J. said as Romeo sat and bobbed his head while 2Pac ranted on about how *Life Goes On*.

Romeo’s mother was too tired to really spend any quality time with her son but vowed to take the whole weekend off so she could attend the weekend's festivities.

Romeo's visit with the P.O went as expected. However, what Romeo wasn't expecting was having to spend 2 hours in the D.M.V., but was happy when he walked out a licensed driver.

Outside, C.J. tossed Romeo the keys and got in the passenger's seat.

"Where to?" Romeo questioned as he got behind the wheel.

"Head to Woodleaf."

"What's out there?"

"Just drive Cuz, you'll see in 7 minutes."

The duo rode in silence the whole way, except for when C.J. gave directions on where to turn. They pulled up to a triple wide trailer. A Cadillac DHS, Chevy Cavalier, and a GSXR 1300 Hayabusa sat parked in a small cemented area. *Nice lil set up*, Romeo thought as he took the whole scene in.

"Whose spot is this?"

"One of my homies just moved here. He's from the Kitchen too!"

"Who? Big Screw?"

"Naw Loc, just come on." C.J. said as he got out the car.

C.J. pulled out an extra set of keys from his pocket and tossed them to Romeo. "Welcome home Cuz."

"You mean…this—"

"Yeah, this is yours Cuz."

Inside, C.J. gave Romeo a quick tour of his new home, then grabbed two 40's of Old English out of the refrigerator. After they sat down at the kitchen table, Romeo asked, "Damn Cuz, what all this set you back for?"

"That's not important. Your loyalty to the cause is! You, Dub, Lace, and Creecha got the exact same setup that I got. Minus the equipment, that is. We all got 15 acres of land in our respected states. Everything is registered under a non-existing corporation."

"Did you do this all by yourself?"

"Naw, me and the wife did; with the help of Popi."

"Wife? Popi?"

"Yeah, I married Ms. Ingles from Edgefield."

"You mean Super Bo…Damn! My bust Cuz!"

"No need for that Cuz, you didn't know. It's not disrespect. Shit, plus I know my wife is blessed with a bangin' ass body." C.J. said almost boasting.

"I used to wonder about you two, but I shrugged it off. It wasn't my business no way. Anyway, who the hell is Popi?"

"You remember the old Columbian everybody used to call Popi? Well he set me up with his wife. She had 1000 keys delivered to my front door inside of some statues. She charged me $4,000 a key, and I knocked them off for $15,000. I moved a thousand a week, for 6 months straight. You do the math."

Romeo sat trying to calculate the numbers in his mind. Seeing his homie struggling, C.J. blurted out, "Cuz, I made $286,000,000 in six months! Now, I'd never try to buy your friendship or loyalty. Those things can't ce bought! You've proven your loyalty to me, and your set. Now it remains to ce seen if you'll put forth the same energy to this movement."

"What movement?"

"The one I mentioned in the joint."

"Oh yeah, something about riddin' the world of snitches."

"Exactly!"

"O.K., when do we start. And where do we start. The world is full of that shit right now."

"After the party this weekend, we all goin' out to my pad in

Colorado. I'll give everybody the rundown and layout then. You know as much as the rest, so don't trip. Enough about that for now. Let's get cack to the Inn. O.K., look in the trunk of the Caddy."

Romeo popped the trunk.

"Damn! Who,…I mean...What the fuck?"

"It's a mill in cash. Leave it there, or take it in the crib, but just hurry the fuck up so we can get back to those freaks!"

Romeo opted to leave it in the trunk. He jumped back in his Cavalier and followed C.J. back to Salisbury.

C.J. rode off content with how everything was falling into place. Romeo smiled as Scarface rapped about how *It Feels Good To Be A Gangsta.*

It damn sho' does Romeo said to himself.

***　　***　　***　　***

C.J. and Romeo arrived in time to catch the Crip Walkin' walk off. All the women were stuffed in the Jacuzzi with Creecha. Dub, Lace, and RoRo all took turns reppin' their sets, and culture. RoRo moved like a second coming of the legendary 'Dancin' Sugar Bear. Everybody was in their own zone. No one suspected that this would be their last weekend together. Although the mood was jubilant, an eerie veil hung over the entire room.

CHAPTER 14

To ensure that no unexpected visitors showed up for the party, they made it an invitation only affair.

C.J. rented Club Rascals for the weekend. They also had a cookout at Dan Nicholas Park where they all partied into the wee hours at the club. During both days it felt like an old-fashioned family reunion. However, the last night brought out the freak in everybody.

On Sunday night it was the original crew, a few turf-rats, as well as a couple other cats who hadn't worn out their welcome.

Big Screw had flown in for the festivities himself. But just as quickly as Screw would appear, he would vanish in the same manner. That was just his style. *Move like a Phantom* he would always say. Big Screw had become one of the most elusive gangstas of all time, making him yet another street legend.

When the stragglers eventually got their bellies full and minds twisted, they started making their exits.

C.J. pulled Romeo to the side and told him. "A Cuz, go holla at'cha mom and let her know you'll ce cack by next weekend. Tomorrow, we start our journey. It's a 30-hour drive, but we'll all take turns at the wheel, so we'll try to make it in 24."

"Yo Cuz, I was thinkin'…Mayce I should bring RoRo." Romeo proposed.

C.J. shook his head in disagreement.

"Naw Cuz! You gotta do your homework first, on family too! Once you've observed the lil nigga, if you still feel like incorporating him into this movement, then his life will ce in your hands."

Romeo tried to understand the logic in C.J.'s statement, but his mind kept reciting the last part of what he said. *His life will ce in your hands…*

C.J. had peeped the uneasiness in Romeo over the past couple of days. C.J. saw first-hand the bond between Romeo and his son. It truly was unbreakable. He also saw the fire in RoRo's eyes. They were the eyes of a heartless killer. *This could be a problem*, C.J. told himself. *Yes, we need ruthlessness, but one must also know when to slaughter, and when not to.*

This is why C.J. told Romeo to go see his mother before they left. If things didn't go according to plan, and Romeo all of a sudden had a change of heart, then this would be the last time Romeo's mom would see her son alive. C.J.'s resolve was very simple: *I won't hesitate to murder whoever stands in the way of this movement. Man, woman, child, friend, or foe. If you cross me, then you gotta go!*

***　　***　　***　　***

C.J. rode shotgun while Creecha drove. They took I-85N to I-

40W. As they rode, C.J. chopped it up with his comrade while the other three gambled on *Madden 2012* in the back of the Hummer.

C.J. and Creecha switched places in St. Louis. C.J. needed the isolation, so he told Creecha to take a nap.

"I got it from here homie." C.J. assured.

"You sure?" Creecha asked before he drifted off.

"Yeah." C.J. said patting his I-Pod, "Face and Pac will keep me goin'."

CHAPTER 15

The crew pulled onto C.J.'s property Tuesday afternoon, shortly after 3:00pm.

C.J. had upgraded his double wide into a triple wide. He'd also purchased a ranch in Mesa, AZ that he and Shaneka occupied as their main place of residence. This was done to keep their lives separate from the movement.

In Arizona, C.J. was just Clevon Johnson; the entrepreneur who had major success in real estate and commercial cleaning. In Denver, C.J. was a *turf* legend. And in Limon, he was just a *country ass nigger.*

Shaneka opened the door upon their arrival. She met C.J. on the front deck with a hug and a brief kiss, then greeted his guests with a sisterly hug.

The interior of C.J.'s house had an Amazonian effect to it. *The decorator must be from South America somewhere.* Romeo thought.

Not wasting any time, they all strode into the master bedroom.

C.J. moved the dresser that sat cater cornered. Pulling the carpet back, he lifted a trap door that exposed a descent of some 20 steps beneath the Earth. The quartet was in awe, as they took in the scenery.

Once they were all in "Headquarters" they saw so much equipment, and heard so many beeps and bleeps, that they knew that this movement was even bigger than any of them would have ever imagined.

There was a small room that could've passed as a music studio directly in front of them. A club-sized bar sat adjacent to the butter soft leather sectional that could seat 20 people. Directly in front of that, was a projection screen. Then to the immediate left was a blue-felted pool table, a foosball table, and an air hockey table. Another room encased an indoor swimming pool.

"Damn, this shit tight!" Creecha said astounded.

"Hell yeah!" Dub cosigned.

Romeo and Lace just looked at each other and smiled.

"Mrs. Johnson, get us some drinks, will ya?" C.J. said to his wife.

Shaneka asked everyone what their drink of choice was, then left to go fill their requests.

"Have a seat homie," C.J. instructed.

The gang all sat around, shootin' the shit, while they waited on their drinks to arrive. Once they had their drinks C.J. looked at Shaneka and said, "Baby, go ahead and get things set up."

Without a word, Shaneka turned and walked towards the studio looking room, placed her palm on a monitor, and the door retracted. Once she passed through the door, it closed behind her.

C.J. stood and raised his glass.

"Today, we etch our names in stone."

They all raised their glasses and toasted to the future. C.J. continued after they all downed their drinks.

"We, with the exception of Creecha, made a pact several years ago. Now that Creecha has joined the movement, today we'll find out for sho' *who's who*. I've spent a lot of money and have taken life threatening risks in order for this meeting to take place. I've also ensured that we were all financially stable in our own personal lives, as well as for what we're about to set off. I'm quite sure ya'll are tired of the delay, so here it is.

We're about to start ridding the world of all these hot ass rats! However, before we do that, we must clean up our own front yards first. The room that my wife just went into is soundproof, so no one will hear your responses. My wife no longer works for the Federal Bureau of Prisons (F.B.O.P.). She is now a federal agent, with C.I.A. credentials backing her.

We're all goin' to ce asked the same questions, while ceing monitored by a polygraph machine. Once this matter is concluded, we'll start mapping things out. Creecha your situation is different, so your questions won't ce the exact ones everybody else gets."

Creecha only nodded.

"So who wants to go first?"

Since everybody just looked at one another, C.J. volunteered himself, "Fuck it, I'll go. It was my vision that created this…so I guess it's only left that I go first."

C.J. stood and waved for Shaneka to buzz him in.

After he took his seat, and the sensors and heart monitor were hooked up, Shaneka began with her interrogation.

"Firs', state 'cha name."

"Clevon Johnson."

"How ol' are ya?"

"38."

"Do ya know ya informant's name? If so, please state it."

"Yes. The fools name is Donald Linworth."

"If the opportunity presented itself, would ya kill 'im?"

"Yes!"

"Would'ja be remorseful if somebody else killed him?"

"No."

"Does this cause really matter to ya'?"

"Yes!"

"Thank you, Mr. Johnson. Your results will be brought to ya at the conclusion of this matter. Please send the nex' man in."

The quartet tried to read C.J.'s facial expression as he exited the room, but as usual, it was an impossible task.

"Next man!" C.J. said going to pour himself another drink. Creecha went next.

"Please state 'cha name fo' me."

"Quentin Heaggins."

"How ol' are ya?"

"48 years young."

"Why are you here?"

"To help out a great friend."

"Would'ja kill anybody for this friend?"

"Without blinkin' an eye Ma'am."

"I take that as a yes. Correct?"

"Yes Ma'am."

"Thank ya Mr. Heaggins. Your results will be ready shortly."

Romeo entered the room next.

"Please state 'cha name."

"Jerome Myers."

"How ol' are ya?"

"36."

"Do ya know ya informant's name? If so, please state it."

"Yes. Jake Rivers."

"If the opportunity presented itself, would you kill him?"

"Yes."

"Would'ja be remorseful if somebody else kilt him?" "Hell no!"

"Does this cause really matter to ya?"

"Yes, it does."

"Thank ya Mr. Myers. Your results will be ready shortly. Please send in the next man."

Lace entered next.

''Please state'cha name."

"Marcus Lacy."

"Do ya know ya informant's name? If so, please state it."

"Yeah, I know. It was my stankin' ass daughter's mother!"

"Please state her name."

"Valerie Black."

"If the opportunity presented itself, would'ja kill her?"

"Of course not! That's my kid's mom."

"So, you'd feel remorse if somebody else kilt her on your behalf?"

Lace pondered on the question for several seconds, then blurted out an unconvincing "No!"

"Thank ya Mr. Lacy. Your results will be ready shortly." A queasy feeling started to churn in the pit of Laces stomach as he stood up.

"This shit's crazy." he mumbled as he walked out of the interrogating room. "Yo Dub, you up homie."

Before Dub could get through the door, Lace spoke through clenched teeth. "Cuz, somethin' ain't right. I can feel it." Dub gave him a confused look then stepped into the "Room of Truth".

Creecha gave C.J. a strange look as the Duo pretended not to notice the exchange. Romeo's back was turned, so he missed it.

Shaneka went through all the formalities, then started her interrogation.

"State'cha name fo' me."

"William Andrews."

"How ol' are ya?"

"38."

"Do ya know ya informant's name? If so, please state it."

"Yeah! It was that bitch-ass buster Nutso from Grape St.!" Dub screamed.

"Calm down Mr. Andrews! Ya' bout to fuck up ma equipment!" Shaneka said in an equally aggressive tone.

"My bad Ms. Johnson."

"Shaneka will do."

"All day Shaneka. Let's get this shit over with."

Shaneka waited until Dub's heart rate subsided before she continued.

"Now Mr. Andrews, I take it that if given the opportunity, you'd kill this Nutso. Am I co'rect?"

"Damn right you are." Dub replied in a much calmer tone.

Shaneka skipped her next question and then asked, "Does this cause really matta to ya?"

"Yes, it does." Dub answered sincerely.

"Thank ya. You can leave now."

Dub removed all the sensor pads, then got up to leave. "Dub?"

"Yeah Shaneka?"

"I trust ya as much as my husband does."

Dub threw up his set, then walked out of the room. The door

closed immediately after he got on the other side.

Shaneka turned off the equipment, gathered the test results, then went to make everybody a new round of drinks. She included herself this time.

After each man had their fresh drink, they all toasted to the future.

"To the strong, and demise for the weak." They said in unison, then clanked their glasses together and swallowed their drinks in a single gulp.

C.J. spoke to the entire room.

"As ya'll know, my wife is an expert at giving' and readin' these tests. Everyone in this room knows how important this movement is to me and those who hustle to survive; how important it is for those who took their time like men, although they were given basketball score numbers. For those that'll never see the streets again, I've dedicated the rest of my life to riddin' the world of hot ass snitches and their families that have violated the code of silence! This is my callin' and that's why I've rewarded my comrades with tokens of my appreciation. This here is the key to our success." C.J. said sweeping his arm at all the monitors and equipment.

Before he could finish his speech, Lace fell to the floor. Fully aware of his surroundings, he asked "What the fuck's wrong wit me? I can't feel shit!"

C.J. looked down at his fallen comrade and said, "Shaneka was instructed to put a paralytic agent in everyone's drink that failed the test; including mine!"

"How did I fail C...Cuz?" Lace asked sorrowfully as tears began to escape their duct.

Shaneka leaned forward and answered, "Ya failed by accepting betrayal ova the movement. You can't be down with this you weak ass niggah!" then kicked Lace in the face as hard as she could. Everybody looked on in shock at how gangsta Shaneka really was, but then they all took back their surprise once they remembered who her husband was and how he got down.

"C…Cuz" Lace pled as blood seeped from his freshly inflicted wound.

C.J.'s whole demeanor changed from cold to freezing; worse than anyone in the room had ever witnessed. "Look bitch! You ain't for the movement, so fuck you!" C.J. spewed.

After he paused for a few seconds C.J. calmed his nerves and said, "I ain't gonna kill you, but *we* are goin' to kill your bitch! As a matter of fact, where's the money I gave yo' bitch ass?"

"It's in a safe at my crib. Why Cuz?"

C.J. kicked Lace in the same place Shaneka previously did, deepening the laceration.

"Don't Cuz me you buster ass bitch! Since yo' bitch ass must know, I'm goin' to set up an anonymous account for your daughter."

"If you ain't gonna kill me, then why you gotta set up an account for her?"

"Cause now she's considered an orphan! Ya'll help me drag his bitch ass to the pool!"

"Please ma-man. I can't move!"

Creecha and Romeo both grabbed a leg. Dub held the door while C.J. grabbed both arms. They carried Lace into the pool room then tossed him in. Lace's screams subsided, as he was submerged.

Dub spoke "Cuz, I ain't trippin', but I thought you said you wasn't goin' to kill him."

"I'm not. He'll kill himself whenever he decides to breathe again." C.J. informed

They all walked away from the pool to go celebrate the movement, and the death of a traitor. No one spoke on what had just taken place, but it continued to play out over and over again in each of their minds.

CHAPTER 16

At 2:00am C.J. drug Lace's corpse down to his hog pen. Dub, Romeo, and Creecha all followed all followed behind C.J. puzzled, until they heard the hogs squealing. They then knew that Lace was going to be their next meal.

Everyone was in their own zone as they watched the hogs tear the flesh from Lace's bones.

"Yo' Cuz, do they eat bones too?" Romeo asked.

"Yeah! But I'm gonna throw his in there." C.J. said pointing to an acid pit several yards away.

Once all the flesh was torn off of Laces bones, C.J. used a yard rake to drag the bones over to the fence and pulled them over. The ligaments kept the skeleton intact, making it easy to pull everything over at one time. After tossing Laces' remains in the acid pit, they all went back inside.

***　　***　　***　　***

"So what now Cuz?" Dub asked.

"We'll clean up our shit first then we'll work on the rest of the country. Eventually, we'll go international."

" So what...we gonna just kill everybody that's a snitch? I mean...I'm wit' it, I'm just curious." Romeo inquired.

"First and foremost, we must always cover our tracks. Creecha is goin' to train us to ce assassins; not killers." C.J. said in a tone a college professor would use. "There is a difference, you know."

"What's the difference." Dub asked.

Creecha spoke up, "Killers get caught, assassins don't! Killers are sloppy, assassins are precise. Killers brag and some want to get caught for the recognition. Assassins want their causes justified but seek no attention. Killers act on instinct. Assassins are impulsive. My job is to make sure that we all get away; plain and simple. I'll also train you for C.Q.B."

"What the hell is C.Q.B.?" C.J. asked.

"Close quarter battles. You never know when you'll have to use your hands or a small instrument to conquer your opposition. I'm going to teach you how to break down and assemble three different sniper rifles. The Galil, SOCOM II, and the Walther Wa 2000. You'll also learn to fire them properly, along with an MPS and a Stoner SR25. The AK-47 has nothin' on that badboy!" With a devilish grin, Creecha added, "We'll begin training once our initial agenda has been taken care of."

"The firs' order of business is Valerie Black." Shaneka said, handing C.J. a manila folder.

"This is the bitch that cost Lace his life." C.J. said showing his team a glossy 8x10 photo of Valerie. "She's a professor at the University of Memphis. She lives close to the campus, on Buford Ellington S. Dr. For now, we'll make these murders appear like random acts of violence. We don't want things to look orchestrated. We should ce finished with the preliminaries within a weeks' time. We're headed to Ten-A-Key in a few hours. This is it homies. I'll holla back in 7 minutes." C.J. then grabbed Shaneka's hand and headed up the stairs.

An hour later, he returned. Descending the stairs with an armload of blankets C.J. said "We're a team, left?" The trio appreciated the fact that C.J. would leave the comforts of a woman to be with his team right before the first battle got underway. C.J.'s hospitality was also held with high regards, but it was his vision that they all admired; plus, his GANGSTA.

They loved that shit!

CHAPTER 17

When they arrived in East Memphis, rush hour was in full swing. Commuters were burning up Buford Ellington. The quartet rode past Valerie's residence slowly, so they could scan the house with a high-resolution TR Thermal Imaging Monitor.

"No one's in there." Creecha announced, holding up the monitor so that everyone could see it.

"If someone would have occupied the residence, green and yellow dots would have appeared showing all of their movements. Red would mean that they were stationary."

As Creecha finished explaining the functions of the monitor, an off-duty campus police officer drove past them and turned into Valerie's driveway.

"Fuck! Who...what the fuck is that motherfucka doin' goin' over there?" Creecha said banging his fist against the steering wheel.

"Calm down homie. That's our way in. Turn around Cuz. We'll flash these credentials on dude, then sit and wait on her to get home. This is plan C." C.J. said smiling.

"What happened to plan B?" Creecha asked.

"You know bees are only good for makin' honey."

Creecha made a 3-point U-turn in the middle of the residential street, then pulled the Crown Victoria alongside the campus police car.

Hearing the car doors slam, Jerimiah Layne opened Valerie's front door and was greeted by four middle aged Black men. Two were dressed as street thugs while the other two were dressed in tailor-fitted suits.

The two dressed as thugs appeared to be law-enforcement agents because they had badges hanging from around their necks. The other two produced identical looking badges from their inside breast pockets.

Holding out his F.B.I. replica badge C.J. spoke up. "We're here to see a… Ms. Valerie Black."

Not sure if the badges were real or not, Jerimiah closely examined Dub's badge as if he really knew what he was looking for. He didn't dare look in Creecha's direction too long. *That's one ugly motherfucka* Jerimiah thought.

"What's this about?" Jerimiah asked.

"Look rent-a-cop! This is an ongoing federal investigation. Do I need to call headquarters and have them call your supervisor to inform them that you're interfering with our investigation? As a matter of fact, do you want to be included in this conspiracy?" Dub said in a tone above normal.

Needing his job, Jerimiah didn't question the thugged out cop. Even though things didn't seem right, he wasn't about to get caught up in something that didn't pertain to him. Jerimiah had enough problems of his own. What Jerimiah did know was that whoever these guys were, they were not to be fucked with.

"Well...as you can see, she's not here officers." Jerimiah indicated by pointing to the driveway.

"We'd like to wait for her inside. That's if it's not a problem." C.J. said in a mild tone.

Against his better judgement, Jerimiah stepped aside allowing them to enter.

The quartet entered the foyer, taking in the moderately decorated house. *Hardwood floors for a hardheaded bitch!* Romeo thought. They all sat at the dining room table and waited on the star of the show to arrive.

CHAPTER 18

Valerie pulled up to her home frustrated.

"What the fuck could they want now?" She said as she grabbed her briefcase and stepped out of her Range Rover. "They ain't 'bout to fuck up my groove. Shit, Mr. Short Dick just got paid and I need my cut. They gotta go!"

Hearing the front door open and close, everyone remained still.

"Jerimiah, I didn't kno—"

Valerie's voice was caught in her throat as the faces before her caught her off guard. She gave C.J. and *I know you* look. The other faces, with the exception of Creecha's, started to register. Before Valerie could make a retreat, C.J. stood up and introduced himself as Agent Marrow.

C.J. extended his right hand, then produced his fake credentials. Valeria reached for C.J.'s hand, but a left hook caught her square in the jaw, knocking her out cold.

Confused, Jerimiah made a move towards C.J., but stopped abruptly when a piece of cold steel met his temple.

"Don't play hero Homie. This ain't your fight Cuz." Dub said coldly.

"Ya'll Loc's?" Jerimiah asked after hearing Dub's dialect.

"All day!" Romeo boasted.

Not knowing what umbrella, they fell under (or caring) Jerimiah broke his shirt open, exposing his *gang-blasted* upper body.

"Five Deuce Hoover here!" Jerimiah said throwing up a Hoover *'H'*.

Creecha walked over and pulled Jerimiah's shirt down over his shoulders. C.J. nodded confirmation that he was properly blasted up. Then the long line of questioning came pouring in.

"How long you done known this bitch?" Dub asked.

"Do you know why we're here?" C.J. inquired.

"What's crackin' with this cop shit?" Romeo asked.

"Cefore I get into all that, where ya'll from?"

"Dig it Homie, til we figure *you* out *we* askin' the fuckin' questions, understand?" C.J. said giving Jerimiah a look as saying *You'd better!*

"Yeah...I can dig it, but on some *'G'* shit, what's crackin'?"

"Gimme your license and your story. If you check out, you live. If not, *two* motherfuckas are dyin' in this bitch today!" C.J. said with a slight menace. He then looked at Creecha. "Strap that bitch up." C.J. instructed, then tossed Creecha some plastic restraints.

After securing Valerie, Creecha slapped her viciously across the face.

Before she could scream, Creecha knocked Valeria out cold again. He then reached under her skirt and pulled down her panty hose grabbing her thong. Creecha snatched them in an upward motion, causing the thin material to tear into Valerie's pussy. The excruciating pain caused her to wake back up, only to pass out again from shock.

Creecha stuffed Valeria's thong into her mouth and used the panty hose to secure it in place. They all looked at an unfazed Jerimiah.

"Talk nigga!" Creecha yelled.

"O.K. we— the Hoovers had East and West Memphis on lock with the syrup and pills. But the day they raided all of our spots; I was outta town handlin' some other shit. To make a long story short, I was never on wire or camera. I stayed in the cut, but the MPD kept harrassin' a *'G'* ever since those raids, and the feds keep lettin' me know that they're watchin' and will eventually get me. They're just waitin' on me to slip. They pop up everywhere I go, so I said *Fuck it! I'll get a job.* That's how I met her." Jerimiah finished his statement by pointing down to a wiggling Valerie.

"So what's crackin' wit' yo' homies?" C.J. asked.

"They gave my lil bro thirty for ceing head of the conspiracy. The rest got anywhere from ten to thirty. The bitch nigga who testified is roamin' around out here right now! If I touch him, then they'll come snatch me up cefore the bitch nigga's heart stops. But cefore I leave this Earth; I will cut that rat bastards tongue out of his snitchin' ass mouth!" Jerimiah said in an aggravated tone.

"Give me 7 minutes. You'd better hope your story checks out. What's your brother's name Homie?"

" Robert Layne."

C.J. exited the room and speed dialed Shaneka on his mini Stu3 MX3030 com satellite phone. He gave her the names and info he needed, then hung up.

While waiting on his wife to call back, C.J. gave himself a personal tour of the upstairs. There were two bedrooms. The bigger one was overly feminine. He figured it to be Valerie's.

The next room brought on a wave of emotion for C.J. There, tacked to the wall above the canopy bed, was a poster of Lace, C.J., Dub, and Romeo. The picture was taken nearly a decade ago. They all had on their khakis, creased to perfection. They were all looking away from the camera, their way of blocking out their surroundings with their own thoughts.

Lace had written *"Can't Stop, Won't Stop 4 the 2000's!"* across the bottom. He remembered clearly Lace saying, *"I'm goin' to send this one to my daughter. We look li-"*. The vibration of his phone stole C.J. away from a pleasant memory of his former homie. Regaining his composure, C.J. condemned, "Fuck you Lace. I hope yo' bitch ass dies a thousand more times while you're in hell!" Then hit the talk button on his phone. "Yeah?"

"Yeah, Robert Layne is servin' a 30-year sentence. Did not cooperate, no form of government assistance. Jerimiah Layne is currently under federal surveillance. Both are Hoovers. Anything else I can assist you with today, sir?"

"No Ma'am. You have been of great service to a much-needed cause. Thank you very much." As much as C.J. wanted to tell his wife how she could *really* assist him, this call wasn't for that. C.J. made a mental note to call her later and have phone sex with her. After hanging up he looked at the poster one last time and said, "Bitch ass nigga!" then walked out of the room.

The laughter coming from downstairs caused C.J. to descend the stairs two at a time. The stench in the air was horrendous. Jerimiah leaned against the wall and wondered, *What the hell did V do to piss these niggas off so bad?* as the trio continued to torture Valerie.

Romeo and Dub both held separate legs while Creecha repeatedly touched Valerie's clit with a mini high voltage stun-gun. He had already burnt off all of her pubic hair.

Seeing C.J., Creecha hit her clit again. Everyone laughed hysterically as Valeria winced and flopped around like a fish out of water.

"What's this, a fish fry?" C.J. asked, using his rarely exposed sense of humor. This caused the room to erupt into an even deeper form of laughter.

C.J. walked over to Jerimiah and said, "You are who you say you are, so you're good on that. But...you see the problem now is, you've seen too much for us to just let you walk outta here."

"What'cha mean I saw too much? Look Cuz, I ain't no snitch. You just said that I checked out, so what's crackin'?" Jerimiah asked with agitation as well as aggression.

"Do you know why we're here?" C.J. asked.

"Naw, not really. I just know that the bitch had to have pissed you off in the worst way. But I ain't did shit!"

"You're left Cuz. You ain't did shit…*yet.*"

"What'cha mean yet?"

"It's like this: The bitch testified against our former comrade. Her daughters' father."

" O.K., that's where I know ya'lls faces from! From the poster in Marcia's room." Jerimiah started to remember.

C.J. nodded, then continued. "Yes. You see, you know too much, and today we're about to catch a body, or *two*. However, that depends on you."

"What's crackin'?"

"Well, you can eliminate this snitchin' bitch and we can handle your problem, which is really the *world's* problem. In return for your loyalty, you'll ce able to quit that two-dollar ass job and come work with us and for yourself. You'll have your own business as well as having your surveillance lifted."

"It sounds good, but how do I know that this shit's legit?"

"It's a win-lose situation."

"Win-lose?"

"Yeah, you win our loyalty and all the extras that go with it, *or* you lose your life. It's that simple."

"So twist this bitch, and I'm good?"

"For life."

"I'm in. Gimme a strap."

"Naw, that's too fuckin' noisy. Use your belt and strangle that bitch!"

Without hesitation, Jerimiah took his holster and removed the leather belt that held his pants up. He casually walked over to Valerie and kicked her in the head, and then sadistically began to whip her across the face. Jerimiah's hand moved in a blur as he raved on about Valeria being just like the nigga that got his brother 30 years. The leather cut into her once pleading eyes, causing a yellowish discharge to mix with the blood seeping from her previously filled sockets. The once baritone voice turned into a demonic cry as Jerimiah continued to lash away at what was once a beautiful face.

C.J, Dub, Romeo, and Creecha stood stone-faced during the grotesque event happening before their eyes. Creecha, a sadist himself, got an instant erection and nearly climaxed on himself watching the whole ordeal.

Jerimiah snapped out of his frenzy and said, "My bad, you said to choke the bitch."

Jerimiah took his bloody belt and looped it around Valerie's neck. He was careful not to get any of her oozing blood on his clothes. Jerimiah tightened the belt as far as he could, almost severing the carotid arteries.

Jerimiah sat down above Valerie's head, placed his feet on either shoulder, then pulled and leaned back until her convulsing body no longer moved.

With Gangsta adrenaline pumpin', Jerimiah stood adroit.

"Now what?"

Creecha checked her vitals, then nodded his head.

"Yep. She's as dead as dead can get."

"O.K., now you have blood on your hands, are you ready for the next level?" C.J. asked.

"I'm listenin'."

C.J. gave Jerimiah his cell number.

"Go ahead and leave Cuz. This way our car will ce the last seen leavin' here. That's in case she has—"C.J. stopped and looked down at Valerie's corpse. "In case she had nosy neighbors."

Jerimiah threw up his *'H'*, straightened his clothes, and headed for the door. Before he could make it out the front door, C.J. called him.

"Yo Cuz, call me in a couple hours and we'll discuss everything."

"Sho' ya left!" This time before Jerimiah could make it out the front door Creecha caught up to him and said, "That's my kind of shit you just did! Welcome to the movement." Creecha extended his hand.

Although he'd just committed an act of savagery, shaking Creecha's hand sent icy chills throughout Jerimiah's entire body.

Exiting Valeria's house felt like exiting his mother's womb to Jerimiah. It gave him a sense of freedom. However, Jerimiah began to question that freedom to himself.

Am I really free? It feels like I just signed my life away. Was it for a good cause? Damn! All I wanted was some pussy. Pussy: the real root of all evil.

***	***	***	***

Backing out of the driveway, Jerimiah spotted Marcia Lacy sitting in her Honda Accord waiting to fill the space he'd just abandoned.

Jerimiah pulled alongside her car then rolled his window down.

"How's Momma actin' today? She ain't trippin' is she?" Marcia asked.

"Naw, she's coolin' as we speak."

"If she's cool, why you leavin'?"

"I got corners to turn lil lady."

Licking her lips in a seductive manner Marcia then asked, "So when you gon' have me screamin' like you have my mommas ol' ass?"

A spitting image of her mother, Jerimiah had been wanting some of that 19-year old pussy ever since his first time in Valerie's house. "One day baby girl, you just might get that. But right now, I gotta slide."

"Oh well, your loss. I'ma beast wit it." Marcia said flicking her tongue in and out of her mouth, clacking it's barbell against the back of her teeth.

"Damn!" Jerimiah said rubbing his full-blown erection. *I should've been fucked her hot ass.* He thought as he pulled off, then frantically began dialing C.J. 's number.

The call wasn't needed because Romeo had watched the two engage in their conversation from the living room window.

After alerting the others of the woman getting out of the car and heading towards the house, Creecha shot through the foyer and waited behind the front door for the woman to appear.

The door opened, and Creecha sprang into action. He reached around the cracked door and snatched the woman by the wrist through the doorway. Before Marcia could scream, Creecha whirled her around and snapped her neck all in the same motion.

Marcia's face and ass were pointing in the same direction before her lifeless body hit the floor. The trio came running through the foyer as Creecha was unbuckling his belt.

"Naw Creech!" C.J. warned.

"Naw hell!"

"Creech! That was Lace's daughter."

"Yeah nigga. *Was!*"

"Spare this one Homie."

"Nigga, do you know when I was in Desert Storm, so many of my brothers…homies...comrades, real fuckin' men!" Creecha paused as if his soul had returned to the war.

"You know, some nights, some went to get some Saudi pussy and when they stuck their dicks in 'em…the bitch...the bitch would blow them *both* to pieces. Clean off this fuckin' Earth! Wasn't a damn thing to send home, but the usual stories 'bout how good of a man he was. We sent home so many empty caskets wit' flags over them. The smart ones like me…" Creech emphasized by slapping his chest with both hands. "We killed them bitches, *then* fucked 'em!"

The lust that had previously filled Creecha's eyes were now tortured and hollow. "Don't start judgin' me Homie...I survived! I went in a child and came home a man. I owe this much to my brothers who lost their lives behind some funky ass cunt, so let me be!"

"Creech! We don't have the time, and I'd never judge you Homie. But for now, we gotta get the hell up outta here!"

"But—"

"But nothin'! Next time, but not now! We got two dead bitches on our hands, so let's get the fuck outta here. Now!"

Both men stood toe-to-toe, and eye-to-eye. Neither flinched. Creecha was the first to break their stare. He looked down at Marcia then kicked her in-between the legs, and said, "Stankin' ass cunt!"

The crew wiped the place down and left. As they rode off, if you were to add up all of their thoughts, the equation was simple. *Finally, murder for a reason.*

No more bangin' on colors. We're bangin' for the *'Beast that gotta eat!'* For the ones that's been caught in the trap. For the ones being hunted right now, ***this movement is for you!***

CHAPTER 19

Jerimiah met up with C.J. later that evening at a local strip club. They had come to celebrate their new alliance and solidify their pact. Meanwhile, the MPD Homicide Division was trying to investigate a double homicide, and at the same time the MFD tried to extinguish a brush fire caused by a burning Crown Victoria.

C.J. and Jerimiah made small talk as different strippers entertained them. Although these strippers were above average looking, and damn near become any of the patrons *"Wifey",* their main focus was on a heavily jeweled loudmouth at the bar.

Several flunkies stood around this man, hanging onto his every word as he let imitation pimp and gangsta slogans escape his lips.

Ever since the Hoovers fell (with his help of course) Jason Porter had been on top of the world. Once a low-level crack peddler, Jason got busted on a possession with intent to sell and deliver. Afraid of going to prison. Jason agreed to help bring down the Hoovers in exchange for his charges being exonerated and the chance to play 'Big Willie'. The Feds agreed to this just as long as Jason helped to bring down every illegal operation in Memphis.

Thinking that his entourage were some real-life goons, Jason felt extremely confident and safe as he continuously cut his eyes in Jerimiah's direction. *Who's that sucka with J-Roc* Jason wondered. *Maybe one of those square ass niggas from his job.'*

Jason's thoughts immediately dismissed any and all possibilities of a threat as a young stallion sashayed past, with a garter belt full of $1 bills.

"Damn bitch! You phatta than a mufucka!" Jason said while slapping her across the ass with a handful of $1. As the stripper turned to face the violator, the alarm to Jason's Chevy went off.

"Damn, I just put those 31's on my shit. Who's fuckin' wit my shit?" Jason yelled out loud, but to no one in particular. "Yo Skeet! Go see who's fuckin' wit' my shit. If the sucka even blinks wrong, murder that mothafucka!" he yelled above the music, trying to impress the stripper.

Trying to look the part of a serious goon, Skeet screwed up his face and said, "I got'cha Homie."

Skeet then adjusted his pants so that the stripper could see that he had a gun, and gangsta walked towards the entrance/exit.

"Damn baby. Ya'll must be them niggas. All gangsta an' shit!" the stripper said walking up between Jason's legs.

"Baby girl, I just came here to have a good time. But when a nigga tries to interrupt that, then he gots 'ta get dealt with." Jason said in his best authoritative voice.

"Let's have a private party Boss Playa."

"Just us?"

"Yeah. Unless you can't handle all this." she said grabbing Jason's wrist, then directed his hand down to her extremely moist pussy.

"Damn!" Jason said while parting her pussy lips with his fingers. Two fingers slid in with ease. She squeezed his thick fingers with her inner muscles, causing Jason to have a premature ejaculation in his pants.

C.J. and Jerimiah watched their money work her *Magic*.

After leaving Valerie's, Jerimiah spotted Jason's Chevy Caprice at McDonalds. He pulled into the parking lot, then went inside.

While standing in line, Jerimiah overheard Jason bragging about treating his whole team to a night at the strip club. Jason didn't even order because what he *really* wanted wasn't on the menu. It would be at the strip club later that evening. Jerimiah hurried and called C.J. He just hoped that these niggas were as real as they say they were. If so, Christmas had come early.

Creecha, Dub, and Romeo had already snatched the consolation prize into their Caravan. Now they were waiting on the grand prize to come out while C.J. and Jerimiah watched the entire situation unfold.

Jerimiah had fucked *Magic* on several occasions. He'd met her one evening when he was called out to deal with a car that had broken down in the middle of traffic, causing a serious traffic jam.

Jerimiah arrived at the scene with an attitude, but his mood quickly lightened when he saw the most voluptuous feminine specimen he'd seen in years.

The hood of the car was raised with thick smoke billowing out. "Fuck the smoke. Look at that ass!" he mumbled as outraged commuters blared their horns. To gain control over the situation, Jerimiah told Magic to put the car in neutral so he could push the car over to the curb. The angry commuters rode past screaming obscenities; some flipped them the middle finger.

Magic sat in her car with her arms folded across her perky 36-C's. The tiny University of Memphis t-Shirt fit as if it were painted on her skin. Tears streamed down Magic's face as she poured her heart out about her lifetime of misfortune: From her town whore mother; her pimp father Kool Aide (who is now serving a 30-year sentence for violating the Mann Act); to her dope-fiend uncle who began molesting her from the time her father was arrested until her mother walked in and caught her brother in the act.

Magic's mom reacted was a quick blur. She pulled her straight razor from her bra and began slicing and dicing her brother's face. Every incision caused the flesh to tear beyond repair.

Screaming at the top of his lungs, Magic's uncle bear hugged his sister and tried to run her into the wall, hoping she'd drop the razor. So much blood was in his eyes that he misjudged where the wall should've been. Normally, the windowsill would have slowed the pair's momentum. However, fear and adrenaline mixed with pain caused them to crash through the window.

Magic's mother and her Uncle fell several-stories to a painful and horrific death. Magic ran to the window to see her mother's body twitch for its last time. When her movements stopped, it seemed as though her mother smiled up to her as if to say *Finally, I did something right.* Magic's Uncle head had burst open and looked like a pumpkin after being stomped on. Through teary eyes Magic said, "Thank you Momma" and walked away from the hole that had claimed her mother's life.

Jerimiah heard her, but he wasn't really listening. The only thing on his mind was to fuck this beautiful and distraught woman. He comforted Magic with mellifluous words. Over dinner, Jerimiah told her that she was too beautiful not to have a man.

Magic explained that men only wanted her for her body and would rather struggle to make ends meet than to live the life of a whore as her mother once did.

It took several hours to convince Magic that she could sell fantasy and not her body at the strip club. "Yeah, you'd give lap dances and dance on tables, play the stage a lil bit, but you don't have to fuck! I don't want these nasty dick niggas all up in my chick." he preached to Magic.

"Oh, so I'm yo chick now, huh?" she asked playfully. "Damn skippy, you mine!"

"Well if I'm yours, why you gonna let other niggas look at what's *yours*, as you say?" Magic searchingly asked.

"Cause a man ain't got shit if the next man ain't lustin', fantasizin', or dyin' to sample what's his. It's all illusion, baby!" Jerimiah said smiling at how quick he'd come up with that answer, and even more so after he saw how hard it had Magic smiling.

That, and promising to get her car fixed, is all it took to get her back to his apartment. That night, Magic earned herself a pre-owned Honda Accord. Her and Jerimiah have been sexin' now for the past eight months since.

"Can she get him outside?" C.J. asked Jerimiah.

"Do Crips wear blue?"

C.J. smiled at the mention of the color that once defined who he was. Now he defined the color.

C.J. watched as Jason made his way towards the restroom, leaving Magic enough time to sashay over to Jerimiah. She straddled his lap, and began working what her mother gave her: *A.T.A.— All That Azz!*.

Pretending to lick Jerimiah's ear Magic whispered, "I made that fool cum on himself. He went to clean up, then we gonna leave."

Thinking quickly, C.J. called out to the van. "Yo Creech, this nigga just went in the bathroom…Yeah...Yeah hurry up…One other niggas wit 'im. Yeah hurry up!''

"Yo Magic, go work the stage wit yo' phat ass." C.J. insisted.

Magic looked at C.J. as if he'd lost his mind.

Catching the vibe, Jerimiah said, "Yeah baby, hit the stage and juice that niggas whole crew."

"But I thought yo—"

"What the fuck did I just say dammit!" Jerimiah yelled, then pushed her off his lap. Confused, Magic headed to the stage but made a mental note to check Jerimiah about stuntin' in front of his friend.

Magic walked over to the DJ's booth and had DJ Climaxxx to put her anthem on. '*Shake what'cha momma gave ya!'* came blaring through the eight 12 inch woofers.

As Magic shook her assets, Creecha came through the door wearing a pair of dark Dior sunglasses and a Rasta hat with synthetic dreadlocks flowing down his back. He could pass for a true *Rude Boy* from the mean streets of Trench Town; Kingston, Jamaica's most notorious hood.

No one paid Creecha any attention as he looked for the sign indicating the restroom. Magic had every set of eyes in the house glued to her. Creecha even stole a glance before he went to fulfill his obligation.

*** *** *** ***

Creecha walked into the restroom and peeped the scene. One man stood leaning against the wall talking on the phone. The other man stood in front of the hand dryer, allowing the air to dry his pants. Knowing time was of the essence, Creecha palmed the man's head that was talking on the phone and thrust backwards. A sickening crunching sound came out once the back of the man's head hit the wall.

Jason attempted to scream, but Creecha hit him with a knife punch to the esophagus. Jason slumped to the floor holding his throat. Creecha reached down into Jason's pants, encircled his dick and balls then said. "You's a bitch, sucka! Welcome to the world of retribution bitch!"

Creecha tightened his grip, turned his wrist to its near breaking point, then snatched with all his might and separated Jason from his family jewels.

Next, he grabbed Jason by both of his ears and slowly twisted his head until his neck snapped.

Picking up the once functioning organ, Creecha walked back over to the first victim, opened his mouth, and stuffed Jason's bloody dick and balls in it.

"Wrong place, wrong time, and definitely the wrong nigga to be hangin' with, Sucka!" Creecha said into the dead man's ear as if he could really hear him.

After washing his hands, Creecha wiped everything he'd touched, exited the restroom, and stole another glance of Magic working her *magic*. *'Damn!'* Creecha said as he walked over to the bar and ordered a double shot of Henny. When he got his drink he threw it back and swallowed the 'Yac' in one gulp. C.J. and Jerimiah had already left the club.

Dub and Romeo sat in front of the club waiting on Creecha to come out. They were close enough in case they would have to go in there and set it off like St. Louis did in the movie *Players Club*.

Creecha came boppin' out the exact same way he bopped into the club. Dub pulled off before Creecha could even get the door closed. At the exact same time that their tires screeched off, Double A was leaned over, throwing up at the sight of Jason's bloody dick hanging out of his brothers' mouth.

Jerimiah followed the van out of the parking lot, but then passed them and indicated for them to follow him. He led them into the upscale section of Arlington. There, they doused the van and a semi-conscious Skeet with gas. Dub made a trail from the van to Jerimiah's Expedition and dropped a lit cigarette. They were only a half a block away before they heard the explosion.

They decided to call it a night. Each of them got separate rooms at a small hotel. When Jerimiah was about to get one, C.J. pulled him to the side.

"A Cuz, go home and go to work at the usual time tomorrow and we'll get up some time next week."

"I'm wit ya'll Cuz."

"Dig it Loc, what we gotta take care of now is personal."

"So what...I ain't down now?"

"Cuz, you are officially on the squad, but this here is somethin' we made a pact on many blue moons ago, and we gotta see it through. We can't move forward without rightin' the wrongs that started this movement."

Not sure if Jerimiah fully understood, C.J. put his hands-on Jerimiah's shoulders and further explained, "What happened earlier was the beginning of the movement. You just happened to ce in the wrong place at the left time. Now one of our former comrades' death has been vindicated. Your brother...well, we can't get him out; at least not yet anyway. But trust me homie, everything is going to fall into place. As of next week, you'll have your own business and $1M in cash. You'll ce off the radar, and you'll then help us rid this country of this rodent problem. Call me next Friday, and everything I've just said will have already come into existence."

Jerimiah nodded and walked out of the hotel lobby trying to absorb everything C.J. had just explained; especially about the million in cash.

CHAPTER 20

The next morning C.J. caught a cab to Herbs Discount Autos. Herbs motto was: *"The longer the buck, the better your luck."*

After browsing the lot, and finding exactly what he was looking for, C.J. had the cab driver take him to the First Union Bank, then back to Herbs.

Herb arrived at 9:45 am. Upon exiting his Lexus LS400, Herb eyed the black man standing on his lot with heavy suspicion. His nerves told him that he wasn't a henchman for his bookie, but something in his gut also told him that the man was extremely dangerous.

"Hey, hey, hey, there fella." Herb said walking towards C.J.

C.J. turned away from the Dodge Caravan and looked at the balding, fat man in the loud green polyester suit. He almost laughed at Herb's appearance.

"If ya look too long, it might end up gone." Herb said snapping his fingers,

"Just like that." Adding emphasis to his pathetic sales pitch.

"We both know this piece of shit ain't worth $9995.00. It's a 2001, meaning it's already halfway to being a classic. Plus, the shit has over 125,000 miles on it. So I'll tell ya what, since it only worth a few grand I'll give you $4,000 for it right now, and that's being generous."

This nigger knows his shit Herb mumbled under his breath while nodding his head and stroking his chubby jaws with his fat fingers.

"Tell ya what my friend. We are friends, right?" Herb said with a slight bop. When Herb went to put his hand on C.J.'s shoulder, an eerie wave shot through his arm causing him to snatch his sweaty palm back.

"Um...yeah. I'm a fair man my friend—" Herb said while trying to shake the queasy feeling out of his protruding belly. "Tell ya what I'm gonna do for ya. I'll knock off a grand. How 'bout that?"

"I've got $5,000 on me. Do you want it, or do I need to go across the street? I saw a nice Cherokee over there for five thousand. It's your call *my friend*." C.J. said using Herbs lingo back on him.

After pondering for a minute and wanting to call C.J.'s bluff, Herb said, "Naw my friend. I can't let this baby go for that. Sorry." Then started walking towards the office.

After taking the usual 10 steps, Herb realized that C.J. wasn't on his heels trying to renegotiate. He turned around to see C.J. standing on the sidewalk, waiting to cross the street to Dans Discount Autos.

Not wanting his arch nemesis to make the $5,000 sale Herb screamed at the top of his lungs, "Hey pal!...Hey wait up." As he trotted towards CJ.

C.J. had no intentions of going across the street to Dans'. C.J.

saw the greed in Herbs' eyes, so all he had to do was play the stall game. He'd won.

C.J. never turned around. He kept up the charade as if he were really going across the street. Herb jogged around so he was standing between C.J. and the busy street.

"O.K. pal, ya got me by the balls. I'll let'cha get her for $6-grand."

"I only got 5."

"Geeze...ya killin' me!" Herb said slapping his forehead.

"I'd never do that!"

"You're doin' it now!"

"That's why I'm going over to Dans. I ain't tryin' to hurt'cha."

"Man, ya got the cash?"

C.J. responded by pulling out a knot of Dead Cracks. (Dead Crackas)

" Hol' up. Are you crazy? Don't pull that out here!", Herb said looking around, making sure that none of Mr. Ablos' henchmen were somewhere lurking in the cut. Herb was about $150,000.00 in debt to Mr. Ablos, and he needed the money to try to hit a ticket, a number, or flip it. With this $5-grand, there was still hope that Herb and his family would survive to see another day.

"You got people around here that'll kill ya for a third of that!" Herb added thinking about some of the gruesome acts that the Mosalini Brothers had inflicted over Mr. Ablos money.

Stepping around C.J., he motioned for him to follow him.

"We'll handle this in my office."

One hour later, C.J. was pulling off the lot in his Caravan. "Damn! This fat bastard must really be somebody." C.J. said to himself as a stretched Mercedes limo drove up accompanied by two S550 Benzes. Little did C.J. know, he was Herb's final customer.

CHAPTER 21

The quartet decided to head back to North Carolina and put things into motion. C.J., Creecha, and Dub settled in at the Embassy Suite of Charlotte the following afternoon. Romeo went back to Salisbury to do some research on Jake River's whereabouts. It didn't take long to get the information that he was looking for.

When a sperm donor becomes neglectful, the baby momma becomes easy prey. After a trip to the Salisbury Mall, and some fresh out the penitentiary dick, Tracy told Romeo everything about Jake and his whereabouts.

Dub rode to Statesville with Romeo so that there was positive identification. Fire shot through Romeo's veins when he saw Jake leaning against a red, candy-coated six series BMW, talking on his cell phone, with a petite cutie standing between his legs.

Dub noticed the look on his comrades face as they drove down the Blvd. They both looked Jake in the face on their way back up.

Romeo called RoRo and asked him what kind of arsenal did he

have. All RoRo said was, “Come through,” then hung up.

***   ***   ***   ***

Romeo pulled up on Knox St. where RoRo and his comrades stood in the yard fuckin’ with some Pit Bull puppies.

Lil Noochie drew down on the van with his .357. When RoRo saw who was in the van, he walked over to Lil Noochie and slapped the shit out of him.

“What the fuck, Cuz?!” Lil Noochie asked, really needing some clarity about RoRo’s actions.’

“You see who the fuck that is? That’s my fuckin’ Pops! The Big Homie Romeo, fool!”

“Damn Cuz I ain’t know!”

“Well now you do!”

Dub and Romeo sat and watched the whole situation unfold.

“The Lil Homie is destined for greatness. I love the lil nigga’s gangsta.” Dub said admiring the way RoRo handled the situation.

Romeo boasted with pride from hearing Dub speak so highly of his son, which was something that Dub rarely did.

RoRo got in and asked what kind of heat they needed?

“I need somethin’ that’ll do plenty damage.” Romeo told his son.

“ Shit, I got grenades, choppers, 47’s, and 74’s. I got s—”

“Shit, ya’ll niggas are strapped for war, ain’t ‘cha?” Dub said cutting RoRo off.

“Yeah, you know how us Crips do. Plus, these fake ass slobs out here real thick.”

After hearing RoRo use the word Slob, Romeo thought back to when he was first introduced to gang bangin’. A Crip named Screw came from Colorado and put 81 Kitchen Crip on the East Coast. No Bloods surfaced until Lil Wayne and Baby started their fake ass Blood movement.

The Crips were on West coast time, while the Bloods were claiming a 5-pointed star. That was over a decade later. Plus, Romeo was locked up, and Big Screw just up and disappeared. Only Romeo knew of his true whereabouts.

"Let me get an AK and a grenade." Dub told RoRo.

Romeo got out and hit Dub up. RoRo tossed a small duffle bag into the passenger's seat.

"You might wanna hold this Big Homie." RoRo said handing Dub a pineapple grenade. Dub really was diggin' how RoRo carried his Crippin'. *He's turned up fo' sho'!*

"Good lookin' Lil Cuz." Dub said throwing up a *'C'* out the window as he was pulling off.

*** *** *** ***

CJ, Creecha, and Dub headed to Statesville later that evening.

C.J. and Dub went into the Blvd. Grill while Creecha rode down the Blvd. Creecha stopped and bought a $20 rock from one of the youngsters, promising that if it was good, he'd be back to buy a quarter ounce. The young pusher smiled but the greedy man leaning on the Beemer was all ears.

"My man…" Jake said walking towards the van. "It's the best in the Ville, and I got it for the low-low."

"Well, I'll let you know in a minute what'cha workin' wit." Creecha said then drove back up the Blvd.

C.J. and Dub jumped back in the van while Creecha drove and scanned the area for any police. After devising a clear escape route, they headed back down the Blvd.

Jake saw the approaching van and allowed dollar signs to cloud his better judgement and reasoning. Two men now occupied the van which could only mean more money.

C.J. was driving with Creecha on the passenger's side. Dub laid on the floor in the back of the van, clutching the AK-47 with an extra clip duct taped to the first.

As they got closer, Jake started walking towards the van. Before he could reach into his pocket, he saw Creecha's arm come out the passenger window in a throwing motion.

The entire scene became a blinding blur of heat with shards of metal flying everywhere. Jake attempted to run but tripped over his own feet.

Dub moved with the agility of a cat. "Run them pockets bitch, not yo' feet!" Dub said when he sprang up from the back floorboard.

Hoping that this was just a mere robbery, Jake quickly removed all the contents of his pockets. Even though Dub was a *'C.J. Made'* millionaire, he couldn't resist taking a snitches' money. *Hell, he'll never get to spend it anyway* Dub reasoned as he let off a volley of tumbling rounds in the direction that was now smoking from what remained of the Beemer.

Realizing that he didn't have time to waste, Dub turned the *Chopper* on Jake and sprayed his body with a side to side motion, making the weapon earn its nickname.

Jakes upper body turned over as he attempted to push himself up, but his bottom half couldn't cooperate. His brain couldn't send a message through the nervous system because the two halves were no longer connected.

During Jake's last attempt to get up, Dub sent three consecutive shots to the back of his head, leaving only a stub on Jakes neck.

After picking up the contents that Jake had pulled out, Dub dove back into the van. C.J. drove into the direction as the approaching sirens. *So far, so good.* C.J. thought. *Ain't no turnin' back!* echoed from C.J.'s subconscious mind, sending chills throughout his entire body. He remembered the first time he'd heard those words. C.J.'s mind drifted back into his childhood.

*** *** *** ***

C.J.'s mother kept stressing his father to buy her some new furniture.

"Woman, this shit ain't even a year old yet!" Cleon snapped.

"Look, you said that my every wish is your command...so what? You goin' against your word?" his mother questioned. Cleon turned and walked away from his wife.

He entered the kitchen where young C.J. sat eating a bowl of Trix.

"Son..." Cleon began, not bothering to sit down. "Whenever you tell somebody that you're going to do somethin', *then you do it!* Ya hear? You do it. You less than a man if you don't. You understand, don't 'cha?"

C.J. nodded with a mouthful of cereal that he stopped chewing. Something wasn't right in his father's demeanor. "Yeah son, I promised your momma the world, and that's exactly what I plan on givin' her. Or die tryin'! You'll be proud to say your ol' man was a real man."

What happened next, shook C.J.'s little skeletal system. Cleon leaned over and kissed the top of C.J.'s head: a gesture that his father originally said was for girls and sissies. C.J.'s father then turned and walked back through the beaded doorway. He stopped and turned back towards C.J. and said.

"Ain't no turnin' back." He pulled out his Saturday Night Special (.32 cal), inspected it, then stuck it back in the back of his belt.

Seeing the distant look in his father's eyes, C.J. chewed the soggy cereal and swallowed hard.

"I love you C.J." his father said and walked away. Both father and son knew that that was their last encounter.

C.J. got up and put his bowl in the sink and mouthed, "Ain't no turnin' back". This would become the motto C.J. vowed to live and die on; just like his father did.

As he drove, C.J. turned to The Secret Garden on 101.9FM. Luther crooned about dancing with his father again. C.J.'s heart ached. *I miss you daddy* he said to himself. Dub and Creecha's telepathic senses heard C.J.'s thoughts, but neither said a word. They all rode in their own zones, and each one knew from then on wasn't no turning back.

CHAPTER 22

The first 10 calls went straight to voicemail. Frustrated, C.J. hit the duress button on his phone that sent a loud shrilling sound through Romeo's satellite phone.

Romeo jumped up out of Tracy's sloppy wet pussy after he heard his phone going berserk.

While fumbling with the phone, trying to figure out how to turn the annoying sound off, Tracy pushed Romeo back on the bed and started sucking her own nectar off of his dick.

Finally hitting the talk button, C.J.'s voice boomed through the earpiece.

"Look Cuz, we won the game. We got two more games in the playoffs that you gotta play in, then we all go to the championship." This translated to *"We got that mother fucka! Now we got two more hits that you going on, then this movement will officially be underway."*

"Are you ready?" C.J. asked.

"Uh-mmm Oh yeahhhh I I're—"

"Ro!"

"Yea...Yeah...Cu Cuz?" Romeo moaned. Surprised at his own actions, Romeo shouted, "Yeah Cuz!" while trying to snatch his dick out of Tracy's professional throat.

"Ce ready by ten! And Cuz?"

"What's crackin'?"

"Bust one for the team."

"Sho' yaleft." Romeo said, then guided Tracy back down so she could finish getting her throat pregnant.

CHAPTER 23

Shaneka had already given C.J., Donald Linworth's "aka" *Jonny Suttons* precise location. Donald operated a car detailing business off of Academy Blvd. in Colorado, Springs.

They arrived at headquarters the following night at midnight. Jonny Suttons file was sitting on the kitchen table. After studying his new identity, C.J. scowled and handed the 8x10 glossy black and white photo to a now frowning Dub. After memorizing the rodent's face, he passed it to Romeo. Creecha looked over Romeo's shoulder and studied the soon to be dead man's face.

"I'll see ya'll when ya'll get cacked." C.J. said to his comrades as he held the door opened for them to exit. They all knew that this was retribution for C.J. Soon the wounds would start to heal.

The trio left for the Springs immediately. To kill time, they hung out at the Citadel Mall until it was close to closing time for *Custom Fx.*

Romeo called and personally spoke to Jonny about installing some neon lights under his car. He was told to bring it in around

7:30 PM, so he could take a look at it.

The trio pulled their Yukon Denali in front of Bay-1. Romeo exited the SUV in his navy blue F.B.I. windbreaker and walked into the opened bay.

Jonny slid from under a PT Cruiser in oil stained Dickie coveralls.

"Jonny Sutton?" Romeo asked, extending his fake credentials.

"Yeah?"

"I'm agent Mathis. Are you here alone?"

"Naw, my man Curt is over there under the Lac."

"I need a few words with you in private, so I can bring you up to date on our program."

"Yo, hol' that shit down. Curt don't need to know my business."

"Alright then, do you have somewhere where we can go speak in private.?"

"Yeah, follow me."

Romeo turned towards the Denali and signaled one, then pointed down. He spelled out the word LAC with his finger, then jerked it to the left. He then turned and caught up to Jonny before he could make it into the office.

Dub and Creecha jumped out of the Denali and ran in the direction that Romeo had just indicated.

Dub couldn't believe his luck. He walked right over and hit the green button on the hydraulic lift control. The Cadillac slammed down on Curt so fast that he didn't even get a chance to scream.

The sound of the Caddy slamming down caused Jonny to jump. "What the fuck was that?" Jonny said as he went to investigate. Romeo hit him in the neck with a high voltage stun gun, causing Jonny to drop to the floor and grab his neck.

Romeo put the stun gun away. Jonny was so stunned that an agent would abuse a star witness like this, but soon realized that this man wasn't an agent. Romeo was a one-man jury that just sentenced him to death.

"Where's the money?!" Romeo demanded.

"Th...th-the sa safe...in th…the corner." Jonny winced. Romeo turned his head for a split-second giving Jonny enough time to exert all of his energy into making a break for his only chance at living. Jonny thought he'd made it when he snatched the door open, but he was only met with a crowbar across the nose. Jonny grimaced in pain as he fell back into his office.

Feeling like an ass, Romeo immediately began Crip Stompin' Jonny. After his head swelled to twice its normal size, Creecha walked over and delivered two dead blows with the crowbar. One to the throat, and the other to the center of the forehead, causing several different colored liquids to seep out of the wound.

After wiping the crowbar off on Jonny's coveralls, he waved for Romeo to follow him.

"Lets go rookie." They made it back to Limon by 10PM.

*** *** *** ***

When they arrived, C.J. already had Norman Walters, "aka" *Nutsos* file out. He informed them that they'd celebrate after they cleaned up the last piece of the original mess.

Feeling the energy, C.J. pulled out a bottle of Jonny Walker Blue and passed out 40's of Old English.

"We'll leave tomorrow evening and catch that bitch ass nigga slippin' Friday mornin'." They sat and drank while watching classic UFC fights. No one was permitted to use their cell phones because alcohol makes a person's lips break a lot of street codes, especially when the *Root to all evil is* on the receiving end talking about how wet her pussy is. That's when most men will boast about their gangsta ways, but all along violating the original code of silence.

CHAPTER 24

On their way to California, an omen fell over the Hummer. Snoop Dogg had just introduced his newest protégé', Roe Wood, who was from Tennessee. C.J. turned the volume to its max as Roe Wood started going into a tirade about C.J.'s vision.

I make examples outta you snitch niggas/
Now here I come, pullin' these triggas/
Witness protection don't work/
If I can't find you, then ya family's in the dirt/
5K.1's for niggas that bitch up/
187 nigga! Yo' times up!/
You saw too fuckin' much/
Since you opened yo mouth, and wanna hide, then it's yo momma I'ma touch/
Ain't no trial for yo bitch ass/
You guilty bitch, now eat this blast/
All ya'll niggas is bitches/

If ya are or hangin' with snitches/
I got my shovel, so I'm diggin' plenty ditches/

Snoop grabbed the microphone. "Yeah, that is a lil freestizzle from Roe Wizzle fo' shizzle. Look for the homies CD to drizzop niznex mizunt, on the fizif. Now back to the original platform that the O.G.'s walked on."

The Big Payback came blaring through the eight 15 inch woofers.

No one spoke. Their souls were getting replenished by the food coming out of the speakers. Once the Godfather of Soul went off, the quartet was completely rejuvenated and ready to eliminate the last rodent of the first chapter.

*** *** *** ***

They pulled into 'Hub City', Compton the following afternoon. C.J., Creecha, and Romeo met some of the A.B.C. (Acacia Blocc Crips) legends. C.J. got a kick out of one of them. This particular one walked around and smoked cigarette after cigarette. He had the entire pack of Kool's gone in less than an hour. All the while smoking, he would walk behind his homies and kick over their heads. He'd then laugh, covering his mouth with a crooked finger pointed at you but veering off in another direction. You have one like that on every set.

Dub kicked it with Big Karen for the rest of the afternoon. After the trio left, the Acacia homies started to fade out, but Dub and Big Karen had crept off to go get a sneak fuck in. This was something that the two of them had been doing since Dub learned that his little snake could spit venom. No one ever said anything, but the whole Hub City knew about their rendezvous.

***　　***　　***　　***

Watts, California

The next morning, Jessica Walters ran out to her father's Impala to crank it up. She did this every morning so she could play with the hydraulic switches. Ever since Nutso had put the hydraulics on the Impala, *Baby J* wanted Nutso to drive her to school. This morning was no different.

Nutso ran out of the house wearing a purple Lakers sweat suit with the new Kobe Bryant's.

When he got in the car, Baby J all of a sudden remembered that she hadn't fed her hamster.

"Daddy, I'll be right back. I forgot to feed Rocky!" she exclaimed while jumping out of the car and running back into the house. Nutso didn't protest.

Although pissed, he always gave his baby her way.

Nutso was glad Baby J had gotten out when he saw the fiend approaching his car. He looked around to make sure *One Time* wasn't out creeping.

The fiend walked up to the driver's side door, looked around, then dropped a crumpled $10 bill in Nutso's lap.

"What's crackin' fool? You bangin', shermin',...what cha need?" Nutso asked going into his CD bag, where he kept his stash of drugs.

"Let me get a wet stick?" the fiend answered, while rubbing his hands together.

Typical head Nutso reasoned. As he pulled the cigarette from the pack, Creecha was already making his move. He dropped a 4" icepick from his sleeve and sprang into action.

"Here you go—" was all Nutso could get out before Creecha grabbed his lips with a death grip and plunged the icepick into his ear to the hilt. He pulled the icepick out two inches, then jabbed it back in twice; both in different angles.

Creecha slid the bloody pick back up his sleeve and laid Nutsos' head on the steering wheel. Just as Creecha turned to walk away, a real fiend approached.

"Yo homie." Creecha called to the fiend.

"What fool?"

"He said to give 'im five minutes so he can get his shit together." The fiend only nodded, then stood on the sidewalk for a minute, then approached the car.

Jessica came running out of the house in time to see Sidney running away from the car.

"Da-deee!" Jessica screamed when she saw her father's head leaning against the steering wheel with blood leaking out of his left ear. "Sidney killed my da-deee!" Jessica wailed, getting the attention of the gangbangers shooting craps on the corner.

When Big Trop looked in Jessica's direction, then saw Sidney running down the street at full speed, he pulled out his .44 Magnum and took aim. Sidney heard the cannon erupt, then felt a thump on the back of his head as his soul left his body. He was now headed to *Dopefiend Hell.*

C.J. and Romeo heard the blast as Creecha rounded the corner. They all smiled when their comrade dove into the back seat.

"Let's go get Dub, it's time to celebrate." C.J. informed his crew.

*** *** *** ***

They parked the stolen Nova at the Compton Swap Meet, then hailed a cab back to Acacia to pick Dub up so they could go celebrate.

When they got back to Acacia, Dub was nowhere to be found. C.J. guessed he was probably with the big girl that had his eyes sparkling earlier.

They waited around with the A.B.C.'s who showed mad love. They even crunk up a couple grills and threw 40's in an ice filled trashcan.

Dub came wheeling the Hummer around the corner a few hours later, and as sure as shit stinks, Big Karen stepped out the Hummer trying to look as nonchalant as possible. However, the truth was written all over both of their faces.

That night, they found out that the crooked fingered prankster was a reputable and had did time with the legendary Big Screw many years back. He was also a notorious killer, but you'd never know it by his antics. Those that had crossed him, were no longer around to tell about it.

The crew all partied in the *'Hub'* for the rest of the day. Late evening, they loaded up the Hummer and headed back to the Centennial State.

Deciding to take a more scenic route back, they got on I-10, then jumped on I-25N. They ended up getting rooms at one of Albuquerque's most luxurious hotels.

They rested, then celebrated the *work* that they'd put in. C.J. called Jerimiah and told him to catch a plane out to Albuquerque the following day. He ended the call with,

"It's time"

CHAPTER 25

The following day, they picked Jerimiah up from the airport. Next, they hit the mall full throttle.

A friend of Dub owned an extravagant strip club. After a phone call, the club was shut down for a private party during that whole weekend. Each of the 50 dancers would receive $10,000, plus tips. The owner Tricky, pocketed $100,000. It was a no holds barred affair.

The first 25 dancers earned their money that Saturday. 10 straight hours of the freakiest and kinkiest shit ever imagined occurred. However, the unfathomable happened on Sunday. The second group brought the thunder down from the sky, and fire shot straight up from hell.

One chick named Jaws stole the night. She danced with a 6ft. albino Boa Constrictor. No one got too close to the stage. She licked the snakes tongue every time it stuck his tongue out. Laying down, she allowed the snake to crawl all over her entire body, always stopping its head at her plump pussy. The snake must've thought that Jaws was the Garden of Eden, because her pussy was as fat as the apple that changed the world.

Tricky told his guest, “Get your money ready fellas, here comes the shit niggas only dream about seeing.”

Two stallions walked out onto the stage, one carrying something that looked like a bulletproof vest. The other, pushing a machine. They all sat back with curiosity swelling both heads; *big and small.*

The one with the vest, laid it across Jaws’ body, obstructing the view, until the other chick turned on what was actually an X-Ray machine. Jaws’ entire skeletal system illuminated.

Standing on either side, each chick grabbed one of Jaws’ legs, and pulled them apart. Jaws caressed and stroked the snake as it explored the entrance of her cave. Somehow, she worked his entire head into her pussy.

The X-Ray machine only showed Jaws’ skeleton and a long vertebra going between her outstretched legs. Eventually, the illusion was that of a skeleton getting fucked by a long skeleton dick. The snake started trying to pull back out, only to be pulled in even further. When it tried to open its mouth, Jaws lost it..

“Ohhh shit! I’m ‘bout ta cummmmmm!” she screamed over the music. That was the DJ’s cue to turn the music off for the finale.

“ Ahmmm! Sheeeit!”, she moaned while sweating profusely.

Holding her head up, Jaws’ stared into the eyes of the murderous patrons which were filled with euphoria. Jaws’ pussy muscles contracted against the boa constrictor, causing the snake to start palpitating. The scene was violently erotic.

Muscle against muscle. Beast against beast. A real struggle for the top position of evil supremacy.

The snake quit fighting after another minute and went still.

Tricky reached up and grabbed the slain serpents tail and snatched its cum soaked head out of Jaws' hole of death.

Tricky turned towards his guest and asked, "Now do you see why they call her Jaws?"

C.J., having such an inquisitive mind asked, "Why didn't the snake just wrap around her and squeeze her to death instead of dyin' himself?"

"The same reason so many humans die behind it. They get a taste and they will do anything to keep it! Niggas…they talk all this gangsta shit about hatin' snitches, but once a nigga hits his homeboy, a brother who he grew up playin' in the sandbox with, in the head, he doesn't do shit. But let a nigga look at his bitch or talk to her, just like that—" Tricky snapped his fingers, "He kills a nigga! Went out like a sucka, and over what? Some mothafuckin' pussy! The only thing a bitch is good for is a good nut and to bring me money. Call me what you want: gay, racist, or even a sadist because the only thing I love is old dead white men, and those evils slits bring 'em to me! Plenty of 'em!"

"The root to all evil." C.J. said evenly.

"You got that right my man! The yin, it's evil as fuck, but what it brings is great! Just as long as it jingles, or folds in my pocket, I'm great." Tricky said winking at C.J.

As C.J. sat and absorbed the jewels he'd just heard, Tricky said "Now gimme a quarter."

C.J. looked confused but complied.

"Now, I don't feel bad." Tricky said flipping the quarter, then put it in his pocket.

C.J. smiled. Now he understood the reasoning behind the quarter. *The game was to be sold, not told.*

The rest of the night was spent drinking and fucking until they couldn't do any more of either one. Drained, they thanked their host and hostesses then returned to their suites with the dancer of their choice. *No one* took Jaws.

Monday afternoon, they sent their C.O.P. (Choice of Pussy) on their way. Once the strippers left, over Meat Lovers pizza, C.J. unveiled his vision.

"We are now ready for the next level. Creecha here, is going to work with us on an individual basis. I won't compare this to Navy Seal boot camp, cause I don't know the full extent of their vigorous training. But I can say this: *This will ce a full-fledged Gangsta Camp*. I'll let Creecha break it down for you. My initial part is done. I poured the foundation of an unbreakable force, an unstoppable force. Real solid men! I gave every one of ya'll a million in cash, a crib, and a few vehicles so there wouldn't ce a delay in our movement. The money is to start a business. Preferably a cleaning service. We want to undercut all business owners in our field, so we'll have access to mobilize without drawing any suspicion. *The best quality of work, for the lowest price* is our motto." C.J. paused to see if everyone had grasped what he'd said so far. Feeling that everyone was on the same page, he continued.

"We'll make house calls. All the contracts will come from Headquarters. There's not much we can do for the soldiers that have already fallen. Our job is to see that no more fall to this nasty plague of snitchin'! Our First Lady will fax us everything that we'll need."

C.J. gestured to Jerimiah. "You'll ce filled in on the rest once we get to Headquarters. O.K. J-Roc?"

Jerimiah nodded a confused nod wondering how C.J. knew his street name without him ever telling him. He then realized that C.J.

had access to everything else, so he just shrugged it off and left it at that conclusion.

"So here's the breakdown: we go to their people and holla at 'em about bringin' their people home. The ones still in the county, that is. Our fee is $10-grand, and their loyalty. Any wrong move of the family, or fallen soldier, they die! *Plain and simple.* We'll murder their asses too! Straight like *that*!" C.J. indicated by snapping his fingers.

"They gotta pass a test that we all passed. Yours is comin'." C.J. said looking at J-Roc, then continued. "This is the only way to clarify things. Here's an example. Say Stud is locked up and headin' to trial. We go by Bella's, Studs ol' lady, unannounced. We'll let her know that this is in regard to Stud. We bring in our vacuum cleaners, shampooers, and all the extras. A polygraph machine will ce built into one of them.

If Bella passes the test, she lives. Then we'll go assassinate the Buster tryin' to ruin Stud's life. We collect our fee, then wait on our new member to win trial. He won't ce able to start right away cecause he'll ce under heavy scrutiny. We will employ him, and after the heat dies down, he'll come in and put in his share of work.

If she fails...well, we can't leave any witnesses. We must ask specific questions and give guarantees, cause a nigga will flip the script when he gets out. He must know what will happen if he ever crosses or bites the hands that freed him! If not, our whole movement will ce in jeopardy. That's why the First Lady will only ce sending info on cats that's already on some loyalty shit. Our movement is goin' to ce an epidemic, and it won't get compromised by no fuckin' body!"

C.J. took a pause to regain his composure, then he put the icing on the cake.

"No talkin' is permitted unless the machines are all on. There's a noise distributor that distorts any and all listenin' devices. We will write things down, and once everything is agreed upon, then we'll leave. There must ce a clear understanding as to what to expect. Sometimes the wife, or whoever, may not have the money at the time. That's cool. He can work it off when he gets out, or we'll give her a job doin' somethin'. Are ya'll diggin' where I'm comin' from?"

Creecha, Dub, Romeo, and Jerimiah all acknowledged that they were all with C.J..

"O.K., for the next year Creecha will test us to see exactly what we're made of. Ce ready when your time comes." C.J. warned.

Creecha stood up and added. "Most of the shit ya'll gonna learn, hopefully you'll never need to use it. But it's always better to know and not have to use it than vice versa. I've enjoyed be...I mean *cein'* around you Crips and I appreciate the introduction to ya'lls world." Creecha's demeanor then turned ice cold.

"*Now it's time to welcome ya'll into mine!* A certified assassins world! Experts with the hands, feet, mouth, and can use anything from a blade of grass to a missile launcher as a weapon. As C.J. said, for now, we're all we have. The number one rule is no man left be...I mean *cehind.* I'ma get ya'll dialect down cefore I leave this Earth. I never thought I'd love another group again after…

After my entire platoon got blown off the face of this Earth! Why? They…they left one-" Creecha dropped his head for what seemed to be an eternity. When he raised his head, he didn't even try to wipe the tears that were streaming down his face.

"They left me cehind. Me!" Creecha screamed as the tears took different courses to his chin, thanks to the shrapnel that tore chunks of flesh out of his face.

"I'll never leave none of you cehind! Never! I'll go down myself cefore I let anything happen to any of ya'll. Ya'll my team, and I'll ce damned if I let another team get away from me! Man enough of this sentimental shit, I love ya'll motherfuckas! Now let's get back to Headquarters so we can get this shit crackin'." Creecha turned and smiled at C.J.

"You like that, huh? Let's get this shit crackin'!" this time Creecha burst into some sort of demonic laughter.

A laugh that could scare Satan himself.

CHAPTER 26

Shaneka was at HQ when they all arrived.

"That's off limits!" C.J. informed J-Roc when he noticed how J-Roc gawked at his wife.

Holding his hands up in surrender, J-Roc said, "Yo Cuz, no disrespect intended."

"None taken since you didn't know. But now that you do…" C.J. let the warning linger in the air as he ascended the steps of the deck.

J-Roc shook the negative thoughts from his mind, rationalizing the situation and concluding that he would've handled it the exact same way.

***　　***　　***　　***

After the initial line of questioning was completed, Shaneka made their drinks. C.J. made a toast.

"To the future of takin' our streets back!"

They all clanked their glasses together and swallowed their poison.

C.J. spoke again.

"In this very room, our former associate chose to love the bitch that you murdered over this movement. Yeah, my wife was instructed to put a paralytic agent in anyone's drink who failed their test. No one was exempt." C.J. said staring directly at J-Roc.

Unmoved, J-Roc assured "Then I have nothin' to worry about."

C.J. went on.

"Now that we all know exactly where each of us stands, it's time to get our country back in order. Romeo, you need employment so Creecha is goin' to *hire* you to work for your own company."

"What?" Romeo questioned.

"You need a front, so whatever business you decide to open up Creecha will ce your acting employer, just so you'll have a check stub to show your P.O. You already got a stable place of residence, so with this your P.O. won't have any reason to fuck with you."

A sly smirk crept across Romeo's mug as his brain shuffled through the whole concept.

" Plus..." C.J. further added "You get to get your training out of the way first. Jer—J-Roc, here's the confirmation number and the keys to both safety deposit boxes. They are in Clarksville. You have a triple wide trailer, just like this one, minus the equipment in Hopkinsville, Kentucky. I heard they call it Hop-town."

J-Roc agreed while gathering up all three keys.

" Hold up Cuz, you have two cars and a bike as well, so here." C.J. said, giving J-Roc a ring with five more keys on it.

" Damn Cuz, you a dream come true. Sheeit, with treatment like this, I'll kill the whole fuckin' world fo you!"

"You see, this ain't for me, you, none of us individually. Naw Loc, this is for the survival of mankind! You see, with people like us and your brother off the streets, who do we have to guide our youth? No fuckin' body!" C.J. screamed without looking for a reply. "Yeah Cuz, with all the real G's gone, you got kids lookin' up to these suckas who's fakin' it to make it. These kids are growin' up thinkin' it's O.K. to snitch, just as long as they don't tell on their homies. Then you got these fools jumpin' on cases, goin' back for time cuts, then put niggas onto cases that they can jump on.

I...*we've* seen it and heard this shit with our own ears. They eat rice bowls together after one of them comes back from ruinin' another man's life. These bitch ass niggas even say, *why do 10 when you can give 5 to a friend!* So this ain't for me Cuz. This is to purify the streets again. We'll never have to indulge in street hustlin' again. But for those where street hustlin' is their only means of survival, we're pavin' the way for them. Hopefully, one day they'll have other alternatives. But for now, *we're* their only hope.

Each one of us is goin' to ce a commander over his own region. There are 5 of us, and there are 50 states. We get 10 states a piece. It's a lot of territory to cover, but this...this is what separates the men from the boys. The real from what we're about to end. Many people have thought about doing what we've put together, but didn't have the team, and or the will to see it through.

This ain't just a Crip movement; this involves the Bloods, GD's, Vice Lords, Stones, Kings, N14's, even those 13's. Hell, every fuckin' body is suffering' cehind the same rat infestation. So eventually, some of them (hopefully all of them) will embrace this movement. I know some will consider this to ce genocide, but what is genocide? Genocide is the planned extermination of an entire kind. People exterminate all things that invade their comfort zone, so that's all we're doin'. We're riddin' the world of unwanted creatures. Creecha, we only need one Creecha around." C.J. said smiling at his comrade.

Shaneka cleared her throat, suggesting to her husband to wrap up his long drawn out speech.

"All day baby." he said acknowledging her request.

"Her' ya'll go." Shaneka said passing out everybody's plane ticket. They loaded the Hummer and headed to Denver's International Airport. Once everyone boarded their flights, C.J. hit the Eastside to pick up his two daughters and granddaughters.

Both daughters were now strippers. That was a lifestyle C.J. never wanted for them, but with a Cokehead for a mother, what choice did they really have? No one really cared about them but C.J. However, daddy had been gone for so long, that their survival instincts had to kick in.

Both of their daughter's fathers had been murdered. One by a rival gang member. The other by Denver's most notorious gang: the Denver Police Department.

To ensure that their lives became successful, C.J. had their very own club built. They knew all the ins and outs of the business, so they could run a club with their eyes closed. Only the most erotic, and exotic would be employed here.

With a new beginning, and all of his women within an arm's reach, C.J. could now focus on cleaning up the streets. C.J. stood by the motto: *"Take care of home first."*

" Arizona, here we come." he said as he zoned out, preparing for what was about to go down.

CHAPTER 27

Romeo was a natural when it came to marksmanship. RoRo came to every session, and like father like son, he was a natural as well. Creecha loved the enthusiasm in the youth, but what he really admired about RoRo was that he reminded him of himself.

Whenever they were at the clothing store on Long St.; in the back-storage room, Creecha would demonstrate how to disarm, hit pressure points, grapple, hand-to-hand combat, as well as use everyday utensils as a weapon.

Both father and son exceeded Creecha's expectations in less than a month. Creecha called HQ to confirm that Romeo was officially ready. To celebrate, Romeo took Creecha to Sugar Bears strip club in Greensboro. Although they enjoyed themselves, Creecha didn't party too hard. He knew he'd have time for playing later. For now, his main focus was to get everybody prepared for the upcoming war.

Creecha left the following afternoon, flying into Memphis. J-Roc was still working security at UM. He'd been picked up for questioning about the double homicide the evening he returned from HQ.

Valerie's nosy neighbor, Sasha, had called MPD upon discovering her neighbor's bodies. She described J-Rocs security car and another assumed to be police car.

"Looked like the Feds." she told the homicide detectives. J-Roc was released after being interrogated for over 5 hours. The detectives drilled J-Roc about the other assumed to be police, but since his story coincided with Sasha's, they had to release him. So now the question was, *who were these mysterious so-called Feds?* Nashville's office had no knowledge of any of theirs visiting Valerie's home. Before leaving the precinct, J-Roc was informed that he was not to leave the state without notifying the MPD. He immediately called C.J.

C.J. told him not to worry and that all tracks had been covered. C.J. then called Creecha and told him to go ahead and train Dub next. Dub would be waiting on him at the LAX when he got there.

Dub was a natural as well; that is once he stopped shooting sideways like they do in the movies.

The time had finally come. C.J. told Creecha to go home and enjoy his family for the next 6 months or so, while the heat died down on J-Roc. But little did they know, the real heat was about to get turned up.

CHAPTER 28

"Collins! Get your dumb ass in here now!" the Chief of the Colorado Springs Police Department screamed.

"Yeah Chief?" Officer Collins replied as he walked through the door of the Crime Lab.

"You dumb fuck! You pushed the button at the garage, didn't you?"

"Yeah Chief...I had to see if the victim was still breathing or not."

"Well asshole, Carter here…" Chief Hagar said pointing to the Senior Lab Technician. "Has lifted what seems to be three sets of prints, but our data base decryption system can't separate the three. If there really are three...hell, who knows! But I can say this: your fuck up got the Feds crawling all up in my ass! Behind you, you asshole!"

"Chie—"

"Shut the fuck up! One of those guys was in witness protection! The other one…fuck the other guy, you really fucked up bad."

“Who was who, Chief?”

“Why does it matter numb nuts? The one in the office was in the program. He was federally protected.”

Letting his mouth outthink his brain, Collins blurted out “Well, if the one under the car wasn’t in the program what are you so ma—”

Before he could finish his statement, Chief Hagar swung a haymaker at Collins which made him stumble over a swiveling chair.

The overweight chief grabbed Collins by the lapels of his jacket and screamed through coffee stained teeth. “You dumb son of a bitch! You fucked up the only lead we had! I swear...I swe-” Chief Hagar let Collins go and clutched at his own chest.

Carter had seen the Chief overexert his heart on many occasions. Reaching into Hagar’s breast pocket, Carter pulled out the tiny bottle of nitro glycerin and popped a pill into Hagar’s mouth. After a few minutes, the Chief stood up and walked out of the room, then straight out of the entire precinct. Collins walked out next, staring dumbfoundedly at his hands. Meanwhile Carter sat and smiled at his own craftiness.

After finding out that Donald Linworth “aka” Jonny Sutton was in witness protection, he purposely sabotaged the evidence. The three prints easily separated.

Each lifted and ran through the national database. Officer Collins, the dead man, Curtis Pendergrass, and the man assumed to have committed the gracious act.

Corey Carter’s father and older brother were each serving a 45-year sentence for running the biggest Meth operation in Mid-West history.

Leon Baker, a local Meth-Head, cooperated with the authorities to dismiss a simple possession charge. All Corey had to do now was locate this William Andrew's character and proposition him with a job to rid the world of Leon Baker.

*** *** *** ***

Compton, California

Dub sat on the hood of his '63 Impala talking to Karen. In the middle of a sentence, the clouds that were suspended above their head opened up and allowed a bright beam of sunlight to shine directly on them.

"Damn baby, this is a sign for us to quit hidin' our love and show these fools what's really crackin'." Karen said, hoping Dub would finally agree to them living their secret life out loud.

"Naw baby girl, that's a sign sayin' somebody or somethin' is lookin' over us." Dub replied, hoping that statement would quiet Karen down about exposing their love affair.

"Like a guardian angel?"

"Exactly!" Dub said, not knowing his real angel's name was Corey Carter.

CHAPTER 29

"Damn Daddy, you did all this for us?" Chenelle (C.J.'s second oldest daughter) asked as she looked around inside the 10,000 sq ft. club he'd bought for her and her sister.

"This is only the ceginnin' Nelle. Wha —"

"Dayumm. Daddy hooked us up!" Nesha the oldest daughter said interrupting C.J. and high fiving her sister. "I just left from downstairs, and I counted 250 dressin' booths. We gonna get paid girl!"

"Damn right we are!"

"Daddy?"

"Yeah Nesha?"

"I know you got a wife, a new baby, and plenty of money, but...what's our future with you? I mean...is this a way to buy us off?"

"Watch yo' fuckin' mouth!" C.J. snapped. "No one is above anyone else in my family! Shaneka is your stepmother. Shit, she's your only mother. And she's a damn good woman! Without her, none of this would've been possible. You will respect her with the respect that you would demand for yourself! As far as splittin' my love, I don't have to! My love is one. You, Nelle, Niyah, Nee-Nee, your baby sister Cleondra, and my wife!"

"I didn't mea—"

"Check yourself! I'm your father, and a few things you better never question. One, my manhood! Two, my Gangsta! And third, my loyalty to what's mine! I did this to take ya'll away from the life that could've taken you under. So why keep you in the same atmosphere? So you don't forget where you came from.

You've seen that lifestyle from the inside lookin' out, now it's time to see it from a new vantage point. Not everybody has somebody to help pull them through. Now that you have an advantage, ya'll can help better somebody else's life. Your last might ce someone's first. Just so—" C.J. stopped when his *Emergency Only* phone vibrated on his hip. He held up a finger for them to give him a minute.

"Yeah?"

"Baby, we gotta talk now!" Shaneka yelled.

After clicking Shaneka off, C.J. told the girls "It's time to go!"

The look in C.J.'s eyes, and the tone of his voice, had Chenelle and Nesha dead on his heels as he exited the club.

***　　***　　***　　***

Shaneka was pacing back and forth in their horseshoe driveway when C.J. pulled up.

"What's up Neek?" C.J. asked his wife when he jumped out of the Hummer.

"Hey Shaneka." both Chenelle and Nesha said greeting their

stepmother.

"Nelle. Nesha." Shaneka said acknowledging her stepdaughters. "Let me holla at'cho daddy real quick." Without a word, Chenelle and Nesha went into the house. Shaneka hopped in the passenger's seat, while C.J. got back behind the wheel.

"Baby, all the field offices got faxes on the demise of some top confidential informants. They 'bout ta start questionin' people from ther' jackets."

C.J. smiled a sign of relief.

"Baby, did'ja her' what I just said?"

"Is this what got your thong all up in a bunch?"

"Maybe you're not undastandin'. They 'bout ta question you and your team, and I—"

"Listen, let em' come. We all have alibis on where we were when them fools got touched."

"But they —"

"Cut nothin'! Hop yo sexy ass in the cack and let me ease yo' mind."

Still unsure about the circumstances, but trusting her man's judgement, Shaneka obliged. Plus, he was speaking in his Panty Wetter dialect.

C.J. pulled the lavishly laced SUV a full 100 yards down his driveway and parked. He climbed in the back to an eagerly awaiting Shaneka who was naked from the waist down. C.J. didn't even fuck his wife. He just lapped away all of her worries with his tongue.

As Shaneka started to climax, all of her doubts, insecurities, and worries vanished, leaving both her conscious, and subconscious mind completely clear. Yeah, her man knew exactly what he was doing.

*** *** *** ***

"O.K., you're sayin' you have a double homicide at a...Ms. Valerie Black's residence, and another double homicide at some sleezy strip club, yet you have no leads or suspects?"

F.B.I. Field Agent Salvatori Kelly asked.

"Well...we...um, you see, our prime suspect was seen at both locations. At the Black's residence, a neighbor...a Ms. er, um...Sasha Turner observed our perp leaving the scene, followed later by a group of African American males, supposedly some of your men. At the smut club, he was sitting in a booth with this man…" Captain Strickland replied, pausing to show Agent Kelly C.J.'s mug shot.

"And…" he added "This same man is on a poster in the younger victim's room. Coincidental...maybe…but my hypoth—"

"Is you ain't got diddly squat! If you knew what the hell you were doin I wouldn't be here now, would I?"

Unthreatened, Strickland shot back. "You are here because I called you. Nothing more, nothing less! All I wanted to do was pool our resources together and maybe come up with some kind of link, or whatever, and solve some homicides. But nooo! You uppity, dick up the ass, cocksuckers from the Bureau swear your agency is all that and a fuckin' bag of chips! So I'll tell you what, Mister *F.B.I.* man, get the fuck outta my office! As a matter of fact, get the fuck outta my precinct! Tell ya boss, if he wants to send somebody into my jurisdiction, next time, please send a professional." Strickland said, then got up and walked out of the conference room and left Agent Kelly looking dumbfounded and wondering how he was going to explain what just happened to his superior.

"Damn!" was all Agent Kelly could muster up before walking out of Captain Strickland's precinct.

CHAPTER 30

"Pop!"

"What's crackin' RoRo?"

"Let me show ya somethin' real quick."

Romeo came out of the master bedroom of his new triple wide to see what had his son so anxious and excited.

"Yeah?" Romeo inquired.

"Welcome home Pop!" RoRo said while pushing play on the DVD player.

Romeo was expecting to see some freaky shit, but what appeared on the screen, was the last thing he had expected to see. The recording was low budget, but everything soon became high definition with quality sound.

The room looked like the inside of an abandoned crack house. Two naked bodies were suspended 2 ft. above the floor. One male, one female.

"Look what we got here!" RoRo's voice chimed in. The camera followed his every step as he began commentating.

"What we have here is a disrespectful slut, and a stupid ass nigga!"

RoRo mimicked his every word as Romeo watched the rest of the disc.

"Yeah bitch, you tried to play an O.G. for this bitch ass busta, but guess what? Today is ya lucky day. All my homies want some of that ho pussy, and when they get finished and Big Dog gets some, you get to leave. Unfortunately, fo' yo' bitch ass, nobody wants to fuck you!" RoRo told Alonzo.

" Ma…man, I sa..wee." Alonzo pled through crusty, swollen, bloody lips.

"Do ya mean it?"

"Uh-huh."

"Well today is your lucky day too! Mousey!"

Mousey quit fondling Laura and pulled out his straight razor.

"Ma…ma...man wha da puck?" Alonzo pled when Mousey grabbed his dick. In one clean swipe, Mousey separated Alonzo from his manhood. Looking around, while still holding Alonzo, Mousey's diabolical mind switched into overdrive. He picked up a piece rebar, and jammed it into the dismembered organ, like a skewer. Then, in one powerful thrust, Mousey rammed the rebar deep into Alonzo's ass.

Shock took over Alonzo's body as he began slipping into a place where his soul would have to answer for all of his deeds.

"He got his wish Pop." RoRo said into the camera. Then he turned back to Alonzo and said, "You fucked yourself when you decided to fuck with the Kitchen, you bitch ass nigga! Hey Pop? You get it? He fucked himself." Then doubled over into a hysterical laugh.

After a few minutes, RoRo regained his composure and said, "I need to do standup O.G. Ain't I a funny mother fucka?"

Laura looked on in horror and said more prayers than a priest says *Hail Mary's* in a lifetime.

"Ya'll hurry up with that bitch, so we can ce out!" RoRo said in a somewhat aggravated tone.

"Big Homie, this…shit...like...that!" Smoke said as he rammed Laura's pussy with all his might.

"Hurry up fool, so we can stab the fuck out!" Smoke pumped a few more times and shot lil Smoke babies all up Laura's cum filled pussy.

"Come on RoRo, come get yours baby." Laura said, shifting her legs, trying to push out all the cum that the lil homies had shot up in her.

"Bitch, I wouldn't disrespect my Pops by stickin' my dick in that trash bin you call a pussy!"

"Well...wh…who's Big Dog then?" Laura questioned.

RoRo pulled out a zippo lighter, with a bulldog on the front saying, "I'm the Big Dog!"

The confusion on Laura's face turned into a petrified grimace.

Taz started pouring gasoline over Alonzos hanging corpse, and then over a screaming Laura.

"RoRo! You said...you said, you was gonna let me leave!"

"Yeah. You leavin' this Earth, bitch!" he said striking the zippo and backed towards the door as Taz made a trail. The camera stayed zoomed in on Laura, and when RoRo touched the flame to the gas trail, Laura immediately began doing the Salisbury Shake. The way she moved and shook her ass, Puffy would've instantly became jealous.

Once she was completely engulfed, the quartet jumped into the Deuce and a Quarter and watched as the abandoned house erupted into flames.

RoRo was still commentating while they passed a blunt around. All of a sudden, a running fireball shot through the front door and leapt on the hood of the Buick. The quartet screamed like a bunch of children watching a horror movie for the first time. Taz snatched the car in reverse as Laura's flesh continued to melt away from what it was designed to protect.

Her adrenaline eventually failed once the flames went out. You could hear a loud thud over the roar of the fire when Laura's charred remains rolled off the hood.

Romeo looked at his son in bewilderment. *Did he inherit those traits from me, or did my absence cause those animalistic tactics to emerge?* Romeo asked himself.

Seeing the footage, and the smile on his son's face, told the whole story.

RoRo was really turned up on his Crippin'! Nothing else was said except for "Play that shit again!" Romeo told his son with an approving smile. RoRo happily complied.

CHAPTER 31

After a full week of running William Andrews name through DMV, USFPO (United States Federal Parole Offices) and a worldwide criminal database linked to Google, Corey took a leave of absence, and nervously planned a trip to Compton, California.

Corey pulled up onto the 1100 block of Acacia St and was immediately approached by the G Homie with the crooked finger.

‘‘What’s crackin’?” G asked.

“Um…yes I’m looking for William Andrews. He goes by Dub-1.”

“Look here cracka, gimme one of those smokes.” G said spotting a half pack of Marlboros on the passenger’s seat.

Corey complied.

“Have you seen him?” Corey asked.

Lighting the cigarette, G said, “I don’t know no damn body by that name.”

“Look this is—”

“You one-time fool? Cause don’t nobody ride through here callin’ out full governments!”

"Excuse me?"

"People's names Cuz, so I suggest you get the fuck up outta here!" G said taking a deep pull off the cigarette and threw down the butt.

"Gimme another smoke."

"Not until you te—"

Corey stopped midsentence when he saw a man fitting Dub's description getting off of a Multistrada 1200 Ducati. A chubby chick remained sitting on the back.

Corey tried to get out of his rented Solora, but G pinned his body against the door. Dub saw the move, and his instincts told him to run. However, instead he held fast. Corey hopped out of the passenger's side, only to be staring down the barrel of a .45 Desert Eagle.

"Dub!" Corey screamed.

Hearing his name, Dub started to make a break for it, but then stopped mid-stride and looked up and down the street, expecting a raid of some fashion.

After seeing no out of the ordinary movement, Dub approached the man that G held hostage.

"You know me fool? From where?" Dub asked, while running the white man's face through his memory bank.

"Yes, I know of you...can you please tell your friend to take that big ass gun out of my face."

"Not until you tell me your business here, homie."

"Well I work for the Colorado Springs Police Department. I'm a lab technician; forensics, blood, lifting prints off of hydraulic lifts...you name it. But I assure you that you're not in any trouble."

Dub waved G down.

"Let me holla at 'im Cuz. But if he blinks wrong..." Dub threw up a 187 with his fingers.

Corey walked around to the driver's side and got in. Dub got in the passenger's seat.

"Hey man." Corey called to G.

"What?"

Corey tossed him the car keys, took out a cigarette, offered Dub one, then tossed the now smiling G the rest of the pack.

"You just made a friend for life, white boy." Dub said as they watched G light a cigarette.

" Firs—"

Dub cut Corey off by putting his finger up to his lips, then reached over and snatched Corey's shirt open.

" Man lis—"

Dub cut him Corey again by instructing him to pull his pants down, then take his shoes and socks off. Once Corey passed Dub's inspection, Dub said, "Come on...but leave yo' shoes in the car and pull your pants up too!"

Inside Karen's house, Dub asked "What's up?"

"Well Dub, I saved you from getting the needle. Now, well, I would like to be compensated for my good deed."

"I don kno—"

" Umm, I believe that you do. In fact, I know it! I lifted your prints off of the lift in the garage where a double homicide took place a couple of months ago."

"I'm listenin'."

" Well, when I lifted the prints, I forged my report and now your prints no longer exist in this case."

" So you ain't got shit on me?"

"On file, no. Right now, you could tell me to kiss your Black ass and kick me out of your house, and there wouldn't be a damn thing I could do about it except leave. But I'd never kiss a man's ass!"

Dub liked the cockiness of the white boy.

"You still ain't tellin' me shit!"

"O.K. Dub, I know your handy work, and I need you to do it again. But not for free. I'll gladly reward you handsomely for this deed you're about to do for my family."

"I'm listenin'."

"This piece of shit got my brother and father 45-years *apiece.* Our family has money—plenty of it. The problem is, my father and brother are suffering behind the wall and our family suffers outside of it. Meanwhile...this cocksucker walks the streets, content with his treachery. This son of a whore must pay severely! I'm here to offer you a half a million dollars to make our family's walking nightmare disappear."

Dub pondered on the deal he'd just been offered for several minutes, then spoke. "Keep your money. You saved my life Homie, so it's only fair that I help you in any way I possibly can."

Corey got up and headed to the front door. Confused, Dub asked, "Where the fuck are you goin'?" but the question fell on deaf ears because Corey kept on going.

He returned less than a minute later with a small Nike gym bag. Feeling more comfortable, Corey went and sat at the dining room table. He pulled out an 8x10 photo of Leon Baker and handed it to Dub. Dub studied the junky's face, then looked Corey directly in the eyes. They were the exact same eyes that his family had when Nutso took the stand on him over a decade ago.

***   ***   ***   ***

Dub and Nutso had grown up together, that is until Nutso's mother died. When she died, Nutso ended up moving to Watts with his father. Even though Nutso had been born and partially raised on Acacia, he still ended up joining the Grape St. Crips, knowing there was bad blood between the sets. Dub and Nutso still kicked it, just not on either of their turfs. Nutso became Judas when he got caught with 200 gallons of PCP.

***　　　***　　　***　　　***

Dub snapped out of his reminiscent state when Corey handed him a picture of the 7-Eleven that Leon slept behind on Nevada Ave.

"So my friend, are we on the same page? I mean…the two guys in the garage got handled...except for the minor slip that could've been major, but I fixed that. This junkie piece of shit will be like long stroking some good pussy. Super easy. Oh yeah, here." Corey said handing Dub the gym bag.

Dub opened the bag and found five $10,000.00 bundles.

"Naw, keep this Homie."

"You were getting that whether you accepted the offer or not. It's a token for your time, I won't take it back."

" Well white boy—"

"It's Corey. Corey Carter."

"Yeah, that's right."

"I never gave you my name. I just told you what I do, and who I work for."

"All day, you got me on that one. But yo...you ever had some Black pussy?"

"No I'm afraid not."

“Are you racist or a separatist motherfucka?”

“No, actually I think Black women are the beautiful creatures on the face of this Earth.”

“So you want some?”

“ Hell yeah I do!”

“Well partna, I’m bout to take yo ass to get some killer pussy. Yeah, this Black pussy actually *kills*.”

“I’m not trying to catch the virus. No...no thank you.”

“Naw Cuz, it ain’t no shit like that. Man, when do you have to go back to work?”

“Actually, I have 10 days left of vacation time. Why?”

“Well, we’re goin’ to New Mexico. This $50-Gees here…” Dub said patting the gym bag, “Will be well spent, trust me.” Dud added, leading Corey back out to his rental.

When they got outside, Big Karen and G were leaning against the Solora. “Yo K, I gotta go handle somethin’. I’ll ce you in eleven minutes.” Dub told his favorite sneak piece.

“You gonna stab out on me for some cracka?”

Dub got in the Solora and rolled the window down.

“K?”

“What?”

“You remember that sign we got not too long ago?”

“What about it?”

“Well this is Corey.”

“And?”

“Get yo panties outta that bunch, cause without Corey here, we wouldn’t exist! He’s really my guardian angel!”

Dub then turned back to Corey and said, “Let’s go!” Corey pulled off content, but ignorant to the full extent of the alliance that was just formed.

CHAPTER 32

Not even 15 minutes after Corey pulled off, the Alphabet Boys simultaneously swarmed Dub's, Lace's, C.J.'s, and Romeo's addresses. None were home, but business cards were left at each residence, by each agency's head officer.

Lace's girlfriend informed the agents that he hadn't been home in a couple months.

"Yeah that niggas' probably laid up over that bitch Val's crib."

Once enlightened of Valerie and Marcia's demise, Tanya smiled inwardly thinking. *Now I ain't gotta share him with that bitch! I'll just have to give him a baby...Yeah, that's what I'm gonna do to get his mind off those bitches.*

Agent Morgan patted Tanya's shoulder when a lone tear escaped her right eye. The agent had mistaken the tear for sadness, but it was really a tear of joy.

***　　***　　***　　***

Chenelle called C.J. immediately after the agents left.

"Say what?" C.J. asked in a higher octane than his usual.

"Yeah, they said that you need to contact...umm, Agent Shepard."

"All day baby girl. Ya'll good?"

"Yeah, but Daddy about earlier…Nesha di—"

"That's over! I said what I had to say, now let me go so I can call that fool. Uhh, what's the number?"

Chenelle gave C.J. the number.

"All day Baby Girl. See ya later and hey…"

"Yeah Daddy?"

"Give my grandbabies a kiss for me. When I get there, I'll take all my ladies out for ice cream."

"O.K. All day." Chenelle replied and hung up.

Chenelle sat and wondered if the rumors she'd heard about her father were really true. *Couldn't be* she reasoned. If her father was as heartless as they say...then he damn sho' wouldn't say things like *kiss my grandbabies*, or *I'll take all my ladies out for ice cream*. Now her heart yearned to be a little girl again, and have her daddy take her and Nesha out for ice cream.

No man had ever showed Chenelle and her sister any affection until their bodies started to develop. Even then, it was only lust, which they'd both mistaken for love. *Daddy's home now, and I'll be damned if anyone ever takes him away from us again! Fuck the Feds!* Chenelle muttered through clenched teeth, then started making phone calls.

***　　　***　　　***　　　***

C.J. called Romeo.

"Yeah they just left Ma' Dukes crib. What's crackin'?" Romeo asked nervously.

"I don't know yet, cut the First Lady is on top of it. I'll hit you cack once I know what's crackin'. Just lay in the cut 'til I call cack."

"All day, Cuz."

" Sho' ya left!"

*** *** *** ***

Dub answered on the first ring.

"Uhhh!" in a squeal that could've passed for Maxwell on *This Woman's Work.*

"I'm glad you got time to live out your mic dreams!"

"Damn Cuz, I was 'cout to get at you. Yeah they raided the block lookin' for a 'G'." Dub said pushing Slutatious' forehead back, then pulled his slobber drenched dick out of her mouth.

"Well I holla'd at"

"Ahhhh, Ohhhh Gawd!"

"Who…what the fuck was that?" C.J. asked.

"That's my man Corey. Jaws got a hol' of 'im."

C.J. could only feel sorry for whoever poor Corey was. After witnessing the demonstration she'd put on the snake, he knew that no man would ever be the same after being sexed by Jaws.

"Yeah Cuz, I need to holla at you about 'im too!"

"Why, somethin' wrong? You need him checked out?"

"Naw Cuz, nothin' like that. Let's just say he cleaned up what I messed up…we'll chop it up when I get cack from the Springs."

"That's what's crackin'. Shit, dig it, I'll ce at HQ, day after tomorrow. Stick around, we'll rap then."

"All day Homie, let me get cack to this vicious mouth game." Dub said rubbing the head of his *Compton Cottonmouth* on Slutatious juicy lips.

"Fo sho'."

"Ahhhh shit! Shit! Shit!" Corey screamed as he released his nut in Jaws eagerly awaiting pussy, then fainted. Jaws giggled and motioned for Dub to come get some.

"Hell naw! Not meeee! That...that's too mu...much pussy for meeee!" Dub screeched as Slutatious locked her lips around the head of his dick and sucked away any chance of this load making a baby.

Damn! We ain't even spent a gee yet. Dub thought. He looked over at Jaws one more time who was now working Corey's limp dick with her other set of jaws, and teasing Dub with her ass in the air, making her pussy lips pucker as if she were blowing him a kiss. Then she sucked her outer lips inward, with the suction of a high dollar Hoover vacuum cleaner, and blew them back out, causing them to vibrate like two pieces of bologna frying in a pan. Seeing that, Dub's big head out thought his smaller one. He opted out and rolled a blunt.

CHAPTER 33

"What's good, Babe?" C.J. asked into his *Wifey* phone.

"My people said yo' thangs coincidental, and circumstantial. They ain't got shit, but ya know how these fools are. Let the team know ta go see them people A.S.A.P.!"

"Thanks Babe."

"Naw niggah, thank me ta'night. I got somethin' fo' yo' ass ta'night anyway."

"All day. Love ya girl."

"Love ya mo."

After they hung up, C.J. immediately called Agent Shepard.

"Shepard here."

"I hope you had a warrant when you invaded my premises."

"Ahh yes. Mister Johnson I presume."

"You damn right this is Mister Johnson! What the fuck do you want?"

"Calm down Mister Killer…I mean Mister Johnson."

"That statement just cost you your job chump!"

"And those murders just got you the needle! Now, if you want to talk to me, come see me at 8am tomorrow, or we'll come back and snatch your Black ass up! Your choice. Oh yeah, bring that pretty lil redbone lawyer of yours with you, and your sexy ass wife. I'll—"

Before Agent Shepard could finish, C.J. hung up.

C.J. immediately called Creecha. "Time to go to work. HQ, day after tomorrow."

***　　***　　***　　***

The following morning, C.J., Shaneka, and Attorney Ann Gatlings arrived at the F.B.I. office in Tucson at a 7:45am. Shepard arrived at precisely 8:00. Stepping out of his car with a cup of Starbucks coffee, and a cigarette dangling from his mouth, he approached the trio.

"Mister Shepard, smoking on government premises is a violation of Bureau policies. Do I need to—"

Ann was cut off by Shepard waving his hands in surrender.

"Hey, we're all friends here, right?" Shepard responded, then let the cigarette fall from his lips, and grounded it into the concrete. This time Shaneka stepped up.

"That's a violation that'll get'cha reprimanded!"

Frustrated and visibly pissed off, Shepard shifted "Lets focus on the major and skip the minor."

"From what I see, you are the only violator of any law here." Ann said in a chastising tone.

Shepard tried to rush past the trio, purposely throwing his shoulder into C.J.

"That's assault on an unarmed man. Wow!" Ann said, already

plotting on what she was going to buy once she won this case.

Realizing the mistake, he just made was major, Agent Shepard turned and looked directly into Ann's hypnotizing greenish-gray eyes and offered, "Look, maybe I jumped the gun. We can overlook this matter and let bygones be bygones. What do you say?"

"It seems to me that you're trying to solicit, and or bribe my client. No, we'll do this interrogation and then I'll go to your supervisor and have him charge you for every offense you've committed today. Some are *minor* you say, but then we do have a couple majors. Your record is already tarnished, and that camera won't lie in the courtroom." Ann said, pointing to the camera mounted above the entrance.

Agent Shepard knew that his career and marriage were about to end behind his antics. Both had warned against any new infraction. Agent Shepard nodded and said, "You win. Let me go get the reports out of the car."

Agent Shepard stepped back into the government issued Ford LTD, lit another cigarette, and thought about all the injustice he'd brought on while serving *Justice.* Agent Shepard then thought about his failing marriage, and then how much his kids and coworkers hated him. Pulling his Glock .40 from his shoulder holster, Agent Shepard stared at the trio as they stared back at him.

I ought to kill all three of them niggers right now, but naw. My record is bad enough. I gotta at least be halfway right when I go meet the good lord.

Taking one more pull off the Camel, Agent Shepard plucked the rest on the floorboard, and stuck the barrel of the Glock .40 in his mouth. He stared directly at Shaneka and mumbled, "You sexy black bitch!" then pulled the trigger.

Immediately after the interrogation of the Memphis murders, and now Shepard's suicide, C.J. called his team and assured, "Go see them folks, we straight!"

*** *** *** ***

Romeo called Agent Gates, then his newly acquired family attorney Kathy Berdino. C.J. suggested that they all get female attorneys because a woman will fight harder to prove herself in any field dominated by men, or she can use her sensual powers to gain a victory. *As long as you win* was another one of C.J. 's mottos.

They all met up at the Project Safe building at 3:00pm, the following day. Agent Gates was a no-nonsense type of guy, plus he hated to see his race wasting away through genocide. Agent Gates hated gang members especially. Although he ran with the local crew as a youth, Agent Gates somehow escaped his fate and the stereotype placed on all young Black men. He went on to attend Johnson C. Smith University and graduated with a Bachelor's Degree in Criminal Justice. The rest is history.

Now a mentor and a Federal Agent, Gates' only concern now was to preserve the youth by giving them a better alternative in the streets.

Once they were all in the main conference room, Gates didn't waste any time.

"Look, straight up no chaser Mister Myers, we don't have shit on you…but it's protocol to give you a chance to clear your name. Whichever you do, talk or walk, it's on you. Understood?"

"Mister Gates, if you have nothing on my client, then I move to have the questioning to cease." Attorney Berdino quipped.

"Well, if he has nothing to hide, then I don't see any harm

here, do you Mister Myers?"

There was a quick telepathic exchange between the attorney and client, then Romeo broke the silence.

"What am I here for?"

"Well, there was a double homicide in Memphis not too long ago. You wouldn't happen to know anything about that, would you?"

"Yes."

Everyone in the room looked at Romeo astonished.

Gates leaned forward and encouraged, "Go on." then turned on his tape recorder.

"Um...Mister Gates, I'd like to speak with my client in private for a moment."

"Naw, that won't be necessary, Ms. Berdino." Romeo told his attorney, then turned back to Gates.

"I was watchin' CNN and I saw the murder scene. What got me was they flashed pictures of a friend of mines' daughter and her mother, sayin' they were the victims. Whoever did it better not sleep light."

"Your friend, what's his name?!:':'

"Marcus Lacy. But I call 'im Lace."

"When was the last time you saw your friend?"

"The day I got out of the halfway house. He came to a party they had for me."

"They who?"

" My friends and family."

"That was the only encounter you had with him?"

"Yes."

"Do you know a Clevon Johnson, and a William Andrews?"

"Yeah. They're my homies from the pen."

"Did they attend the party?"

"Yes."

"Have you ever been to Memphis?"

"Naw…Hol' up, I know you ain't sayin' I did that shit!" Romeo screamed, and jumped out of his chair.

"Calm your client down Ms. Berdino."

"Mister Myers, please sit down!"

"Hell naw! This fool is tryin' to fuck my—"

"Look Myers, like I said, I ain't got shit on you. You volunteered all that, now sit yo' ass down before I call your P.O. and get your ass violated!"

Romeo plopped back down in his seat and crossed his arms across his chest. Agent Gates studied Romeo's body language, but it was undeterminable, so he couldn't make a final assessment of guilt.

"Listen Myers, I have to let you go for now. But next time...if there is a next time, it won't be this social. Whoever did this heinous shit, I will do everything in my power to see him or her get the needle. You're free to go. For now that is."

Romeo stood up and kicked his chair backward. Gates grabbed Romeo's wrist and said, "For now!" then let it go.

CHAPTER 34

"I'm marrying her and that's that!" Corey snarled.

Dub looked into his pussy whipped eyes and said,

"Check ya self—"

"No! Check *yourself*! That woman just sucked the soul out of my body. She made me cry mannn!" Corey said grabbing Dub by the shoulders and shook him as tears began to stream down his face.

Dub pulled away and scornfully started, "You hella crazy Cuz! Do you think a bitch li—"

Before he could get the rest of the snide remark out, Corey punched him in the mouth.

"Bitch ass cracka!" Dub roared as he began to punish the under matched Caucasian.

Slutatious and Jaws heard the commotion and came running from the adjoining room. Jacinda Ellis, "aka" Jaws, came trying to save her meal ticket. Meanwhile, Joy Savers, "aka" Slutatious, came as a supporting cast act to just be nosy.

"Dub! Get'cho hands off my man!" Jaws screamed, trying to stop Dub's vicious assault on Corey.

Dub backhanded Jaws with a closed fist, causing a sickening crunch to emerge from her nose. Blood began to spew from her nose as she ran back into the other room. Slutatious knew exactly what Jaws ran to the other room for.

"She's goin' to get her blade." she warned, as Dub stood over an unconscious Corey, breathing like a madman.

"AAHHHHHHH!" Jaws screamed as she ran back into the room, swinging her straight razor above her head. For a brief moment, Dub was caught in a sadistically state of lust when he saw Jaws bloody breast swinging side to side.

As her arm came forward, Dub snapped out of his state of mind and his survival instincts kicked in. He side-stepped and caught Jaws with a solid blow to the back of the ear, discombobulating her equilibrium. Jaws staggered to her left and fell face first into the glass coffee table.

The shattering of the glass brought Corey out of his stupor. Through busted lips, Corey let out a wounded animal howl.

Dub looked over at Slutatious who was standing on a chair, covering her mouth with both of her hands.

"Dig it S, we gotta stab out, so go put your clothes on." Seeing she wasn't moving, Dub screamed, "Now!"

Slutatious stepped down nodding hysterically.

Corey laid on his side, reaching for Jaws.

"Whyyyy man? You ru...ruined my life!"

Dub just stared at the poor excuse for a man.

"You lil bitch. You killed her, not me!"

"You ca...can save her, pl-please man...then…then we're even!"

Dub look at Jaws, who was past the stage of survival. Blood squirted from several severed arteries in her neck. Dub decide to put her out of her misery.

He snatched a cushion off the sofa and pressed it against her face with his foot. When her body no longer contorted, Dub lifted his foot and said, "I saved the bitch from sufferin', so now we even!"

Slutatious came running back through the door in time to see Dub pull his Calico from his waist band, snatch the cushion he'd just ended Jaws' life with, and put it over Corey's face. The retort was muffled as Corey's soul left to go join its mate. Slutatious could only wonder what her fate would be as she looked on in horror.

"Help me wipe the place down so we can get the fuck up outta here!" Dub instructed. Slutatious could only nod a nervous nod, then commenced to wiping things down with the tail of her shirt. Dub started wiping down everything he thought he might have touched. *Can't ever ce too careful* he thought as he started wiping everything behind Slutatious too.

When they were done, Dub said, "We gonna walk up outta here all hugged up and shit, then...you just wait cause—"

"What'cha gonna do with me?"

"Look, it's damn near $50,000 in this bag. It's yours. You just forget everything you've seen. Deal?"

"I already forgot."

"Good then, here you go." Dub said tossing her the bag. Dub and Slutatious hugged and kissed their way down to the lobby, then walked over to the front desk. The desk clerk was busy chatting on the phone when Dub asked, "Where's the manager?"

Annoyed, the desk clerk stated, "Back there." and jerked her thumb over her shoulder.

Dub walked around the desk and cold cocked the clerk.

"Watch her, I gotta run back here." Confused, Slutatious walked up and leaned on the counter, trying to act as nonchalant as possible.

The manager looked up from the safe, and asked, "What…who the hell are you?"

"Look, this ain't a robbery. I just need the surveillance tape from last night and this morning. If you don't give it to me, I'll find it myself, then kill you. You have a choice here."

Weighing his options, the manager said "The discs are over there. I just changed the one from last night."

"Go get it and eject the one runnin' now."

The manager did as he was told. Once Dub had the discs, he sent a slug from the Calico through the old white man's head.

Out front, Slutatious was still leaning on the counter watching the clerk take an early day's nap.

"Come on, let's go." Dub said in an even tone.

As they headed for the front entrance, Dub quickly ran back to the front desk. He leaned over and put a slug through the clerk's head.

In the car, Dub looked over at Slutatious and said, "Shit, no witnesses, no crime, right?"

"Shit, Dub…there are four dead bodies in there."

"Yeah, but don't nobody know who did any of it, but us." he said looking at her sternly.

"My nigga, I don't know shit."

"Then it's all good. Like Cube said, *today was a good day.*"

"I know that's right." Slutatious said, but both having ulterior motives for making their statements.

"Hey Dub?"

"Yeah?"

"You can drop me off at the bus station, and I'll catch a bus back home."

"Where's home?''

"Wilksboro, North Carolina."

"Oh yeah?"

"Yeah, and I can start a lil escort service with this." Slutatious said patting the bag of money. "I can't go back to Tricky, especially not after he finds out he's lost Jaws. That was his hottest commodity. He knows we left together."

"I'll take care of Tricky."

"Yeah, you do that. I don't want no part of the rampage he's gonna go on!"

Dub pulled into a 7-Eleven parking lot.

"Do you want somethin'?"

"Just a Slurpy, and a condom."

"Cool." Dub said smiling.

10 minutes later, Dub came out carrying a hefty sized bag and two Slurpies.

"Damn nigga, you went grocery shoppin' at a corner store." Slutatious half-joked. Dub didn't even reply, he just drove off.

They rode for a while until Dub saw what he was looking for. Looking at Dub with nervous eyes, Slutatious asked "Why we goin' down a dirt road?"

"The same reason you asked for a condom. So I could bang that pussy cefore I take you to the bus station."

"Yeah, I do need some good dick before I take this long ride." Slutatious said, but was thinking, *Yeah, he can get one last nut, cause I'm puttin' the PoPo's on him, and Tricky's ass. Then I'll go back to New Mexico, and run Tricky's spot like it should be!*

Dub broke her out of her zone when he grabbed the back of her head and pushed it in his lap. Slutatious knew her head game was tight, so she decided to give Dub an All-Star performance that would make Superhead change her profession.

After bustin' a quick nut, Dub said "Get out them jeans, I need to ce inside you." Staring at Dub all starry eyed, Slutatious started to comply, but ended up passing out.

Dub sprang into action. He jumped across Slutatious' unconscious body and pulled her out of the passenger door into a shallowly wooded area.

Dub then ran back to the car to get the roll of toilet paper and both bottles of lighter fluid that he'd just bought from 7-Eleven. He pressed the toilet paper against Slutatious temple, then shot through it. The toilet paper suppressed the blasting sound that the handheld cannon usually made. Slutatious' life ended with the sound of a loud cough.

Dub then doused Slutatious' body with the lighter fluid. He even stuffed her mouth with the remains of the toilet paper and saturated her pussy with the rest of the fluid.

"Won't find my DNA now!" he said lighting a Newport.

Feeling that the fluids had had enough time to fully saturate Slutatious' sexy ass, Dub dropped the cigarette then hurried back to the car.

"Damn, what a waste of some bangin' ass head!"

When he got in the car, Dub pulled out a bottle of Visine and smiled.

"This shit really works." he said putting a drop in each eye, then tossed the bottle into the flames that erased all evidence that could've been used against him in a courtroom.

CHAPTER 35

C.J. and Creecha sipped on forty ounces as they discussed the progress of the movement.

"We got damn near 20 bodies and we ain't even got started yet!" C.J. said with a little hint of frustration.

"No war is won over night, Homie."

"Yeah, you right, but-"

"But nothin'! We still breathin', and niggas are still snitchin'! It's time to, how ya'll say it, turn this shit up!"

C.J. loved Creecha's enthusiasm and was glad that he was a friend instead of a foe.

Creecha missed an easy shot in the side pocket. Inwardly C.J. knew that he'd missed on purpose, so he purposely missed an easy bank of the thirteen ball. They both smiled, toasted, then shotgunned the rest of their malt liquor.

That was a strategic move to show that they were on the same page, without uttering a word.

They'd drawn first blood and won the first battle. Now, they hoped that the whole war would have the same outcome.

To break the silence, C.J. tossed Creecha a manila envelope. Creecha opened it, and pulled out two glossy black & white, 8x10 photos, along with both individuals profiles. One man was Hispanic, the other was Black. Both men were honorable to the game and were planning to go to trial. The Black man whose name was Chris Rankin's, his dope-fiend brother Josh was the government's star witness. The Hispanic one, Eric Morales, was set up by his cousin's boyfriend, Jonny Hychen.

C.J. then tossed a second envelope on the table. This one contained the informant's names, pictures, and profiles on their whereabouts. One lived in Henderson, Nevada. The other in North Augusta, South Carolina.

"We'll leave out as soon as Dub gets here. He'll ce here sometime today." C.J. informed his comrade.

Still unclear as to how they were going to do this, Creecha only nodded his agreeance. He was down for whatever.

"Get Romeo and J-Roc on the horn. Tell 'em it's time. No wait!—"

Creecha pulled the phone away from his ear.

"Tell J-Roc to go see Romeo. We'll ce there in a couple days." Creecha looked at C.J. to make sure that that was the actual message to deliver. Once confirmed, he made the call.

***　　***　　***　　***

Dub pulled into Colorado Springs, and left Corey's rental parked in the Chapel Hill's Mall; thoroughly wiped down of course.

Dub then caught a cab out to Limon but got dropped off a half of a mile away from HQ. He and the cabbie had smoke two blunts of Dro' during the ride, so he was feeling real nice. Dub actually felt so good that he gave the cabbie $300.00 for a $90.00 fare. *Fuck it, I got damn near $50-grand here, plus it's rough out here on a nigga workin' a real job. Niggas out here killin' mufuckas for way less than that, so the nigga deserves a lil extra for his pockets'* he reasoned.

Once HQ was in his view, Dub began jogging, then broke out into a full sprint once he hit the driveway.

The motion sensors were triggered, which alarmed C.J. and Creecha. C.J. ran to the window, ready to unleash some pent-up frustration with his .50 cal Gatlin gun. Creecha moved, grabbing two shrapnel grenades out of the cupboard and positioned himself by the front door, waiting on the go-ahead nod to shred the transgressor.

Seeing it was Dub, C.J. waited to see what had his comrade running as if the devil were behind him.

Once reality set that no one was out there but Dub, C.J. walked out on the deck. As Dub ascended the first step, C.J. dove and tackled him back onto the graveled driveway.

Winded from running, Dub couldn't put up much resistance against the *Big brother, Little brother* blows being delivered. Creecha finally intervened.

He snatched C.J. off of Dub in a fatherly manner.

"Inside. Now!" he roared into C.J.'s ear. Creecha then turned back and snatched Dub up by the front of his already torn T-shirt.

"I'ma fu—"

Bam!

Dub's threat ended when a short uppercut caught him in the solar plexus. Before he could fall, Creecha dipped under, and hoisted Dub up over his shoulder. He then carried him inside and slammed him on the floor.

Dub raised his head, trying to figure out what stemmed this attack. *I ain't goin' out like Lace did* Dub told himself. He reached for his Calico but realized that it was in the gymbag.

His nerves shot when he didn't feel the bag on his shoulder anymore.

"Lookin' for somethin' my friend?" C.J. asked, holding up the bag.

Before Dub could reply C.J. kicked him under the chin, knocking him out cold.

"Tie that nigga up!" C.J. demanded.

When Dub came back to consciousness, he was hogtied, but to his amazement, he could still move his body.

O.K. I'm not paralyzed. Dub opened his eyes to a sight that he'd fear for the rest of his life. Two cold-blooded killers staring at him with tears streaming down their cold faces.

Holding Dub's *Equalizer*, and the money spread out in front Dub's face, Dub frantically asked, "Cuz, I know you—"

"Why Cuz?" C.J. asked, interrupting Dub's plea of innocence.

"Cuz, it ain't like that."

"No? Then what's it like?"

"Whatever you're thinkin', it ain't left."

"Is that left? You come runnin' up here full speed, with a bag of money and a strap! Tell me what I should think then, huh?"

"Cuz, you know damn well I ain't on no shit like that!"

"I don't know shit! Who the fuck sent you?"

"Damn Cuz, untie me!" Dub said, squirming to get free.

"I can't do that 'til I know what I need to know, and so far, it looks like you'll ce choppin' it up with Lace real soon. Now is your only time to convince me that you weren't comin' here on no foul shit. Out of respect for your set, you got 11 minutes. Your time is runnin'."

Dub started from Corey coming to Compton, to the reason he came, the double homicide, then the second double homicide, to his 5th body, and burning Slutatious in the woods. Once he got to the part about him and the cabbie smoking dro' it all started sounding like a bunch of gibberish.

C.J. sat with his eyes closed while Creecha pecked away on the computer. Pissed off, but also nervous because his fate was uncertain, Dub let out one final plea.

"Loc, fuck what 'cha thinkin'. Go wit what'cha know, and you know I'd never cross a homie, Cuz…we family. We made a pact and...and I take that shit as serious as I do Crippin'! If you feel I'd cross you…smoke me now…with my own fuckin' strap, or unfuckin' tie me!"

Creecha stood up from the computer and pulled out his straight razor.

"Creech...ma...man what the fuck are you doin'? C.Jayyyyyyyy!" Dub screamed. C.J. never opened his eyes. Creecha raised the razor and came down with the alacrity of a cheetah. Dub didn't move.

"Get'cho ass up, fool!" Creecha bellowed.

Not feeling any pain, Dub opened his eyes. Realizing that he'd been freed from the restraints, he jumped up and punched C.J. in the mouth, sending him to the floor.

C.J. shook the cobwebs from his mind, while Dub stood over him saying "That's for kickin' me in my shit. Now we even!" He then offered C.J. a hand up.

C.J. accepted it. When he stood up, him and Dub stood toe to toe. Creecha intervened.

"We got bigger fish to fry. Once this shit is over...if it's ever goin' to ce over, *then and only then* will I let this go down. I've come too fuckin' far to let ya'll fuck up your *Vision…*" Creecha emphasized by poking C.J. in the chest. "So ya'll drop the bullshit, or I'll kill ya'll both and pursue this with Ro and J-Roc." After looking at both men, Creecha asked, "What's it gonna ce?"

"When this is over, I need to see you Dub."

"You got that all day." Dub said extending his hand. C.J. took his hand and shook it firmly.

Feeling the tension lighten some, Creecha said, "Let's hit the road."

"Where we headed?" Dub inquired.

"Nevada."

"For what?"

"It's showtime."

"About time. Let's get this shit crackin'."

CHAPTER 36

C.J. being the better looking out of the three, knocked on Angie Harmons door.

"Who is it?" she asked

"Universal Cleaners, Ma'am." C.J. responded.

"I ain't fuckin' call no cleaners!"

"Ma'am, we were sent by Chris Rankin."

Angie snatched the door opened and asked, "What kinda game you playin' fool? My man is in Fed custody, so try again asshole! If you came to rob us, too fuckin' late, the Feds took everything!"

C.J. was so taken in by her beauty that for once he thought he'd seen something that could compete with Shaneka's sex appeal. C.J. snapped out of his trance when Angie started knocking on his forehead.

" Hellllooo! Is…N…E…Bo..Dee home?" she asked, moving her hand like a retard.

Beauty and no brain C.J. concluded.

"Don't ever put your hands on me if you wish to keep them! Now if you wouldn't mind, we need to talk, so invite me in, and don't act stupid again." Angie moved aside to allow C.J. to enter her apartment. Before he stepped in, he called Dub's cell.

"Ya'll come up and bring the equipment."

Angie stared at C.J. with a vague expression as he walked past her.

"So wha—"

C.J. held a finger to his lips, silencing her.

He pulled out a small Memo and wrote, "*Your apartment may be bugged. We'll talk on paper, cool?*"

Angie nodded obediently.

Creecha knocked on the door. Angie looked at C.J. for his approval. After a short nod, Angie screamed "It's open!"

Two men appeared, clad in white painter jumpsuits and ventilation masks while trudging two big machines. They didn't even acknowledge the pair sitting at the table. They just went and found two open outlets and plugged in the so-called vacuum and shampooer.

C.J. removed the stacked paper from his clipboard. The first ten sheets were inventory forms, and invoice slips. Next was a mugshot of Chris.

C.J. wrote, *"Is this your man?"*

Angie nodded with tears starting to well up in her eyes. The love evaporated when he slid her a picture of Josh. She jumped up in a fit of rage, tearing the picture into hundreds of pieces. C.J. motioned for her to sit back down. Angie plopped down hard.

Dub held his hand up, indicating that he'd found a bug inside the phone.

Angie looked at C.J., who then wrote down, *"Your phone is tapped."* Angie's eyes lit up when she read the note.

C.J. then wrote, *"Don't worry, our machine is a bug scanner, the other is a noise disorder. Now you know. Now. do you want your man home?"* Angie nodded.

C.J. then wrote, *"How bad?"*

Angie wrote, *"I'll do anything to get him home."*

He wrote, *"Can you get 10 g's?"* She shrugged her shoulders. *"I'll loan you the money, would you pay me back, with interest?"*

"Yes." she wrote.

"Will you stake your life on that?"

"Yes, but what's the catch?"

"No catch. We want our money and a loyal soldier."

"What do you mean?"

"We're on a mission to rid the world of snitchin' and reclaim the streets. But I must ask you this, when he comes home, say things don't work out with the two of you, would your emotions allow you to keep this meeting clandestine?" C.J. searchingly wrote

"What meeting?" Angie assured.

"Great answer. You see, one of our mission's is to strengthen the households of our people. Go see him tomorrow and ask if he's willing to be down with this cause. Please inform him that if he crosses us, he'll die; his mother, and his wife too!"

That statement caused Angie to swallow hard, thinking of the possibility of an early demise.

"Make sure that he's on the same page that we're on. One slip up or mistake, will cause a major tragedy, do you understand?"

Angie closed her eyes, as though contemplating her decision, but was really lost in the idea of being in Chris' arms again.

Agitated with her delay in response, C.J. reached over and pinched one of her nipples that fought her wifebeater for freedom.

"Ouch!" Angie screamed as she jumped up rubbing her tender

bud. She glared at C.J. with a combination of fire and ice. Lust and hate. Both felt the attraction, but they both knew that it was far greater than a nut.

Angie grabbed her sheet of answers and scribbled, *"Don't ever put your hands on me again if you wish to keep them!"* then gave C.J. a look saying, *Two can play that game.*

C.J. smiled his infamous uneven smile that always made women cream in their panties. That's exactly what was happening now. Angie crossed her left leg over her right, allowing the tight denim to apply friction to her throbbing clit.

The two held an erotic stare off for a good minute until a violent shudder erupted throughout Angie's pubic region.

C.J. gave her an *I conquered you* smile. Embarrassed, Angie wrote, *"Don't flatter yourself, I was thinking about Chris that's all!"* They both knew that she was lying, the evidence was still in her panties.

C.J. wrote, *"Remember, no one is to know of this. We'll see—"* he stopped when Angie got up and went to the refrigerator. She returned with four Coronas.

Angie grabbed her pen and paper and wrote, *"A toast to my husband coming home."* Creecha and Dub joined them at the table. They all toasted and guzzled their beer.

Preppy bitch! Fine, but preppy. Dub thought when he saw Angie's pinky sticking straight out as she drank her beer. C.J. swirled his finger around in the air to let his comrades know to wrap things up.

As they headed to the door Angie followed like an obedient puppy. As soon as C.J. stepped out of the apartment, he turned to give his parting words.

Angie rubbed her pinky against his bottom lip. His sense of

smell persuaded his sense of taste to perform its rightful duty. C.J. sucked Angie's finger into his mouth, and when she pulled it back, a long string of saliva came with it, which she broke with her tongue.

"See you tomorrow." Angie mouthed, then slammed the door. Angie leaned against it, holding her head in both hands.

As C.J. descended the stairs, he and Angie simultaneously said, *"Damn!"*

CHAPTER 37

"How you holdin' up baby?" Angie asked Chris through the visitation phone.

"I'm good lil Lady. How you doin'?"

"I'm alright, just missin' you like crazy!"

"How much?" Angie stood up and lifted her skirt, exposing her thumb-sized clit. Since they were both in isolated booths separated by only a 0.5-inch piece of Plexiglass, it became a ritual for Angie to wear a skirt without any panties so Chris would have something to keep his brother's betrayal off of his mind. At least ease it some if possible. So far it hadn't worked, but he still enjoyed the show. Chris' face contorted when Angie sat back down. His first thought was *she ain't gonna ride with a nigga on this.*

Thinking he was about to get a titty shot made Chris retract his last thought. However, he was disappointed when Angie pulled out a mini Memo pad and wrote "Just keep talking, and nod your head, or shake it, O.K. Bookie?" Chris nodded that he understood, so

Angie continued to write.

"I got a visit from these guys saying they can get you out for 10 g's." Chris squinted his eyes and kept talking.

"I know we ain't got it, but they said they'd even loan it to us...with interest, of course."

Again, Chris only squinted.

"Bookie, these guys are for real! They even found a bug in our house phone. They had all this high-tech equipment and shit. They are starting a movement to get rid of all the snitchin' and shit...something about taking the streets back. Plus, they on some uplifting and bringing families closer together."

"How?" Chris mouthed, then continued rambling on about nothing.

"They expect our loyalty to the movement, along with their money, of course. But Bookie listen, you're gonna have to join the movement, O.K.?"

Chris nodded, then mouthed "What's the catch?"

Angie stared Chris directly in the eyes and held his gaze before writing, "They're goin' to kill Josh!"

Chris sat with his eyes closed for what seemed to last an eternity. Knowing that their 15 minutes were almost over, Angie knocked on the Plexiglass and held up her pad.

"R U DOWN, OR NOT?"

Chris looked Angie in the eyes knowing that his next gesture would determine if his mother would lose him to the F.B.O.P., or Josh to unknown assassins. Either way, she was going to lose a son.

He and Josh had grown up thicker than thieves. They stole their first bike together, their first candy bar, together, bought their first car together, put their money together, and bought their first eightball, together. They even lost their virginities to crackhead Rita together. The only thing that they didn't do together, was *experiment* smoking crack-laced blunts. No matter how hard he tried, Chris could never get Josh to stop.

Chris soon found a major plug and ended up taking over the whole West-Side of Spokane, Washington. He migrated to Nevada when the Feds started sweeping the area. Unbeknown to Chris, Josh was picked up in the roundup. With pressure and threats coming from the agents, and the *'Monkey'* on his back, Josh turned informant in less than 24 hours.

Josh called Chris from an unidentified number and told him that he had a game, and asked could he shoot ball today, which translated to, *"I got a sucka that I'm about to pimp."*

The Feds already knew what he was saying translated into because Josh told them everything that he knew. Wanting Josh to make a come up, Chris agreed to meet him and the so called *'Vic'*. The rest was history. Josh was a Judas.

The phone cut off, so Chris stood up and placed the receiver on its hook. He turned his back on his *everything*. *Bloods thicker than water* Chris reasoned.

Angie banged on the Plexiglass as Chris got ready to exit the booth. He couldn't face her. He couldn't allow Angie to see him crying for his brother. Chris turned the knob on the booth's door and stopped. He nodded his head and held his thumb and pinky finger to the side of his face, indicating that he'd call.

*** *** *** ***

Chris didn't call that night. Instead, he did a 1000 Burpees, took a long hot shower, then laid and stared at the ceiling and meditated. By morning, his conscience was clear. *Fuck Josh! He threw me to the wolves, so Rot in hell sucka'!*

After breakfast, Chris called Angie and told her "The day I fell in love with you, is how I feel now." She heard the hidden message. The day Chris revealed his true feelings to Angie, he lifted her chin with a curled finger, and looked deep into her eyes penetrating her soul, and said, "This is forever, ain't no turnin' back!"

They'd been inseparable ever since.

Chris and Angie chit-chatted for the remainder of the call. After they hung up, a wave of serenity swept over Chris, allowing him to drift off into a deep slumber for the first time during his 9-months of incarceration.

*** *** *** ***

C.J. knocked on Angie's door not even 10 minutes after she got off the phone with Chris.

Knock! Knock! Knock!

"What!" she screamed when C.J. knocked again for the third time.

Snatching the half-smoked blunt out of the ashtray, Angie fired it up then headed to the door.

I bet it's those damn Jehovah Witnesses again! Well they gonna catch a contact this mornin' if they wanna talk to me this damn early.

Angie pinched her nipples, instantly erecting them. With the blunt in the corner of her mouth, she snatched the door opened, hoping to turn the early morning nuisance away.

C.J.'s eyes immediately dropped and took in the contours of

Angie's body. The half damp wifebeater was the only thing obscuring her 38C-24-42 frame. C.J. took a step back and mouthed, *"Put some clothes on."* Angie shook her head *no*, then motioned for him to come in. A battle for supremacy had begun. Who would prevail?

Angie backed up, moving with the grace of a Salsa dancer. Grabbing the black slim remote on the living room couch, she aimed it at her Kenwood house stereo, bringing R. Kelly and Ron Isley's vocals alive. The duo serenaded the room about keeping things on the *down-low*; reiterating that nobody had to know.

C.J. stepped inside and closed the door. Angie put the blunt out then seductively pulled the wifebeater up over her head, revealing her half-inch nipples. A staple-marked zipper scar ran from Angie's sternum to just above her mini afro between her legs. Two small indentions were on either side of the zipper.

A .25 C.J. assumed. Angie had no shame showing it. *A badge of honor!* he reasoned.

Seeing the bulge in C.J.'s coveralls, Angie gyrated towards him. When she started stroking him through the thick material, neither said a word.

C.J. and Angie's bodies intertwined the way two Indian Cobras would during their mating ritual. Their eyes stayed glued together, as their hands explored forbidden grounds.

C.J. spun and landed on the sofa, with Angie stretched out across his lap. He leaned forward and whispered, "You're a bad girl." Angie answered him by raising her ass, encouraging C.J. to spank her.

C.J. licked his fingers, and swatted Angie across the right ass cheek, causing her to jerk forward. Pleasure and pain exploded throughout her entire being. Angie never released C.J.'s dick. Her movement caused a mini moan to escape C.J.'s lips.

Angie then undid the bottom two buttons of the coveralls and was surprised at the size of the snake that sprang free. She squeezed the shaft and stroked up to its head. C.J. slid two fingers into Angie's now dripping orifice.

After Angie sucked the nectar off of his fingers, C.J. swatted her ass again. They kept this escapade going for two more songs, then they both released and ended the feud for dominance. They both knew it was inevitable that they'd end up having some form of a sexual tryst.

Now they were content. Although C.J. and Angie knew what had just taken place was wrong, they also kept in mind that they didn't actually have intercourse. This made them have a mutual respect for one another because both C.J. and Angie loved their significant other. Now it was time that they got down to business.

Angie went and put on a satin robe. The two of them then sat and shared a blunt of *Purp* as if they were longtime friends and that their tryst never occurred.

Once the blunt went out, Angie grabbed her notepad and wrote, "He's down for the movement."

C.J. smiled his smile.

Angie quickly wrote, "Quit doin' that you sexy mother fucka!"

C.J. took the pad and wrote, "The feelin' is mutual. I gotta go. I'll ce in touch."

"How will you know when he gets out?" she wrote.

"I'll know. I found you, didn't I? I know his case, so just know that I can find whoever, whenever."

Angie was so turned on to be in the presence of a real *Boss* that when C.J. got up to leave, she jumped on his lap and pinned him back in his chair.

C.J. reached for the remote control and turned the volume up several more notches, then mumbled, “Why?” as Angie rubbed her succulent breasts all over his face.

“Chris has to pay you interest; well this is *my* interest.”

Fuck it! C.J. thought as he pulled out his Colorado Black snake and pulled Angie down to the hilt. All she could do was hold on and enjoy the ride.

CHAPTER 38

"Yo dude, can you spare a five spot?"

Dub looked the junkie up and down then said, "Yeah, but not for nothin'."

"What'cha need, man?"

"I'll throw you a dub, but you gotta wash my ride."

"That's it! Sheiiit, let's go!" the junkie said walking around to the passenger side of the rented Durango.

"You better walk yo' funky ass up the street to the carwash. I'll meet you there."

"No sweat my man. I'll meet you up there." Josh said, then broke out in a full sprint, needing to be there when his vic got there. His fellow junkies would cut his throat quicker than one can blink. There's no loyalty in the world of Junkyism.

Dub had been coming to this same gas station, every day for 2-weeks while Creecha and C.J. combed other areas Josh was known to frequent.

Dub immediately called C.J., who turned around and called

Creecha. When Dub pulled into the carwash, Josh was already standing in an open bay area, jumping up and down so Dub could see him.

Dub pulled in and said, “I want the works.” Dub then hopped out, got $10 worth of quarters, then handed them to Josh. Dub climbed back in the SUV and fired up a Sherm stick while listening to his Compton homie MC Eiht rhyme about it being *All For The Money*.

Josh wasn’t worried about anything happening to him because he had 24-hour protection. There were two federal agents who were always no more than 100ft. away from their star witness. All of the agents questioned their supervisor as to why they just couldn’t hole Josh up somewhere, instead of following him around on a junkie binge.

“Because he’s our only link to Chris Rankin, damnit! I don’t give a fuck what ya’ll got to do, see, or whatever. You just keep that junkie son of a bitch alive long enough to testify against his brother. Shit, after that…he can take a Hotshot as far as I’m concerned!” The agent’s supervisor finally fed up with their complaining.

The two agents assigned to monitor Josh were named Miller and Sheldon. They knew Josh often washed cars for money or drugs. When Miller and Sheldon saw Josh take off to the car wash, they decided to go grab a bite to eat from McDonalds. Agreeing that it would only take a few minutes, “No harm in feeding the gut, right?” Miller asked his partner. What neither knew was, their guts had just put their careers in jeopardy.

C.J. pulled in two minutes behind Creecha. They positioned their vehicles, pointing towards their escape route. Both stepped out wearing long dreaded wigs and crept up beside the Durango, with their MP.5's, with silencers attached.

"Your brother says hello!" C.J. screamed, but was barely audible due to the noise from the heavy-duty vacuums and high-pressured hoses.

Josh was unsure if he'd heard correctly, so he looked up from his crouched position and before his feet cold react, both fully automatic weapons unleashed, damn near shredding Josh into pieces. Creecha ran and cut Josh Tongue from his mouth and spelled "snitch". Besides his lifeless body.

Although Spokane doesn't have many black people, the dynamic dreaded duo basketball went unnoticed as they made an easy escape. Dub stepped out of the SUV, rinsed the suds off, after a quick wipe down if the handgrip pressure washer. He casually backed out and drove off.

CHAPTER 39

"I told you, Boss to pu —"

"You don't tell me shit, you dumbfuck!" Senior Agent Bourke screamed in Agent Sheldon's face. "Have the two of you seen the news?"

Agent Miller, being Sheldon's superior, tried to mediate the situation. "Boss, he ran up the street like he usually does. Nothing was out of the norm, so we wen—"

"You went and fucked up, that's what the fuck you did! When the main office gets wind of this shit, the two of you will be out of a job; *not me*! Hell no...I won't go down for this one."

Miller spoke up. "I take full responsibility for this. Sheldon was only following my lead."

"Well, he just followed you to the unemployment line too! Now get the fuck out of here so I can get this ass chewing from the Mayor out of the way!"

Both men looked at Bourke and were stunned by his behavior. When they got out into the hallway, Miller looked at Sheldon and said, "Fuck him! He told us to watch him and we told him what would be best. But nooo....he gave the dopefiend the rope to hang himself. I believe Bourke is incompetent of handling the position that he holds. Wouldn't you agree?"

Sheldon smiled and high-fived his partner and said, "I'm with you all the way, Senior Agent Miller." Both of them liked the sound of that.

CHAPTER 40

Dub meet up with C.J. and Creecha at a rest area in Oregon. C.J. walked over to the Durango and said, "Dub, go to the crib, and get that shit straight with them people."

"Sheeit Cuz, the party done started now!" Dub shot back.

"Yeah, but as soon as you show face, the better off we'll all ce."

"I fell ya Cuz, cut—"

"Cut nothin'! Shits about to get ugly out here, and we don't need no unwanted attention on us!"

"I know—"

"Trust me on this Loc. We're gonna hit so many places at an unthinkable rate, that it's gonna feel like World War 3 out this mothafucka! *Bin Laden?* Fuck Bin Laden! This country ain't seen shit yet!"

"And I'm wit'cha 'til the end Cuz."

"Then go handle yo' business!"

"All day Homie."

"We'll get up in 18 minutes."

"All day!" Dub replied when C.J. added their set numbers together.

"We need you Cuz, so hurry up and get left cack!"

"Sho' ya left!" Dub agreed. They hit each other up, then Dub gave Creecha a pound.

Before he could pull off, C.J. called his name.

"Yeah I know Cuz. When this is over, we got around to go!"

"Just remember that!" C.J. shot back.

"And I got the clock." Creecha said adding his two cents.

"All day, O.G." Dub blurted out as he pulled off throwing up a *"C"*.

*** *** *** ***

J-Roc was choppin' it up with RoRo when C.J. pulled up. RoRo was explaining the origin of the massive Presa Canario that was snatching at the cow chain that restrained him.

"Chill out Gangsta, they cool!" RoRo told his man-eating beast. Instantly the dog's demeanor turned passive. He then laid back down and began chewing on a cow's leg bone.

Seeing his uncles, RoRo ran over to the Tahoe.

"What's crackin' Uncs.?"

"You know what it is lil homie." C.J. replied.

"Same shit, different day nephew." Creecha added.

"If you lookin' for my pop, he's in the Fish hollerin' at some cat he did a bid with."

C.J. gave Creecha a baffled look.

Seeing that they didn't understand, RoRo clarified his statement. "My bad Uncs. He went to a turf in Kannapolis called Fishertown."

"When...shit, nevermind." C.J. said dialing Romeo's phone.

Seeing C.J.'s name on the screen, Romeo answered.

"What's Cripalatin'?"

"Shit, I'm at your spot. Time is precious." C.J. said, then ended the call. An hour later, Romeo pulled up in his *Triple. C* (Candy Coated Caddy).

He jumped out with a concerned look on his face. He acknowledged the crew with a *'Big C'.*

"That's for Creecha too." Romeo said leading everyone into his crib.

RoRo passed out 40oz.'s to everybody, then took a seat himself. Everybody looked at him, so he spoke up.

"Dig it O.G.'s, I know ya'll look at me like some loose cannon, and that mayce true, but I'd never jeopardize any of ya'll, or the movement. On the turf—" Roro threw up a 'K' with his fingers. "Ya'll trust my pops?" they all nodded. "Then let me earn ya'lls trust too! The same Gangsta shit that runs through Pop's genes have been passed down to me.

I haven't told any of my homies about the movement cecause I....well I just haven't, and I'm not going to. Once ya'll accept my Gangsta, which I'm hoping ya'll will, then I can start puttin' in work and put the homies to work too! I'm ready to step my shit up and do what I gotta do to prove my worth to this movement! These streets is fucked up, but me and my homies instill the fear of God in these fools around here. Money is funny, and it's infested with rattin' ass, bitch made niggas. We want the streets ya'll left us, back! If it takes my life to help clean this shit up, so ce it...But I want in!" RoRo said with pleading eyes. "I'm goin' to fuck with Gangsta while ya'll decide."

"Yo!" Creecha yelled when RoRo grabbed the doorknob.

"Yeah, what's crackin' Unc.?"

" That ain't a good look—you walkin' out on your first official meetin'!"

RoRo smiled then went and dapped everybody up. C.J. looked at Creecha. The exchange didn't go unnoticed, so RoRo reassured, "I won't let you down Unc."

C.J. stared at RoRo and said, "Let's hope not!" Romeo hardened and looked away for a second because all he heard C.J. says, *"His blood will be on your hands..."*

CHAPTER 41

Mona Morales was in her flower bed pulling weeds when a landscaping truck pulled up. She got up and walked towards the F-450. “May I help you?’ she asked, looking from C.J. to Romeo and back.

“Ma’am, we’re here to help you.” Romeo told her.

“Me no understand.”

“We’re here on behalf of Eric.”

“Who?”

“Your husband...Eric.”

“Si, he’s my husband. He’s no here.”

“We know that Ma’am. Listen, we’ll talk in a minute.” Romeo said getting out, then went and unlatched the riding lawn mower.

Mona looked at Romeo like he was crazy. “Me no have money for you!” C.J. waved for him to finish when he stepped out of the truck.

Mona began to panic. “Me call police! Leave! Leave now!”

C.J. grabbed the hysterical woman by the shoulders and stated,

"If we leave, Eric will never come home. If you listen…then he will, *comprende'*?"

Mona nodded and walked back towards her flower bed. C.J. followed.

Romeo proceeded to make laps around the yard on the mower, while C.J. pretended to weed eat as he conversed with Mona.

By the time C.J. and Mona came from the backside of the house, Mona's once fear-filled eyes were now filled with hope. She told C.J. to come back Friday for the money.

Mona would visit Eric on Thursday. She thanked C.J. repeatedly as she walked him back to the truck.

On the way back to North Carolina Romeo opened a conversation with C.J. about his son.

"Cuz, I know you're skeptical about RoRo, but he's the truth! I'll show you once we get back to the crib."

"Ro, I love the lil niggas Gangsta, but can he think?" C.J. honestly acknowledged, but also seriously searched.

"What'cha mean, is my son re—"

"Fuck no! All I'm sayin' is, he's so turned up on this Crippin', and I know he'll use that tool, but can he rationalize a situation and then make the right decision? That's all I was concerned about." C.J. clarified.

"Look Cuz, he's us when we first got put on, but more deadly! This generation doesn't fight anymore, they just use those ratchets. RoRo...he's willin' to listen and learn so he can teach his homies how to Crip properly. Big Screw disappeared after practically raisin' him while we was biddin'. He understands manhood and he's vowed to Crip 'til the casket drops." Romeo then paused and reflected back on how he'd met the Legendary Big Screw.

***   ***   ***   ***

"Who the fuck is that?" Romeo asked his crew as they shot Craps on the side of the Brookview store.

"I 'on't know." JB replied as he got up to go check things out. The rest stood up and followed suit.

Screw sat behind the wheel of a navy blue '63 Lincoln that sat on 13" Dayton's.

Screw was a slim, but muscular cat with a bald head and appeared to be between 20-25 years old.

When he saw the group approaching, Screw hit a switch, slamming the car to the ground. He stepped out of the car, and threw his hands up in Doughboy fashion, from Boyz-N-The Hood.

The crew all looked at Screw as if he were crazy. Seeing the handle of his 9mm in the front of his pants, Cee-Lo and Ced pulled theirs out.

Robin, a sexy ass redbone, known for only fuckin' with major niggas, emerged from the store with two 40 oz.'s of Crazy Horse, and a box of Philly blunts.

Seeing Screw reach for his gun, Robin said. "I know ya'll ain't on that bullshit with my friend here."

Everybody knew Robin had street cred due to her gangsta ass brothers and uncles.

"Yo', these busters just walked up on my ride like they 'bout to rush me or somethin'!" Screw said, still maddoggin' the miniature mob.

"Ya'll need to stop with that bullshit fo' somebody gets killed out here!" Robin stressed.

JB, the muscle of the crew stepped to Robin. "Fuck that nigga! He ain't from around here!"

"No he ain't! And he damn sho' ain't from the West-Side neither. He's from Colorado, if you must know!"

"Colorado!" JB laughed. "Ain't no niggas in Colorado!"

The whole crew erupted in laughter.

"You really from Colorado?" JB snickered.

"I'm from 81 Kitchen Cuz, cut I live in the Mile High City." Screw said with a scowl on his face.

Standing in front of Screw with her hands on his chest Robin pleaded, "Lets go baby. Please?"

Screw knocked her against the Lincoln with his forearm and barked, "Don't ever jump in the way of me handlin' my cizness! These marks owe me an apology, or else."

"Or else what?" Wig shouted.

Ignoring the little loudmouth, Screw instructed Robin to get in the car.

Once she was in the passenger's seat, arms folded across her chest, Screw let his 9mm erupt.

Blocka! Blocka! Blocka! Blocka!

The whole mob dispersed and ran for cover.

Before he could get back in the car, Romeo emerged with a .38 and shot Screw in the shoulder.

Boom!

"Ahhh! Shit!" Screw howled in pain, then he sent his last bullets into Romeo's direction, catching him in the chest, and shoulder.

Blocka! Blocka! Blocka!

Romeo laid still on the concrete, thinking to himself how his life was about to end from a one-man army.

Several months later, Big Screw and Romeo met up again. Both respecting the others Gangsta, they shot a head up fade in front of a crowd of nearly 100 people, give or take a few people.

Big Screw and Romeo went toe to toe for nearly two minutes, but to them, it felt more like two hours. Finally, Romeo threw a haymaker that Screw ducked and countered with a vicious uppercut.

Boom!

Romeo staggered backward, and dropped to a knee.

Robins' uncle, Horse, who'd watched the whole event unfold, walked over to Screw and said, "It's over. Ya'll handled that like men."

Screw looked at Horse like he was crazy, then made a move towards Romeo.

"That's it I said!" Horse screamed, as he racked a bullet and pointed his gun at the back of Screw's head. Screw then extended his hand to a still discombobulated Romeo.

Romeo accepted Screw's hand. After being pulled up to his feet, Romeo made clear, "I ain't no buster, and I damn sho' ain't no mark!"

"You got heart Cuz...Yeah, you Kitchen material."

"What?"

"Kitchen Crip. That's my set."

"Oh yeah, how do I become a Crip?"

"You just did!"

The two became inseparable from that night, up until the Feds came and snatched Romeo up.

Screw being a true G, made sure lil RoRo and Romeo's mother never went without.

Once RoRo came of age, Screw put RoRo on the set, along with a selected few of RoRo's comrades. He made sure to instill in them that Romeo was their Big Homie. "I'm just fillin' in 'til the homie gets here." No one heard from Screw again, until Romeo's welcome home party. No matter what the myths, rumors, or lies they may speak of, Screw will always be a true Crip legend.

*** *** *** ***

C.J. could tell that Romeo was in deep thought, so he let his comrade be. They rode the rest of the way in silence.

CHAPTER 42

"Yo, start that shit over!" Romeo said when he and C.J. walked into his house. RoRo was showing his DVD to Creecha and J-Roc for the fourth time.

"Yeah, the lil homie put it in fo' show!" J-Roc said, playfully punching RoRo in the arm.

"Shit, I oughta change his name to *Creech-Creech*, cause nephew sho' does remind me of myself!"

RoRo sat and absorbed all the Gangsta praises from the real O.G.'s. When the disc started again, Romeo stood like a proud father would at either seeing his son graduate or win MVP upon winning the championship game for his team. C.J. stood as well and admired the ruthlessness of the youth, but he was still concerned RoRo's situational skills and ability to critically think. After watching the tape for the second time, C.J.'s doubts started to diminish. The whole ordeal was well orchestrated. *Yeah, I can definitely use a soldier like this for this movement* C.J. finally concluded.

"One more time RoRo. This shits a classic!" C.J. boasted.

"Sho' ya left Unc. O-Dawg ain't got shit on me!" RoRo said in a braggadocio manner, then started the DVD over.

CHAPTER 43

Dub set up an appointment to meet with Agent Brooks in the parking lot of the L.A. County Jail, "aka" the *Twin Towers.*

Dub didn't bring his attorney due to the fact that Andre Brook's grandmother lived on the next block over from Acacia. Both of his brothers were Palmer Blocc Crips. One was deceased, and the other was serving a life sentence in the ADX Supermax in Florence, Colorado.

Although older than Dub, Andre had always admired Dub's swagger. He just never had the heart to do the crimes that were punishable by prison.

Dub got off of his brand new 1300 Hayabusa and hopped in the Suburban with Andre.

"What's crackin' Dre?"

"You tell me Dub."

"Tell you what Cuz?" Dub asked in a confused tone.

Andre studied Dub's face for any signs of fraudulence. "How about those homicides in Memphis."

"I saw that shit on the news. It was...it was my homie from the clank baby's momma, and daughter."

"And you don't know shit about it?"

"Just what I saw on CNN." Dubs repeated.

"Now why would a gangbanger like you be watchin' CNN?...To make sure you didn't leave any clues behind?" Andrew probed.

"Fuck you Dre! Fuck yo' info too! Everybody watches CNN in the clank! If you ever get that cracka stick outta yo' ass, and go holla at yo' bro, you could ask him yourself! Oh yeah...I forgot, that wouldn't ce acceptable to your peers." Dub said, chastising Dre and hoping to strike a nerve.

"Look nigga, don't worry about me or mine. You need to concentrate on why I should let you get out of this truck."

"Check ya self Cuz! I'm getting outta here one way or another! I ain't did shit for one, cause if I had, you'd know. I leave my trademark. You remember when I went to Y.A. for bustin' on that mark from Fruit town. If I remember correctly, that was your best friend's lil bro., Poncho. Sorry about that Cuz." Dub said through a heavy chuckle.

"You arrogant ass bastard! I'm a—"

"I'm outta here! Cause if I don't, I'm gonna forget about the love I have fo' Crazy Von and Rad, R.I.P. So since you ain't got shit on me, fuck you! I'm out!"

Dub reached for the door but stopped when Dre grabbed his arm. "Don't ever touch me again. That's your first and only warning!"

Dre released Dub's arm. Dub hopped out of the SUV but left an eerie aura in the seat that he'd just gotten out of.

Although the temperature exceeded well over 90 degrees today in California, it felt like Antarctica in Andre's Suburban.

***   ***   ***   ***

"What the fuck!" U.S. District Attorney Herman Jackson screamed.

"I had put two—" Bourke tried to explain.

"Do you know what this means Bourke?"

"Yes sir, I do."

"Apparently you don't...ooohh, you really fucked this one up!"

"Sir, we still have the drugs, and Agent Bryant's testimony." Senior Agent Bourke said, trying to reassure the D.A.

"What part don't you get? Agent Bryant never saw the transaction. The wire that damn junkie wore was faulty, so all we really had was the junkie's testimony, who you let get killed."

"But sir—I put my best men on him—they made a mistake."

"No, the mistake was putting you in charge of anything! By the way, Agents Sheldon and Miller gave their statements already. According to them, they asked you to put Rankin in a safe house, but you abused your authority and allowed him to roam free."

Those double crossin' bastards! Bourke looked down and screamed inwardly. Taking a deep breath, he then asked, "So what now sir?"

"There's nothin' we can do."

"Well sir, his initial plea was 360 to life. Now if we offer him 10 years—"

"What th—"

"Sir, please, just hear me out. You'll still get a conviction. It may not be exactly what you wanted, but at least you get a conviction, and we can get some scum off the streets for a while.

You know the election is coming up, what would look better. You giving a man 10 years, or you letting a man go free?"

The D.A. sat silently and weighed his options. Then he realized that he didn't have much of any.

"Listen Bourke, I was going to recommend that you resign from the Bureau and receive your pension, but...what you're sayin makes sense. I'll tell you what, you get his lawyer to go for it, and I'll tear up my referral." Both men sat quietly for several more moments.

Bourke finally broke the silence. "I believe I can get that ignorant ass Placcey to go for it. He's so close to disbarment that he'll do anything to get back in good graces.

***   ***   ***   ***

"I got great news Mister Rankin." Attorney Placcey said with a phony smile plastered on his face.

Chris sat with the visitation telephone to his ear. "If I ain't goin' home, then I don't want to hear it!"

This ungrateful bastard! Placcey said to himself. Gaining control over his emotions, Placcey lied, "I got the D.A. to offer you 10-years. No more, no less. Capped of course."

Chris contemplated the offer but decided to roll the dice and gamble on what his *Everything* had told him. Finally, Chris blurted out, "No!" and hung up the phone.

On his way out of the visitation booth, Chris turned and looked back at Placcey. Placcey was still sitting holding the phone receiver. He looked like a puppy at the Humane Society, about to be put to sleep.

Somethin' is most definitely up! Chris concluded. All of a sudden, a sharp pain hit Chris in the pit of his stomach.

After the pain subsided, all he could say was, "Fuck you Judas!" Deep down, Chris knew that Josh was already on a one-way trip to hell. This brought a huge smile across Chris face.

*** *** *** ***

Later that night…

Chris was on a phone call with Angie.

"Can you believe the nerve of this fool, baby? I mean he just walks up in here on some—" Chris started to rant before being cut off.

"Chris...J-Josh…is….dead!" Angie informed between fake sobs.

"What, wh-wha t the fuck you mean dead. Bullshit! Oh god...he can't be!'' Chris shot back with an equally impressive Oscar performance.

"He got sh…sh-shot at a...oh god, it was horrible! The...th-they cut his tongue out! Baby, he's dead!" Angie added to her already award-winning performance.

Chris slammed the phone down.

Angie smiled at her acting abilities and ended the call. She fired up a blunt of Az., and waited on Chris to call back, so they could continue to outdo Denzel and Halle.

Chris paced back and forth in his cell, trying to draw attention to himself. All of his actions and phone calls would be monitored as the authorities would be looking for any signs of his involvement.

So far, Chris had the winning hand. He just had to keep up this charade until he was set free, *physically*. Chris' soul had already been liberated.

Inwardly, Chris smiled at his brothers demise, and also for having a loyal, ride or die bitch. Freedom was right around the corner.

*** *** *** ***

As instructed, Mona wrote everything down in her Memo pad before going to see her husband. The first sheet was all he needed to read. It read: *"I can get you out for $10,000.00, but you must do what is required."* He instantly agreed.

Shit, I'd kill the Pope and Queen Elizabeth to get the fuck outta here! he thought. For the rest of the visit, they only spoke of the love they had for one another. Neither understood the magnitude of the offer they'd just accepted.

*** *** *** ***

C.J. met Mona that Friday afternoon. After sprinkling manure in Mona's flower bed, C.J. moved to the side of the house while Romeo spread the shit out evenly throughout the flower bed.

On the side of the house, Mona lifted her sundress, and extracted two rolls of money from the garter belts that clung to her massive, cellulite thighs. *Too much meat for me!* C.J. thought. However, Mona began blushing because she mistakenly took C.J.'s demeanor as a lust. Mona knew that Black men loved thick women, but someone forgot to inform her that she had bypassed, graduated, and retired from being thick. Mona was a calorie away from being obese.

C.J. assured her that he'd know the moment that Eric was

released, and he'd be in touch soon afterwards.

CHAPTER 44

"What's crackin'?" Dub asked.

"Just watchin' this lil league game. My nephew is on third base as we speak." C.J. answered.

"Cool, tell neph that I'll catch his next game."

"Sho' ya left Cuz!"

They both hung up.

The coded conversation actually meant...

"What' s up?"

"Chillin at Romeos spot."

"I'll catch the next plane out."

"Cool."

*** *** *** ***

It was decided that Romeo, J-Roc, and RoRo would perform the next hit. Their assignment was in Augusta, Georgia.

Eric Morales was snaked out by his cousin's boyfriend, Jonny

Hychen. Jonny wanted Eric's kingship over the Latin Kings, so he planted a kilo of raw heroin and a M-16 in the trunk of Eric's Monte Carlo, then called the police. He told the dispatcher that he saw someone commit a drive by out of that exact car. That part was true, because Jonny shot at some G.D.'s then went to pick Eric up.

When he saw a cop car, Jonny slammed on the brakes then made a U-turn.

"What the fuck are you doin' J?" Eric inquired.

"Just chill King, I'm gonna get away."

When the second cop gave chase, Jonny purposely fishtailed, causing the passenger's side door to slam against another car, pinning Eric in.

Jonny hopped out and escaped, leaving his King to face life in prison.

Jonny frequented the gay district on Friday nights, and RoRo was about to be the bait.

"Hell naw, pop! Unc?" RoRo pleaded to anyone that would come to his rescue.

"Dig it Ro. You ain't doin' nothin' none of us wouldn't do. You just look...he likes young boys." Romeo said reassuring his son.

Frustrated, RoRo gave in, "Fuck it, I'll do it...just as long as I get to kill him!"

The following Friday night, after making his usual rounds and excuses for going out of town to network for the Kings, Jonny headed to his favorite gay club.

RoRo was sitting in the parking lot smoking a cigarette when Jonny pulled up. The only available parking space was beside RoRo's Caddy.

Jonny got out of his car and looked at RoRo, who was rolling the window down.

“Ain’t you Jonny?” RoRo asked, trying to sound coy.

“Do I know you, homes?”

“ Not yet, but you need to get to know me.”

“Oh yeah...why is that?”

“Because I can be very valuable to you.”

“How so?”

“Why are we talkin‘ out here. It’s dead in there, lets ride and talk, then—”

“Your whip, or mine?”

“We’ll take mine. We don’t want no Kings catchin’ us doin’...” Jonny didn’t need to hear another word. He sprinted around to the passenger’s side and jumped in.

RoRo pulled into a rest area and parked beside a white van. “Let’s get a room.” Jonny suggested.

“Let’s talk first. If I like what I hear, then we’ll go.”

“Alright sweet thing, what do you want to know from King Jonny?”

Before RoRo could respond, the passenger’s door was snatched open.

“What the fu—” Jonny’s sentence was cut short when a plastic bag was thrown over his head and he was snatched out with a hand mashing the bag against both breathing orifices. After a brief struggle, Jonny passed out.

“Yo, he better not ce dead Cuz!” RoRo barked.

“Don’t worry lil homie, this bitch is all yours!” J-Roc said throwing Jonny into the van, then he and Romeo pulled off. RoRo followed.

*** *** *** ***

"Wake yo' bitch ass up if you wanna live!" RoRo shouted, kicking Jonny in the ribs.

"Ahhh!" Jonny howled in pain but held onto the thought that he might live through this. *I'm gonna kill every last one of these Black son of a bitches. Especially the pretty young one...after I fuck him that is!*

"This shit's real simple bitch! You gonna sign a confession stating that you set Eric up, then make a few phone calls to the D.A. and to the arresting officer. Once you've given your full confession, you'll be set free, but you can't live here anymore! You must go back to Puerto Rico. Deal?"

"Are you for real? I mean…do you really think you're gonna get away with thi—" J-Roc cut Jonny's air supply off, causing him to pass out again.

When Jonny came to, he was looking into the eyes of the most ferocious beast he'd ever encountered.

Gangsta lunged at Jonny. RoRo had commanded Gangsta not to bark, but to kill. Jonny's screams were muffled by the sleeve of his Armani shirt that was stuffed in his mouth. Romeo had snatched it off to use as a gag.

"Are you ready to change your mind now, or do I let my puppy loose?" RoRo asked.

"Puppy hell!" Jonny tried to say through hig gag, and feverishly shook his head no.

"No what? Bitch you confusing me. Do you want me to let Gangsta loose?"

Jonny shook his head no again.

"So you ready to take the deal, faggot?"

This time Jonny nodded.

Creecha watched in admiration, while C.J. held his usual

nonchalant stare. RoRo and J-Roc drug Jonny up the stairs, causing his head to bounce violently off of each step.

Once inside, they untied Jonny, then duct taped him to a chair, leaving one arm free to write with.

Romeo used a gloved hand to give Jonny a note pad and pen. “Start writin, Pussy!” Romeo commanded.

After the confession was written, Jonny was instructed to put his thumb print beside his signature, then was handed an untraceable satellite phone. Both the U.S. District Attorney Michael Carol, and Master Patrol Officer Mitch Drums’ numbers were already programed into the phone.

Jonny looked at the phone, and then asked, “Ain’t it a lil late to be callin’ these people?”

“Listen you wet back faggot: either you make the calls now, or you die! It’s that simple!” Creecha screamed from the Lay-Z-Boy in the living room.

Jonny called the first number.

“ Yeah?” Mitch Drums screamed over some loud country music playing in the background.

“Yo Drums, this is Jonny Hychen.”

“Well, I’ll be damned, Jonny Boy. What did I do to ‘zerve this early Christmas prez ‘ent?”

“I just wanted to set the record straight. I set Eric up with that shit ya’ll found in his trunk that day.”

“Waz zat you drivin’?”

“Yeah, and all that shit was mine. Eric didn’t know shit about it.”

“Well I ‘bout figgered that. So what ‘cha try’na do heah?”

“Let Eric go, and take me in his place.”

“So you jus gonna turn ya’self in so ya can free up good ol’

Eric, huh?"

"Yeah."

"Well I'm afraid it ain't that easy, son. It's outta my hands. Them there, Feds got 'im now."

"Well, I'm sendin' ya'll my full confession."

"Who's ya'll?"

"You and Attorney Carol."

"You really serious ain't 'cha.?" Drums asked while instructing someone to turn the music down.

"Yeah. I'm dead serious!"

"What, them Kangs foun' out what'cha did, huh?"

"Yeah."

"Tell ya what, come down in the mornin' an I'll get'cha some protection. Howz zat soun'?"

"Great"

"But cha know, ya gotta gimme what I want too!"

"I will. Look, I gotta go." Jonny said, ending the call.

He then looked at RoRo with mixed emotions. Romeo saw the look, so he hit Jonny on the back of the neck with a 40oz. bottle, causing a deep laceration.

"Damn Cuz, don't kill the bitch!" C.J. warned.

Romeo grabbed a box of iodized salt and poured it over the gash. He grabbed a dirty dishrag and mashed the salt into the wound until it stopped bleeding. Jonny passed out for the third time.

"That's one sleepin' mothafucka!" J-Roc said while laughing his ass off.

When Jonny came to, the back of his neck was on fire. He screamed several obscenities in Spanish until C.J. intervened.

"You the bitch, you faggot ass wetback!"

If looks could kill, C.J. would've died right there on the spot.

"Yeah pussy, I speak Spanish too! Now make the other call!"

"Hel-lo," a groggy voice answered.

"Mister Carol?"

"Yes. Who is this, and how did you get this number?"

"This is Jonny Hychen. And to answer your second question it ain't important. Look, I just got off the phone with Master Patrol Officer Mitch Drums, down there in Aiken."

"What does that have to do with you waking me up at three fucking thirty in the morning?"

"Well, I set this guy up out of jealousy, and I want to clear his name."

"Who?"

"Eric Morales."

"So you plan to take his charges and let him walk, correct?"

"That's the plan."

"Well, listen Mister...?"

"Hychen."

"Yeah, Hychen, shit doesn't just go away because you wipe your ass. Now if you want to play ball on the winning team, I can work out a deal for both you and your friend. I'll have an agent con—"

"Listen Mister Carol, I wrote my full confession and will mail it in the morning."

"So you 're not coming in?"

"No."

"Well no deal. We got a man on whatever the charges he has. I'm quite sure they're multiple, so pal you either come in and do it my way, or what's his face is going down for everything."

"Eric Morales."

“Yeah. Eric Morales.”

“But he’s innocent of the charges.”

“I don’t give a fuck! Just as long as I got a body, or bodies, and most importantly a conviction, that’s all that matters. Now if you’ll excuse me, I’m going back to bed.” Carol said slamming the phone down.

C.J. immediately pulled out his satellite phone and hit the send button. Shaneka picked up and said, “Yeah, I got both of ‘em.”

“Thanks. Love ya girl.”

“I love ya mo’!”

“See ya soon.”

“I hope so!”

They both hung up.

“O.K., let’s celebrate.” C.J. announced.

Jonny hurried and snatched his free arm behind his back, hoping they’d forget. He then sat and plotted his escape and could taste the revenge right on the tip of his tongue.

CHAPTER 45

Jonny watched the *dead niggers* as he thought of them, pass around two half gallons of Paul Masson and Seagram's gin. He smiled inwardly and pretended to doze off.

After an hour, one by one, C.J., Creecha, Romeo, RoRo, and J-Roc all began to pass out. The big ugly guy was the last to go. He just stared at Jonny, who was staring back, but he was staring through slitted eyes.

Jonny watched the drunks for a few more minutes to make sure they were out cold, before he started to free himself. *Yeah, you dumb ass niggers are all dead!* He swore.

Once free, Jonny grabbed the keys to the van from the coffee table and made his break.

Gangsta woke up when the front door opened and let out a low growl. Jonny jumped over the railing at the opposite end of the deck to avoid a winless encounter with Gangsta. He made it to the van and down the driveway in two minutes flat.

C.J. shook RoRo awake.

“Huh...Huh…Unc?”

“Your body is gettin’ away.”

RoRo jumped up and looked where Jonny was previously duct taped to the chair.

“Damn Unc, you let ‘im get away!“ RoRo pouted.

“ Lil homie, I‘m ‘bout to teach you somethin‘ that’ll ce a jewel for you later in life. Come on.“

They jumped in RoRo‘s STS, and C.J. drove off.

“One, you good to drive?” RoRo asked.

“Yeah Neph, I ain‘t drink shit.“

“But I sa—”

“You saw me turnin’ the bottles up. It was all an illusion. You see that faggot is ridin’ off callin’ us everything up under the sun while he’s laughing and plottin’ his revenge. I set the stage, and everybody performed accordingly. O.K., here.” C.J. said handing RoRo a small transmitter. RoRo looked at it dumbfoundedly.

C.J. smiled at his innocence and said, “Lift the face and hit the orange button. RoRo did as instructed, causing a series of bleeps and beeps to run across the screen until two dots were the only things moving.

“That’s him on the top.” C.J. indicated by pointing at the top of the screen. “And that’s us. What you’re holding there is a state-of-the-art GPS tracking device. Only top agencies have access to these, and we have someone who’s up there Neph. Now watch this.”

C.J. pulled out the smallest cell phone RoRo had ever seen. “Yes, I’d like to report a stolen vehicle.”

“I’ll need your name, license plate number, and the make and model of your vehicle, sir.”

“Anthony Meers. My plate number is, 8187-JST. North

Carolina plates. The make and model are a 2006 Dodge Caravan. Yes I'll hold."

The operator came back and said, "Sir, we've located your vehicle. It's traveling Southwest at the present time. If you like, we can shut the engine down and lock the perpetrator inside until the authorities get there."

"Thank you so much Ma'am, I'd appreciate that. Lord knows I need my van."

"Not a problem sir. Someone will notify you as to where you'll be able to retrieve your van."

"Thank you so much!"

"You are very welcome. Have a great night."

"You do the same."

"Unc, the dot stopped movin'!"

"Yeah I know, the OnStar just shut down all its functions. We'll ce there in a minute or two."

Not even a minute later, RoRo screamed, "There it is!" then reached for his Glock 40. C.J. grabbed his arm.

"What the fuck Unc? Don't renege on me now!" RoRo whined.

When they rode past the van, RoRo turned around in his seat. "Come on Unc, he might get away!"

"Have I let you down since you've met me?"

"No."

"Well don't ever question my Gangsta. Ever!" C.J. barked, then made a U-turn and drove back past the van. Looking over at a frustrated young soldier, C.J. said, "Push the blue button."

RoRo pushed the button, and an explosion erupted, causing a large fireball to race behind the Cadillac.

"O.K...damn Unc, I blew that bitch up! Daaammn, that shit was hardbody."

C.J. smiled at the young 'G's' enthusiasm. They rode the rest of the way in silence. RoRo stared at the detonator in awe. C.J. stared straight ahead as if to say *just another day at the office* and one step closer to adding another soldier to the regiment.

Before leaving for Arizona, C.J. mailed both D.A. Carol and Officer Drums a copy of Jonny's confession, and their recorded conversations. He added a collaged styled letter to each package. It read:

"If you go against the truth, don't worry about getting re-elected. It won't happen! Once the press hears you saying that you don't care about the innocent, just as long as you have a body, and mainly a conviction, your career will be over. You have one week from today to do the right thing, or I'm going public. Don't try me! Eric Morales must be home next Wednesday on the 17th.

CHAPTER 46

"You just missed the Big Homie Cuz—" RoRo told Dub. "But Uncs Creecha and J-Roc, and Pop are at the crib."

The whole ride from Charlottes' Douglas Airport, RoRo explained every graphic and gory detail about Jonny, excluding the part about him having to play a faggot to catch a faggot.

They smoked some exotic bud that Dub had smuggled from Cali. After one blunt, they were both twisted.

Dub, someone that's not to be outdone, described all the gory details on how Josh actually got chopped into pieces, and how they'd cut his tongue out. RoRo, another not to be outdone, said, "Wait 'til you see my DVD Unc. I'm a fuckin' star! King Kong ain't got shit on me!" They both laughed so hard that RoRo almost drove right under a transfer trucks bed.

The driver of the truck blared his horn, causing RoRo to straighten up and drive right. He and Dub stared at one another, then burst out laughing at how they'd just cheated death.

*** *** *** ***

Dub watched the DVD four times back to back. Each time, he was even more amazed than the first. He'd never seen a running fireball, or people being burned to death.

J Roc, Creecha, and Romeo stood out on the back-deck smoking *Cali Bud.* Romeo notified them about a Damu that he wanted to bring in. "Creech, you remember the Damu homie, Pig...who ran the Blood car at Edgefield?"

"The one that assisted you with that D.C. beef?"

"Yeah, him. I think it's a great idea to bring him in. Shit, we about to have a Latin King army cehind us...shit, plus we gonna need everybody we can get to cause enough pandemonium so that these suckas would rather go do their bids like men than to risk losing his or his family's lives."

"I'm wit' whatever!" Creecha announced.

"Yeah, me too! I think families need to get touched! U we take out the breeders that produce these rat motherfuckas and their offspring, we'll not only accomplish our goal, but we'll also get this population growth under control…"

J-Roc said looking at his comrades and could sense that they were following him. Thus, he continued to let his *'Chronic'* induced words flow.

"Rats reproduce so fast that it's hard to extinct the species, but we can and will hit harder than D-Con!"

CHAPTER 47

C.J. was greeted at the door by Shaneka, who was wearing only a kimono. He could tell that she was naked underneath by the way the thin material clung to her every curve. Shaneka's nipples were so hard, that the slightest friction would have caused the silk to tear.

"Wher—" C.J. started to ask, but Shaneka silenced him by putting her index finger on his lips. He gave in. This was her show, so C.J. let her lead the way.

Shaneka dropped her kimono, then began undressing her husband. As she was taking off C.J.'s shirt she planted kisses from his collarbone down to his waist.

After removing his pants and boxers, she kissed the cobra's head then stood up. No words were said as Shaneka sashayed towards the staircase. The euphoric scent of *Jasmine* filled C.J.'s nostrils as he followed the sexiest woman on the West Coast up the stairs.

By the time they had reached the top landing, C.J.'s manhood had exceeded its previous full potential. As he suspected, *Jasmine* scented candles were burning atop the headboard.

Shaneka pushed C.J. on the bed in a sensual manner, then straddled his lap. She began planting kisses on his chest, and methodically made her way down to *her* Dick.

Shaneka teased the head with her tongue, then patiently made her way back up to where she started. She repeated the process several times until the snake started leaking pre venom.

Shaneka then re-straddled C.J.'s lap, allowing the snake's head to feel the heat from her wet opening. She rocked backwards, allowing *her* dick full access to what caused Adam to go against God's word.

C.J. grabbed her hips, but just as fast as she slid down on *her* dick, Shaneka hopped right off and turned around into the 69 position. She needed to taste a combination of their mixed essences.

C.J. tried to pull Shaneka back towards his eagerly awaiting mouth, but she held firm and made him watch *his* pussy palpitate and start leaking a thick and creamy substance. C.J. wanted to taste his wife. He needed to taste *his* pussy.

C.J. caught a cramp trying to crane his neck towards the Promise Land, but to no avail did it work. Shaneka was in complete control.

She pulled, jerked, licked, and sucked *her* dick, which had C.J. moaning and groaning.

"Oh shit! Damn girl!"

Feeling his balls tighten, and the cobras head swell, Shaneka quickened her pace. She slammed her lips down to the hilt, causing her to gag slightly. However, Shaneka was determined to finish what she started.

C.J. dug his fingernails into her hips. An animalistic sound came from his gut as he shot thousands of *would've been siblings* to his three daughters down his wife's throat. Thinking that she was finished, C.J. tried to pull away from Shaneka's vice-gripped lips, but her rhythm never changed.

"Ahhhhh Shit!" C.J. groaned as he gripped the sheets for stability.

Once she was satisfied that *he* was satisfied, Shaneka rocked back long enough to allow C.J.'s tongue to make brief contact with *his* pussy. Then in one swift motion, Shaneka spun back to her original position.

This time when she straddled him, Shaneka squatted down on C.J.'s full length. Although a little tender, he was ready for round two.

Shaneka gyrated her hips so that her clit made repeated contact with his pubic hairs. Every 10-15 seconds, she'd rise to the top of *her* dick, exposing *his* phat peach and the cream that it was producing. C.J. had given Shaneka the nickname *'Peaches & Cream'* as a result of how plump *his* pussy was and how thick her cum was.

"Dayuuuum, I've missed this diiiiiiick!" Shaneka moaned as her pace quickened.

Somewhat in control, C.J. started his own unique grind that caused her to convulse.

"That's all you missed?" he asked as he reached up and pulled Shaneka down by the shoulders, not allowing any movement other than his grinding motion.

This was his way of conquering his prey.

"Noooo!" she whined as her walls began to tighten.

Now it was payback time.

"Agggh!" Shaneka screamed but ended up in a low purr.

Without missing a stroke, C.J. rocked himself up and slammed Shaneka on her back and began punishing *his* pussy.

"Fuck yer pu-seeeee ni...niggah! Fu...fuck the shit outta meeee!"

C.J. held Shaneka's legs straight up in the air and violently pounded away. This was more than she'd bargained for.

"Yeah, take your dick girl!"

"Ah...Ahmmmm tay-kin-iiiiiit!" she managed to get out between grunts.

Rocking her up on her shoulder blades, C.J. jackhammered *his* pussy. Shaneka's body started to shake violently.

Once her orgasm subsided, he pulled out and thrusted into her juice slicked asshole.

"May-ka-dat ass cummm!"

His actions were his response. For the next 10 minutes, C.J. pounded away. Pussy juice kept squirting as Shaneka's asshole loosened, causing both holes to fart on his back stroke.

Seeing the tears rolling out of her lust filled eyes, and into her ears, C.J. tensed and released his second load.

He lowered her legs and collapsed on top of her. They laid that way, breathing heavy while their souls held their own conversation.

After they'd caught their breath, Shaneka turned C.J.'s face and locked eyes with him. "Niggah, if you eva cheat again, I'll kill ya!" then she pulled C.J. down to her sweaty breasts and stroked the back of his head. CJ assumed that it was women's institution how she knew of his infidelity. He knew he had to tighten up. They both just conquered their prey.

CHAPTER 48

CNN had been running their top story for over an hour nonstop. Attorney General Earl Hailey, had called an emergency press conference. Standing directly behind him were District Attorney Carol and Officer Drums.

"They say our justice system doesn't work. They say it has failed. They say we only look out for our own. That part is true. Who are our own? America, that's who! They say minorities and people that are poverty stricken don't receive just punishments, nor rewards. Usually, when a person is a gang member, I along with many of you—"

Hailey said using a sweeping motion with his arm to include the audience.

"Have used a prejudice to judge them. No, I don't condone terroristic behavior. But I do believe in justice for all. A man has been wrongfully accused of charges that could've sent him away to one of our Federal penitentiaries for the rest of his life. But justice comes before convictions in this great country of ours.

With endless man hours and efforts, these two fine gentlemen standing behind me, but beside me in serving justice, U.S. District Attorney Carol, and Master Patrol Officer Drums, have found injustice in our system. That's why we've come before you fine Americans today. We're here to rectify the situation. It may cost me my reelection to this eminent position, but I wouldn't be able to sleep at night knowing that I had the power to right a wrong, and didn't exercise it—" Attorney General Earl Hailey said, before he paused to raise a sheet of paper.

"Here, I have a full confession from the person that concocted the allegations against an innocent man. Although he hasn't been apprehended at this very moment, we are pooling all of our resources together to bring this culprit to justice! Thank you for your time ladies and gentlemen. May God bless each and every one of you!" Earl closed out.

When he left the podium, Earl's two flunky underlings were on his heels.

"Fellas, this couldn't have happened at a better time for any one of us. I guarantee reelection for all three of us, or my names not—what's my name again?"

"Earl Hailey Sir."

"You damn right it is! And it's going to be the name of the Attorney General come November. Listen, let's drive some balls sometimes. The two of you got my number, right?" Hailey asked as he climbed into his limo.

"I do sir." Carol said trying to seem important in front of Drums.

"Good, use it. Look I gotta go fellas. Hope to hear from you soon."

"Will do sir." Carol responded.

When the limo pulled off, Hailey pressed the intercom button to his driver. “A, Bateman?”

“Sir?”

“Get Homeland Security to change all of my numbers A.S.A.P.! I believe I will have some unwanted calls coming pretty soon.”

“Yes sir, Mister Hailey sir. Right away!” Hailey threw his head back and stared out of the sunroof.

In a low tone, he stated “Politics! Damn I love this shit!”

***   ***   ***   ***

Eric sat and stared at the T.V. that had just declared him a free man. The four other Latin kings were celebrating harder than he was.

Felix Salazar smiled. Now he inherited the top King position and all of Eric’s commissary. “Yo King…”Felix said patting Eric on the shoulder. “I got this in here King, you just make sure that that bitch nigga Jonny dies.”

Eric never confided in his homies about what was going on with his case, except only that Jonny had set him up. Things were still vague to him. All he knew was that there were some serious dudes out there and they wanted him on their side. He vowed to do everything in his power to ensure that they knew that they had chosen a real solid individual. *Whatever is loyal to me, I’ll give mine back 101%* was a motto that Eric lived by and would most certainly die for.

“Eric Morales! Roll ya shit! Be back in 10 minutes for ya!” the jailer screamed from control booth.

10 minutes later, Eric stood at the pod door with only his bed roll, letters, and pictures of Mona.

Once in the Sallyport, he threw up the 3-pointed crown. “I’ll be in touch.” he mouthed to Felix.

One more piece had just been added to an incomplete puzzle.

CHAPTER 49

"What the hell do you mean he won't take the deal?" Herman Jackson screamed in Placcey's direction.

"Sir...he said—"

"You low-life scumbag public defender! The only reason you still have a job is because you get those niggers to take pleas! You could never win a real case. Hell, you couldn't beat your way out of a wet paper bag!"

Placcey sat perfectly still. After 12 years of belittlement by Jackson and his other colleagues, his nerves finally shot.

Jackson opened his mouth to continue his tirade but was met by a flurry of maddened punches. Jackson's secretary, Erica Horne, heard the commotion and hurried to inquire the status of her boss.

The office was usually quiet, except when she was in there pleasing her boss. For the past 6 years, not only did Erica bring Jackson his morning cup of coffee and newspaper, she also brought him some good head and well-douched pussy.

Jackson's big head, and *little* head, got inside Erica on the same day. Jackson knew Erica was the wife of a junkie, and was supporting his habit, herself, and their two children. He had completely manipulated her after the first week.

Erica opened the door and saw Placcey in a blinded fit of rage, pulverizing Jackson to a pulp. Placcey had him bent over the desk, delivering the ass whoopin' of a lifetime. Erica ran and wet a tablecloth, then threw it over Placcey's head. The coolness of the tablecloth caused the hyperventilating Placcey to faint.

Jackson made a weak attempt to stand, but Erica met him with a swift kick to the family jewels. He dropped back to the floor.

With a scolding finger, Erica pointed at Jackson. "Everything stops now asshole, or I'm going to go public with how you forced me into a life of adultery. Oh yeah, your crippled ass wife will be the first to know. I also advise you not to press charges against Mister Placcey. As a matter of fact, you better not leave this office tonight until everyone else is gone. You got that?"

Jackson let out a low groan in response.

Erica patted Placcey on the left cheek, then gave it a firm smack, awakening him instantly.

"Oh my God! Herman—"

"Mister Placcey don't worry, you didn't do that. He did it to himself. *Didn't you?*" Erica asked Jackson, then viciously kicked him in the ribs. Again, he groaned, but managed to frivolously nod his head. He now realized the roles of power had just been reversed.

"Now, what were you saying about me never winning a case?" Placcey asked, now smiling because he knew that he was finally about to check a box in the win column.

***　　***　　***　　***

Chris' trial was slated to be held in two weeks.

"Mister Rankin, I believe that I can get you off on technicalities." Placcey said into the phone.

"What's the catch?" Chris asked suspiciously.

"No catch. I've gone over the indictment, and I found a couple loop holes that we may be able to squeeze through." Placcey lied.

"So you're sayin' I'm goin' home?"

"I can't make promises, you know that. But I will say the odds are definitely in your favor."

"So…?"

"So don't get too comfortable in there my friend."

There was a brief stare held between the two before Placcey said, "I'll see you in two weeks." then hung up the phone and left. Chris did the same, then went to call Angie with the latest news.

Exactly two weeks later, Chris received a letter from the Public Defender's Office.

"Fuck! I knew that shit was too good to be true!" Chris said snatching the letter from the envelope. It read,

Dear Mr. Rankin,

I'm writing to inform you that there will no longer be a trial. Due to a lack of evidence, the United States has agreed to expunge the accusations against you. Upon receiving this letter, the booking department will already have received instructions for your immediately release. I apologize on the behalf of the United States for any inconvenience bestowed upon you. You are a free man Mr. Rankin.

Sincerely,

Edward D. Placcey.

Chris stood and reread the letter repeatedly, trying to absorb it's contents, but it was in bold and italicize print. It didn't fully register until he heard, "Rankin, roll your shit! You're outta here!" the deputy announced.

No matter where you are in the penal system, "Roll your shit!" were the sweetest words any convict could hear.

CHAPTER 50

Both Mona and Angie received a dozen long stemmed roses the day after their men were released from Federal holding. The cards attached to each bouquet read, “C U SOON!”

*** *** *** ***

Since C.J. was already on the West Coast, he went to pick Chris up, and had Romeo go get Eric.

“Bring RoRo too!” C.J. added.

At HQ, Shaneka gave all three men the polygraph test, and they all passed with flying colors. After their induction, C.J. rewarded the “Final Pieces” of the movement with their loyalty package. They were each awarded with $1.2 million in cash. They’d have to purchase their own accessories. Chris paid his “Freedom Fee” out of his newfound wealth.

C.J. took time with each individual, excluding RoRo, to make sure they knew exactly what they’d just committed to. He and Chris walked out to the hog pen first.

“Hell yeah I know exactly what I’ve gotten myself into.” Chris assured C.J then added, “For a movement like this, I’d gladly dedicate my life to it…even if it costs me mine. You could’ve kept

your money. I'm just glad to be a
part of somethin' that will forever be remembered. Plus, you one hell of a nigga!" Chris said, giving C.J. a knowing eye.

"Dig it Homie, the money is yours, and as fa—"

"Save it! She's a real woman. You are the only other man to have ever been inside that. Yeah, we've been together for 25 years—since she was 13. The minute I got in the car; she broke it down to me. Yeah, it hurt at first, but like I said, you a hella nigga! You asked me for my loyalty...now I'm askin' for yours."

"You have my word comrade. I wish I could say that it nev—"

"It never happened, right?" Chris finished C.J.'s explanation, then extended his hand for a truce.

C.J. accepted Chris' outreached hand, and their pact was sealed, as well as their secret. Forever!

*** *** *** ***

While celebrating, Shaneka started downloading everybody's pictures that had or is receiving government assistance. Those still incarcerated with Rule 35's pending and 5K.1's were going to feel it first.

Shaneka had to eventually turn the computer off to cool down. It had already produced 350,000 snitches portfolios, and according to the system's database there were still more than 500,000 portfolios to go.

Shaneka called the crew in to show them just how much work they actually had in store for them. A combination of frustration and eagerness escaped C.J.'s brow. Anger swept over the whole room.

They sat around, sipping on Hennessey, as James Brown

ranted about retribution. *'The Big Payback'* became their war anthem.

C.J. encouraged his team to spread their wealth. "Start businesses. Employed people are grateful people. Plus, until we get our epidemic under control, we need to get our comrades off the streets. These murders must ce the sickest, most vicious, most gruesome, and most heinous acts that the world as ever seen. There are 8 of us, so to start things off, we'll pair up. Our original four will draw names, and tomorrow we'll get this shit crackin'!"

"Creecha, pull." Creecha pulled RoRo. RoRo smiled because he knew Uncle Creecha was the deadliest.

"Dub." He pulled Chris.

"Romeo." He pulled J-Roc.

"That leaves me and you, E."

"I like that Homie." Eric said, pleased with his partnership

"Oh yeah…" C.J. said grabbing everybody's attention. "Make sure you leave a message and a warning to all!"

"Yo Cuz, what'cha think about hittin' agents, lawyers, D.A.'s, and judges?" Romeo asked.

"Hell yeah! Anything in our way, slaughter it! We gonna hit and we gonna hit hard! We are all required to hit at least two spots apiece, every week, for the next 6 months. Remember, each one of you are responsible for who you bring in. They are not to meet your partner. This way if they fuck up, their blood will be on an individual's hands, and not the teams. *Your* blood will celong to the team. Choose wisely!"

"Tomorrow we'll head back East after I meet my man from Ft. Carson. It'll ce great to find a plug outta Bragg too."

"I got one now, Unc." RoRo boasted.

"All day Neph. Now get some sleep, our future starts

tomorrow."

Again, C.J. slept with the troops, but not before he blessed *his* pussy and sent her back to the desert completely satisfied.

***　　***　　***　　***

It took two of the cleaning vans to transport the arsenal that C.J. had purchased from his connect. They now had enough artillery to set the movement off and stay fully equipped for the first 6 months. It would lead right up to election time.

Once a starter kit was passed out to each group, they sorted through the profiles that were in close vicinities of one another.

"Any questions men?" C.J. asked. No one gave a verbal response. They all knew where everybody stood. They were a unit. A team. A crew on a mission.

"Well then, it's showtime!" C.J. announced. They all pounded up and gave Gangsta embraces before going their separate ways. No one knew exactly what the outcome would be. All they knew for certain. was that a lot of blood was about to be shed.

CHAPTER 51

Gary, Indiana

"Mommy! Mommy! We got some clowns at the front door! Are they here for my birf-day?" Jordan Jr. asked his mother, squealing with excitement.

"Boy, what are you talkin' about? Yo' birthday ain't 'til tomorrow; and what clow—"Rita Millers' voice got caught in her throat when she peeped through the window and saw what J.J. was talking about.

She smiled at the thought of how Jordan Sr. always mixed certain days up. *Thank God he'll be home next year. This boy is gettin' too damn grown, too damn fast* She said to herself as she answered the door.

"We were sent by Mr. Jordan Marshal." Bumpy the Clown informed her.

Just as I thought. "Well ya'll, J.J.'s birthday ain't 'til tomorrow, so come back then. We're havin' a party around three."

"No, he specifically said do a party today. We don't know which crew will be here tomorrow." the taller clown said.

A queasy feeling fell over Rita. Her instincts were telling her to grab her son and haul ass. However, Lil J.J. was giving Rita the puppy dog eyes, and it made her go against her better judgement.

"Well, I guess a private party won't spoil the lil booger too bad."

"Fine. Bumpy, go get a few toys." The taller clown insisted while he took in Rita's juicy thighs. *Damn, this bitch is thicker than a Snicker!* BoBo thought as he continued to examine Rita's entire body.

Bumpy the Clown came running back through the front door, with a large box of surprises.

First, he pulled out a DVR and set it up on a mini tri-pod. Next, he pulled out two pair of slip cuffs, and a carnival sized Louisville Slugger. J.J. stared with anticipation written all over his face.

"BoBo?" the shorter clown said.

"Yes Bumpy?"

"It's party time!" Bumpy turned and swung the miniature bat and connected with the bridge of Rita's nose. The pain was too excruciating for her to scream. Rita simply fell backwards and passed out.

J.J. laughed, thinking it was a part of the act. "Ma...Mommy, ya…you are toooo fu 'neeee!"

"Lil Jordan, I want you to look in the camera and say, '*Daddy, why did you snitch? You caused this.*'" BoBo instructed.

Now nervous, J.J. did as he was told. As soon as he said the last word, Bumpy sent a .45 bullet through the center of J.J.'s forehead, leaving a thumb-sized hole.

While BoBo restrained Rita's unconscious body, Bumpy drug J.J's body over to the sofa and propped him up. He stuck his finger into the hole of J.J.'s forehead, then began scrawling his message to the world. Blood and brain matter were used as the paint, and the wall was the canvas.

When the hole didn't produce anymore *paint*, Bumpy slit J.J.'s throat and continued to scribe his message. It read, *This snitchin' shits about 2 stop! C what U did 2 U R family! U fuckin' Rat! D-Con is goin' 2 exterminate UR bitch ass 2! The Feds can't protect U! C U when U come home BITCH!*

J.J.'s body spasmed once, causing Bumpy to jump off of the sofa.

Rita, tied chest down to the table, sent BoBo "aka" Creecha's mind back to Desert Storm.

"Aaaaagh!" Rita screamed when Creecha rammed his full length into her uninviting asshole.

"Shut up bitch!" he growled as he plunged a corkscrew into her back. Creecha's soul was back in Saudi. He was only *physically* present in Gary. Creecha was literally tearing Rita a new ass.

RoRo watched his murderous mentor in astonishment, then went to search the house for anything of value.

When Rita released her bowels, Creecha released his nut. After cutting her restraints, Creecha proceeded with his next endeavor. He pulled a machete out of the box RoRo had previously brought in and began to dismember Rita's corpse.

Once Rita's head was removed, Creecha delicately sat it on her son's lap. He then zoomed in on the message, then to the aftermath, then back to the message before turning the camera off.

RoRo came running down the stairs with a few pistols, and a huge jewelry box. He placed everything in his box of goodies and pulled out a lighter and lighter fluid.

Creecha threw the machete with pin-pointed accuracy and stuck in the center of the bullet hole in J.J.'s forehead. He then took Rita's boy shorts and stuffed them into his clown suit pocket.

RoRo soaked Rita's genitalia last. Once packed, he lit the trail of fluid, and casually walked out of the front door.

On the way to Indianapolis, Creecha had RoRo burn a copy of the disc then mailed it to B.E.T. studios. He'd mail a copy to CNN later.

*** *** *** ***

If there was one thing for certain, over 90% of the Black Federal prison population stayed glued to the idiot boxes, watching B.E.T., movies, sports, soaps, or reality shows. Creecha knew that Jordan wasn't exempt from that percentage.

"DJ Pro Style, let's get it!" Terrence screamed. The whole dorm was watching this Freestyle Friday. Some handicapped white boy was destroying everybody that stepped in front of him. If he won tonight, they'd retire him as a champion.

News Break flashed across the screen.

"Aw, hell naw!" an irate B.E.T. fanatic screamed. Others got up to go grab something from somewhere, or just took their headphones off. Usually, Jordan would've gotten up and added to the unnecessary tirade about the disruption of Freestyle Friday, but something inside held him down in his seat.

A news anchor woman from Gary, Indiana named Sonya Milestone was standing in front of a charred house with GFD frantically running around in the back.

Jordan's neighbor, Karen Frasier was telling Sonya that she wasn't home, but the neighborhood children said that two clowns were over there before the house caught ablaze.

"We were mailed some disturbing footage today from an anonymous source. Please be aware that what you're about to witness is a very, very heinous act. If you haven't eaten or have just eaten, please turn away from your television sets." Sonya warned in a solemn tone.

Although the faces were blurred out, along with the majority of the graphic sex scene, Jordan knew his home and his family like he knew himself. The message that was written on the wall was immediately burned into the back of Jordan's mind.

The whole dorm was now switching their attention between Jordan and the T.V. Jordan sat there until the next move was called. No one uttered a word, because the majority of them knew that that could've easily been their families getting slaughtered behind their own cowardice antics.

***　　***　　***　　***

Jordan walked up the sidewalk, seeing no one, nor hearing them. Several spoke out of the hundreds out on the move, but nothing could penetrate the zone that he was in.

Making it through all check points, Jordan continued on his journey to the rec yard. Moving in a zombified state, he kept walking towards the fence. The guard in Tower-4 opened and shouted, "You're outta bounds. Get away from the fence!"

But the only thing Jordan heard was his son cry, "Daddy, why did you snitch? You caused this."

The guard repeated his warning, then chambered a slug in his .12 gauge. The entire yard froze when Jordan started ascending the fence. Each movement was in slow motion. Inmates screamed for Jordan to stop, but he Jordan's mind was consumed with the sound of his son's cries, and the sight of his woman being violated.

Boom!

The slug hit Jordan square in the chest, killing him instantly.

His body didn't fall though. Jordan's fingers still clung to the fence, leaving him in a crucified state, while his soul descended into the fires of hell.

CHAPTER 52

"Damn, these motherfuckas must know we're on they ass." J-Roc said to Romeo. They had caught their target's wife coming out of a Beauty Salon, but she jumped in the car with another female. Romeo and J-Roc had been following them for the past two hours.

"Just chill Cuz. The hen will always lead you to the roost—" Romeo stopped speaking when he saw a set of headlights flick on and off twice.

Romeo smiled when he saw the man's face sitting behind the wheel of the rusty buster.

Looking back over at J-Roc, Romeo finished his point. "We just found the rooster."

Denise jumped out of the car while her cousin Bria circled the block. She had come to pick up some money to take to the stash house, but this was one trip that her soul would forever regret.

Romeo and J-Roc put on their hockey masks and pulled their hoods over their heads.

Julius was in the middle of giving Denise instructions on which route to take back to the city when the shots rang out.

Boom! Boom! Boom! Boom! Boom! Boom! Boom!

The twin Mac-11's that J-Roc was firing tore chunks of flesh from both victims' faces. Romeo trained his AK-47 on the front door of the house that the Duster sat in front of.

Assured that they were both dead, J-Roc put his signature on his handy work. He pulled out a Sharpie marker and scrawled a message on the windshield. *"Ya'll snitches can't hide! Look at this bitch! We found him and we will find U 2!"*

J-Roc looked down and saw what allowed their victims to get caught slippin'. Between Denise's legs sat a bag full of money.

"Ya'll ain't gonna need that where you are goin'!" J-Roc said to the two corpses, then snatched the bag out of the car.

Right when J-Roc's arm came out of the car, a Sheriff's car came flying down the street directly at him and Romeo.

Boom! Boom! Boom! Boom! erupted from Romeo's AK-47. He shredded the County vehicle's engine. Knowing backup was in route, Romeo ran up on the Sherriff's car blasting. He continued firing, until nothing remained above the deputy's neck.

Sirens were approaching with rapid speed, letting them know that this episode was over. Four patrol cars flew past J-Roc and Romeo as they barely escaped the crime scene. Little did J-Roc and Romeo know; Bria had watched the whole ordeal take place. She felt as though someone was following her, but she didn't say anything. Denise had always called Bria a paranoid bitch, and she wasn't trying to hear that again today. Instead, Bria decided to keep her suspicions to herself and try to lose the tail on her own.

Instead of circling the block, she simply pulled around the corner. Just as she suspected, Julius and Denise were ambushed. Bria heard the gunfire erupt, and knew whoever was shooting, was playing for keeps. *What can my lil .25 do against that big shit.* she reasoned. It would only get Bria buried beside her cousin. Bria vowed to one day track down the Avalon's owner, she even had their plate number. Unfortunately, they had hers too.

CHAPTER 53

"Hey lil man, is ya daddy home?" Dub asked Malik Lawson.

"I don't know you. What'cho want my daddy for anyway?" Malik asked as he shot another jumper that fell short of its mark.

"I owe him some money."

"Well give it here, I'll give it to 'im."

"Naw, but tell ya what, you go tell him his friends out here with his money, and I'll give you five dollars." Dub tempted the lil youngster.

Malik turned and sprinted to the front door, already spending his come-up money in his little mind.

Ali Frazier came to the door in a slight *nod*, only to be fully awakened by a 1500V jolt from a cattle prod. He slumped to the floor immediately.

Malik instantly sensed trouble, and tried to make a break for it, but Dub stopped his chance of survival when he sent the high voltage through his little neck too. Malik's nervous system shut completely down. He was dead before his small body could hit the porch.

Chris pulled out his survivor's knife and plunged it into Ali's chest. Ali's mouth fell agape, but no sound out of it. Wrapping both hands around the handle, Chris snatched downward. The blade tore through major arteries and shattered the left side of Ali's rib cage. His broken ribs draped from the open cavity.

Ali's fatherly instincts conjured up a weak attempt to help his son, but he ended up tripping over his own hanging intestines and slipped on the blood that once occupied his body.

Dub looked up in the nick-of-time to see a 200lb. Bull Mastiff descending the stairs. The only noise it made where it's heavy paws coming down hard. The dog's eyes were locked on Chris' throat.

Moving with lightning speed, Dub hit the airborne K-9 in the throat with the cattle prod. The momentum hurled the K-9 into Chris, but the only atrocity here would be sore ribs for a while.

Chris pushed the whimpering K-9 off and plunged the knife into its face, and body with a savage vengeance. To add insult to injury, Chris even reached down and castrated the K-9.

The K-9 made several attempts to stand, but his life was steadily slipping away with every heartbeat.

"Let's do it Cuz !" Dub said in an anxious tone.

They decided that one would leave the message, while the other went to look for things of value.

Dub hit the stairs as Chris mutilated Ali's corpse. He sliced through one of the protruding intestines and tied one end around Malik's neck. The smell of fresh feces caused Chris to gag, but he held his composure and put on some latex gloves.

Chris swiped blood from Ali's body and wrote his message. *'5K1.1+ Rule 35 = 187! 4 U and UR FAMILY! U COWARD ASS*

SNITCH BITCHES!'

Upstairs, Dub found 40 kilos of heroin and 40 kilos of cocaine. Not finding any cash, Dub concluded that this had to have been the drug stash house. *The money gotta ce at another spot.* "Somebody's gonna ce mad as shit, but at least they won't get a life sentence." Dub said to himself, as he snatched the sheets off of the pissy mattress, and the one down that was being used as a curtain.

In less than 5 minutes, he had all the drugs bundled up and tossed down the stairs.

"Yo Cuz, help m—" Dub was about to instruct, but then stopped to admire Chris' handy work. In the 10 minutes that Dub was upstairs looting, Chris had left a message to the world, along with making himself a keepsake.

Chris had decapitated the K-9 and skinned it down to its hind quarters. He then dumped all of the trash out of the trash bag and dropped the K-9 's hide into the bag, along with his bloody shirt.

After Chris rinsed the blood off of his arms in the kitchen sink, he wiped it down.

Dub had already taken the two bundles out while Chris regrouped.

"Did you find anything?" Chris asked.

Dub looked at him with disbelief, but soon understood once he looked into Chris' empty eye sockets. Every killer that Dub had ever known, after a brutal murder, their eyes seemed to disappear from their sockets and left an opening to view their empty souls.

"Yeah Cuz, we great! Let's stab out." Dub answered.

When Chris grabbed the trash bag, Dub started to protest, but decided against it because he knew how he felt. Dub had once cut an enemy's arm off at the elbow and would've fought or killed anybody who tried to take it away from him.

"Cool, let's get the fuck up outta here, I'm hungry as shit!" Chris said as they got in the car.

"What can you go for Homie?" Dub asked as he pulled out into the street.

"Sheeit, after that back there, I want a bloody steak, and some fries with a lot of ketchup!" Chris grinned then put his hands together.

They both stared at one another, then burst into hysterical laughter. Once their laughter started to subside while still chuckling Chris said, "Naw Homie, I was bullshiting' about the the steak...but I do want them fries." Again, they looked at each other, and almost died from laughter this time around. A car had to swerve to avoid hitting Dub and Chris head on.

"Reckless niggers!" the driver shouted as she blared on her horn.

Coming back to their senses, Dub fired up a Newport and said, "Lets swing by the C-P-T and drop this work off. We got 40 birds of Boy and 40 of girl."

"Sheeit, we closer to my pad. Let's drop the shit off there and keep the momentum goin'. I'll have Ang bump mine off, or she can dump it all. It's on you!"

"Fuck it. To your pad we go." This time they only shared a light chuckle as the proceeded down the interstate. .

CHAPTER 54

A group of men were shooting dice on the side of an Arab store. Eric pulled into the parking lot adjacent to the young hustlers. He stepped out of the van and put his utility belt on. Nonchalantly, he walked over and began climbing the telephone pole.

After making a visual sweep of the area, he pretended to read the meter in his hand, but was actually texting C.J. the instruction, *Now!*

The lookout man had just walked into the store. The words **Bell South** were printed out in big bold letters on the side of the van. The bottom half of the *'B'* slid partially to the left. Before any of the hustlers could react, 7.62mm rounds tore through all seven hustler's bodies from C.J.'s suppressed Stoner SR 25 Assault Rifle. Creecha had taught C.J. well.

Poom! Poom! Poom! Poom! Poom! Poom! Poom!

With 7 shots, 7 lives were taken, and all under 7 seconds to add.

When the lookout came out of the store, Eric started to

descend the pole. The lookout rounded the corner and was caught in the left temple with C.J.'s mm *'Personal round'*.

Eric hopped in the van and drove over to the dead bodies. He pulled out a can and spray-painted his message above the dead bodies.

'Snitch' and 'Guilty by association!'

Abraham Fields "aka" Hambone was the intended target. He had taken down a cartel known as *The Country Boyz* in Columbia, South Carolina through his cooperation with the Feds. Hambone had been hiding in Myrtle Beach ever since.

C.J. hopped out of the van, and stuffed a piece of clay in Hambone's mouth, then hopped back in. Eric casually drove off.

At the stoplight, C.J. witnessed a dopefiend jog around the corner and take in the massacre. When the light turned green, the fiend was attempting to rob the corpses.

KaBoom!

Hambone's head exploded and took a chunk off of Jerry the Junkies' face. Jerry's body slumped to the ground as his soul raced to catch up with the other eight that had been murdered only minutes before.

"Yo Homes?" Eric said while still watching the road.

"Yeah?"

"What the hell was that?"

"C4"

"I thought so. Yo homes, I'm gonna start callin' you *Cat Daddy* from now on."

Puzzled, C.J. asked, "Why?"

"Cause Homes, you just got 9 lives!" C.J. could only smile at his comrade's sense of humor.

CHAPTER 55

Shaneka, "aka" The First Lady, called to inform her husband that the other three teams had already created a buzz in D.C. "HQ, A.S.A.P!"

The whole team arrived within days of each other. C.J. fired up the grill and barbecued steaks as they celebrated their second-round victory.

As they stood around drinking, and bragging on their own personal barbarism, C.J. started shuffling different strategies around in his mind. Every chapter within Sun Tzu's *Art of War* and Robert Greene's *33 Strategies of War* began to circulate through every cell in C.J.'s brain until he knew exactly which pawn to move next.

When the food was ready, C.J. had everyone to come sit at the Round Table while he explained why he called the troops in.

"Soldiers, I just got word that we already got those son of a bitches in the Hoover Building with their *Tightie Whitie's* stuck in the cracks of their asses! I called everyone immediately." C.J.

emphasized to his team. His old head once told him: *The more you acknowledge a person's importance, the more loyalty they'll show you.* It had proven to be effective thus far.

"Now that we have these fool's attention, it's time to mash the gas, and hit some of the chiefs. Romeo, that was a brilliant idea Loc." RoRo looked over at his father with the deepest admiration.

"Yeah...but I can't take all the credit, Cuz. Creecha and J-Roc helped produce the concept."

"Well, around here, we're all one. No one above the team! And I mean *no one*! If ever any of you feel that I'm not pulling my own weight..." C.J. closed his eyes and whispered, *"Take me out."*

A cold chill swept over the room; the stakes had just been risen. They all knew that any signs of disloyalty, would end many lives…including their own.

C.J. opened his eyes and felt the love and dedication so he continued. "While we have these fools on their heels guessin', the element of surprise is on our side. We are D-Con and we'll send our exterminators to finish off these rats. In other words, soldiers, push your pawns." They all understood because they were all avid chess players.

***　　　***　　　***　　　***

Over the next week, each lieutenant started putting their teams together. Romeo decided to recruit Big Buff and Pig; a civilian and a Blood who were both full-fledge murderers.

Pig was a 5-Star General over the Nine-Trey East Coast Bloods and had eighty young Pups under his command.

RoRo incorporated all of the tiny Locs, Gangsta, and Hoodstas.

Eric got all of the Kings together and organized a truce between them, the Vice Lords, Stones, and the GD's. For a cause like this, no one disputed the coalition that originally began in the Federal penitentiaries. The same with the Crips and Bloods. Although the 13's and 14's had a *"Smash on Sight*" beef, they would set aside their beef for now to preserve the streets.

C.J. decided that he'd make an arsenal connect a rich man.

"What can i get for $5 mil?" C.J. asked.

"Shit, you can get the whole damn base for that!" the connect answered.

"I want every grenade, rocket launcher, pistol, rifle, both sniper and assault, and all the ammo that you can get your hands on in the next two weeks."

"It won't even take that long."

"Yes, it will! I want every fuckin' thing you can get over a 2-week period."

"I'll see you tomorrow with the first delivery."

*** *** *** ***

C.J. took things a step further. He called Popi. "You say you were finished, no?" Popi asked.

"Yes, but—"

"No buts!" Popi yelled and dismissed.

"Just hear me out first, and if you don't like my proposition, I'll walk...and no hard feelings will be harbored."

"Talk!" Popi instructed.

C.J. gave a detailed explanation on why he needed to get back in the game. He talked for the next 10 minutes nonstop, while Popi sat with his eyes closed, trying to absorb everything C.J. spat his way. Popi's eyes opened once again when C.J. said he would commit himself for the rest of his life.

"I, along with my comrades, have organized a truce between every organization, except for the Mafia Families. However, eventually they'll be incorporated into the equation. Whatever you send me...better yet, I'll take one 1,000,000 kilos a month!" Popi sat up straight and asked, "Do you know what you have said my friend?"

"Yes. 1,000,000!"

"One million huh? If you do one-million kilos a month for 5 years, you can walk if you choose. Plus, I will keep the price at $4,000 a kilo." C.J. and Popi shook hands and sealed the deal.

On his way to the door, C.J. said, "I'll ce ready right after the election." Popi only nodded and said, "You have my number."

CHAPTER 56

The streets erupted like a modern-day civil war. Everyone who'd ever received government assistance was targeted. If they couldn't be reached, then their families were slaughtered.

Agents were dropping like flies. Would-be snitches were now recanting their stories. Judges, D.A.'s, and lawyers' families were either kidnapped, or slaughtered too! Some were tortured, some were even mutilated!

On every news channel, morning, noon, evening, and nights, their headlines, in one way or another, involved ***D-Con.***

Every Mayor across the country were either calling Langley, or the Hoover building for assistance. The local law enforcement couldn't stand to lose another officer. The police academy classes had dwindled by over 70%. The entire country was in total chaos.

All the politicians vowed, if elected, that they'd personally put the country's nemesis in the death chamber.

Attorney General Earl Hailey, sat in the Pentagon's main conference room with every Chief from Homeland Security.

"I'll keep this short and simple gentlemen. What we have on our hands is worse than the 9/11 attack. In the past four months, there have been more than 100,000 murders on our own soil. We can't monitor what we are in the blind to. There's a leak in one of our agencies. What makes this so bad, *is nobody seems to know anything*! Someone is trying to control the streets—but who?

The only killings going on now are against prior informants, their families, and law enforcement. 145 field agents have met their demise within the past four months. We've lost 32 judges, and 47 prosecutors. City and county officials are up to 7500. More than 20,000 women and children have died by the hands of this unknown militia! Gentlemen, I'm asking all of you to shed your titles until we get a noose around this epidemic. I wish that I could say shoot first, and if they survive, then ask the questions, but *who do you shoot*?

I've received numerous calls laced with threats to leave the streets alone. One even said, *'eliminate conspiracy charges, and for us to do our job, or they'll slaughter every last one of our rats and their families, and everybody else who takes a part in our corruption.'* I have a press conference in about an hour, and you know how that's going to turn out. Roy!" Earl barked to his top advisor.

Roy Scott, Senior Chief of Staff snapped out of his own thoughts and turned his full attention to his boss.

"I'm glad that you have time to think outside the box. Would you like to share with the rest of us what has your mind in a state of delirium, when we have such a major crisis on our hands?!" The entire room turned their focus to Roy.

"Um-u ...hummm-, we're on the same team boss. My

apologies for my incoherency. Please forg—"

"Shut the hell up Roy! Your mind was probably on one of those titty-bar whores."

Visibly upset for being exposed, Roy stood up and slammed his fist down on the conference table. "Dammit Earl! I gave you

all my apology! Now, if we have something to discuss besides my personal life, then talk! If not, I move to have this meeting adjourned."

The tension in the room was so thick that it couldn't have been cut with a knife. A chain saw would've been more suitable.

Being a true politician, Earl knew how to patronize someone.

"Gentlemen, Roy here is a true example of what we're going to need to fight this inland terror. Plenty of heart, and plenty of balls! Now, if you'd excuse me, we have a press conference to prepare for. Come on Roy!" Still fuming, Roy followed Earl out of the conference room.

Out of earshot, Earl spoke through clenched teeth. "If you ever make a mockery of me again, I'll kick your ass so bad that not even your wife will recognize you!"

"Well, if you ever air my laundry out in public again, you won't have to worry about recognition, somebody will have to identify your corpse, my friend!" Roy shot back, his temple was clinching as he began to stare at his boss.

They both stopped and held a brief stare down. Out of his peripheral, Roy noticed President Moore coming out of a side office, flanked by six Secret Servicemen.

President Moore, the first African-American President, had swag that was undeniable. Both men watched as the President bopped his way out to the podium to make the opening

statement for the mid-day press conference. Both men walked

in different directions. Neither holding the others threat in high regards at all!

***   ***   ***   ***

C.J. had his STU 4 satellite phone on conference line with all of his lieutenants, while they all watched the press conference. RoRo sat in a Lay-Z-Boy chair, smoking a blunt of Cali Bud, while intently listening to the President's opening address.

"Afternoon fellow Americans. I wish that I could've said good afternoon, but unfortunately our country is experiencing a major crisis. We are currently having all of our agencies pool their resources together to catch these perpetrators! We will not compromise with them!" A loud roar of applause erupted, but the President waved them down.

"There's no need for that just yet. After we've served justice on each and every individual responsible for such insolence against our country, then and only then, will we have a reason to applaud. On that day, we'll be able to keep moving forward to continue our legacy as the greatest country on the planet."

The applause became hysterical when the President took off his tailored Armani suit jacket and began rolling up the sleeves of his silk Armani shirt. He then loosened his tie and said, "Now, if you'd please excuse my unusual demeanor, it's time for me to quit talking and get in the trenches with our military and other fine agencies to regain control over our own soil. Without further ado, I now give you your Attorney General, Mister Earl Hailey. Thank you and God bless each and every one of you!"

When Earl stepped to the podium, the crowd simmered. Roy Scott took a seat directly behind Earl. The Attorney General basically gave the same speech that the president gave, which caused the crowd to start dispersing.

Realizing the turmoil that they'd already caused; a lightbulb went off inside C.J.'s mind. *"HQ!"* he said, then ended the call.

*** *** *** ***

A few days after the press conference, all of the lieutenants arrived at "HQ", wondering what was on the General's mind.

After their usual ritual of drinking 40 oz.'s and grilling steaks, C.J. enlightened D-Con on what he'd brainstormed.

"Do ya'll remember how Bin Laden used to send those videos of him holding an AK-47 from some cave, and tellin' America what he wanted, or else what he was gonna do?"

"Yeah, CNN used to run that shit all the fuckin' time." Dub answered.

"Right! Now that we've made a wound, lets pick the scab off and rub salt in that mother fucka!"

Looking puzzled, Creecha asked, "What'cha gettin' at lil bro?"

"Right now, they don't know how or what to prepare for. All they know is, motherfuckas are dyin'! There are 8 of us, so we gonna send them the message in eight different ways. What I mean is—" C.J. paused when he saw the quaint look on all of their faces. "Since they don't know what to look for, we'll continue to lead them out to sea."

"How Unc.?" RoRo asked.

"Simple, all of us knows a foreign language. What we'll do is set up a backdrop in each nationalities' native tongue and pose like Bin Laden did. We'll wear hoods and gloves. We'll use C.I.A.

issued voice scramblers. This'll dissuade them completely."

Catching on, J-Roc said, "I see where you at Cuz. We all send the same message, like we're all in cohorts, then they'll think all these countries got beef with our judicial system."

"Exactly! With the world against you, you can't win. This'll spread them motherfuckas so thin, that they'll have to come to some type of terms."

"Yeah, they'll definitely change that bullshit conspiracy law...anything to keep these bodies from pilin' up any higher across the good ol' U S of fuckin' A!"

"Shit Unc, you ce comin' up with some real *'G'* shit! I'm just glad we on the same team." RoRo said with sincerity.

C.J. looked at his team, then locked eyes with RoRo and sternly said, "It is real. Real fuckin' serious! Let's just hope it's as effective as it is real!"

CHAPTER 57

As planned, the lieutenants all made their videos and sent them to every major news station. They purposely avoided local stations, so the dragnet would stay full of holes.

"The First Lady has sent an update of our success, and so far, we've subtracted a little over 100,000 from the equation. Yeah, those are war casualty numbers men—"

"That's not enough!" Creecha bellowed, finishing C.J.'s sentence.

"Exactly! Now I say we team up again. Either keep the same teams, or we can repick. It's up to ya'll."

"Fuck it, we'll keep the same teams. This tim—"

Ping! The sound rand, cutting C.J. off. He walked off., and his whole team followed him into the *Lab*.

C.J. walked over to his fax machine and started snatching papers out of it.

After scanning the first page, a broad smile spread across his face. "Gentlemen and scholars, we're in business!" C.J. said passing out the papers that were just faxed. The First Lady had just sent the addresses of every Federal judge, D.A., and public defender. For a bonus, she sent Attorney General Earl Hailey's as well.

" Let's get this shit crackin'!" Creecha beamed.

***　　　***　　　***　　　***

President Moore sat at the head of the table in the *Situation Room*, and watched as Earl Hailey paced back and forth, sweating profusely. The election was only weeks away, and the body count continued to rise all across the country. Now that things were hitting closer to home, Earl had become more afraid than nervous.

"Mister President, please declare Martial Law! Please!" " Are you crazy Earl?"

"No Mister President, with all due respect, I think you are. No offense, sir."

"None taken. Look Earl, if I declared Martial Law then we can kiss this election goodbye!'

"And if we don't, we can kiss our asses goodbye...*we*... maybe not yours Mister President. "

President Moore looked at Attorney General Earl Hailey with an eyebrow raised "Meaning?"

"Well, you live in the White House...so you're safe."

"Apparently, your eyes are deceiving your mind. In case you haven't noticed, I'm Black. Secondly, numerous presidents have been assassinated, and even more have had attempts on their lives."

"But—"

"But nothin! The way I see it is we need to pacify the situation."

President Moore said. Earl looked at the President as though he'd lost his mind.

In his usual and calm demeanor, President Moore said, "You see Earl, we go on national TELL-LIE-VISION and say the bill to omit conspiracies has been introduced to Congress, the House, and Senate, due to it being racially unbias."

"You know they won't support that!"

"Exactly! It takes a while for the bills to pass anyway. By then, the election will be over, and we'll have the country feeling safe again. And who lead the charge and won? Us! That's who! And who'll get reelected? Us!"

"I see your angle Mister President, but—"

"No more buts! By the time the smoke clears, our terms will be over. Politics baby boy. This is what we do!"

Earl finally sat down, allowing his mind to shuffle this around. *This nigger has a lot of game with him* he thought, but said, "Lets just hope this doesn't come back to haunt us!"

CHAPTER 58

The day after the latest press conference, the videos started pouring in. Over the next eight days, new footage kept emerging. Then came the footage that put the country into another state of panic.

All eight men, armed to the tee, took turns stating that until the new Congressional Bill against snitching was passed, that everyone who was not affiliated with the judicial system, snitches, or any law enforcement agency would be safe. Everybody else, would eventually die!

C.J. spoke in German, then switched to English. A large portion of the country that were previously afraid, were now petrified.

Those and their families who had and are currently enduring the wrath of the corrupted system, felt triumphant.

Every Federal prison and detention center kept their T.V.'s on the news stations. Those that protested (obviously offended) were either ran off the yard, or were severely beaten, or stabbed.

There was such a huge prison uprising, that the entire F.B.O.P.

went on an emergency lockdown, and T.V.'s were unplugged. No newspapers were given out during mail call, which caused even more havoc.

The Idiot Box, "aka" T.V., or TELL-LIE-VISION, was the vast majority of the F.B.O.P.'s population's outlet.

Kites started sliding under doors at rapid speed. The prison notes were telling everything from who ran the tickets, made the hooch, and who had all the tobacco and drugs. Although most of the information was bullshit, or they already knew, desperation made S.I.S. call interviews.

After several days of the same line of questioning, some added to their stories, in total desperation of regaining their T.V. privileges. Both worlds, free and incarcerated were in total chaos.

***   ***   ***   ***

To make sure their point was taken, the night before the election, several hundred voting locations were rigged with hydrogen bombs or C-4 explosives, and a message was sent to CNN.

"No one is to vote on Election Day. We have people watching every poll. Don't play hero, or you will become a statistic. We have the best hackers in the world working for us, so don't try to vote online. We will know. You've been warned!"

The polls opened at 8:00am. To put the fear of God in the non-believers, at 7:45am the polls were blown to smithereens.

The hardheaded ones that were on their way to vote anyway, prayed as they cautiously returned to their homes. Those that figured that they were either invincible or it was just a mere threat, were proven wrong. The warning was heeded. At the end of the day, all candidates were tied with 0% of the votes. Not one single vote was casted on Election Day.

CHAPTER 59

Another video was sent to the White House. President Moore paced the floor of the *Situation Room*, then abruptly stopped. "Who the fuck are these people?" he asked to no one in particular. Every agency had sent their top Intel Team to give the President all the information that they'd gathered.

After looking around with a frustrated brow, President Moore asked, "No one has anything?" The director of the C.I.A. dropped his head like a scorned child. Hector Campbell, the Director of the F.B.I., hesitated before saying, "Sir...we've received an unofficial word that…well it's a longshot."

"Right now, all we have is that longshot!" President Moore declared, as he looked at the other men and women with disgusted eyes.

"Well sir, our office received a call this morning stating that someone knows the identity of the perpetrator."

"From where?"

"It was anonymous."

President Moore slapped his forehead, then shook his head.

"Sir, the woman said that she would call again with the conditions and terms later this evening. And she will only talk to you this time."

"She?"

"Yes sir. It's a woman."

"O.K., fine. Have a tracer on my—"

"Already done sir. When she calls our office, the call will be transferred to your main line. We'll have her pinpointed within 45 seconds."

"Make sure you do. I'll be in the Oval." The president said as he walked out of the *Situation Room.*

Everybody left behind, sat and stared at Campbell. Campbell just stared at the door that the President had just exited. *I hope this longshot has a scope on it. We can't afford a miss!* he thought to himself.

***   ***   ***   ***

At 5:00pm, Attorney Bob Strader placed the call to the J. Edgar Hoover Building, and asked for Hector Campbell. On cue, the global tracking system was activated. Within 32 seconds, Spencer Brown who was the Chief Technician for the Homeland Security had the call pinpointed.

Once assured that the rabbit was trapped, Hector picked up the phone. "F.B.I. Director, Hector Campbell."

"Yes, this is Attorney Bob Strader, from Strader & Strader…"

Hector made a circle with his finger, indicating for someone to send some agents to that location immediately.

"Yes, Mister Strader, um, we were expecting a woman."

"Ahh, yes, my client. Well the purpose of this call is to...(Boom! Boom!) Ahh yes, I can hear that your men are coming now looking for my client, they'll be in here any—"

BOOM!

"Yes, they are here. Please know that I'll be billing your office for the damages done to mine. I'm going to put you on speaker phone so you can instruct your men on how to proceed with this matter. One...two…-"

BOOM!

"That's the second door you'll—"

"On the floor, now!" Commander Faren demanded.

"This is the Director of the Bureau, Hector Campbell. Whoever's in charge, do not put restraints on Mister Strader! He's in full compliance. There's a plane waiting at a private airstrip just East of Highway 6."

"I know the way; my Cessna is located there." Strader informed the gung-ho agents. "See you in a couple hours." he added, then turned the speaker phone off.

*** *** *** ***

Campbell, accompanied by 10 Secret Servicemen, were waiting at the government's private airstrip when Strader arrived. No pleasantries were exchanged as they ushered Strader to the middle vehicle of the convoy.

For the next 45 minutes, not a word was uttered. Strader sat and juggled his thoughts. His emotions about this trip were now mixed. One part of him was nervous. The other, anxious and excited. He'd soon have his name on the same plateau as the late Jonnie C.

Being an avid gambler, Strader knew not to expose his hand too early, so he smiled inwardly and kept his poker face at a Vegas gambler's level.

After a thorough search, both personal and cavity, Strader was escorted into the Oval Office by two Secret Service men. President Moore, and Attorney General Earl Hailey shook hands with their visitor.

"I'd like to skip all the formalities if we can and get straight to the matter at hand if that's alright?" President Moore said in a defeated tone.

"By all means, I'm on your court Mister President."

"Thank you. Now this woman you're representing says she may be able to shed some light on this crisis?"

"With all due respect sir, it's not that simple. And please don't insult my intelligence with a threat of what'll happen for withholding information. We both know that to defy an Oath of Office is an act of treason, so I can only give you what my client has instructed, and I will not breech our confidentiality for no amount of money nor fame." Strader lied.

The President, a former District Attorney himself, knew this to be true. "O.K." Moore began to ask, "What is it that you client seeks in exchange for this information?"

"She requests that her fiancé gets exonerated on all of his charges." The President held Strader's gaze for a long minute. It was a showdown at high noon stare off.

Finally, the president spoke. "What are his charges?"

"I'm not at liberties to discuss that at this very moment. All I'm at liberty to discuss is the agreement. Nothing more, nothing less."

"Mister Strader..." Earl Hailey stepped in. "Do you know that if these perpetrators aren't apprehended by like yesterday, what our death toll could amass to?"

"Mister Hailey, I am a true Blueblood American. My heart goes out to all the families who have suffered from these heinous crimes, but I can only—"

"Listen you!" Earl began to get riled up.

"Easy Earl!" President Moore intervened.

"Now Strader, do you know that when you withhold information that could, and has been detrimental to our country's livelihood, that we'll stop at nothing to find the culprit? And I mean nothing!"

Strader swallowed hard but remained silent.

President Moore frowned at Strader's continued defiance. "O.K., you want to play tough, huh?" Get him over to Homeland and let Mercer have a crack at him. You've watched the television show *24* before, haven't you?"

Strader nodded.

"Well, our Mercer shows no mercy. He's our real-life Jack Bauer, but 10x more persistent."

Strader jumped up in a state of paranoia. "Look Mis…Mister Pr...President. I cannot breech an oath of confidentiality. I will not get disbarred for anything! Plus...she hasn't given me anything else to go on. I was hired to get her fiancé' exonerated. I don't even know who this guy is." he bluffed.

"For some strange reason, I don't believe you." the President said while picking up the phone. "Price, step in here for a moment."

A slim expressionless white man walked in. "Sir?"

"Yes, Price. Our friend here would like to meet Mercer, would you see to it that they get acquainted?"

"Noooo!" Strader screamed when Price grabbed his arm. "I swear to Gawwwd I don't know who this guy is!"

"Well we can't chance that. Mercer will know the truth once every last one of your fingers have been broken just above each joint."

"Please Mr. President! I swear I don't know any more than I'm telling you! Better yet, let me talk to her again. Give me 24 hours. Please, give me that."

"No Mister Strader, you have one hour. Then you'll have a date with No *Mercy*...I mean Mercer. Price, give him his cell phone then put him in Conference Room 4."

"And Strader?" Strader turned back towards the president.

"You have one hour."

*** *** *** ***

"Listen lady, I've done as you asked, and now I'm being threatened with bodily harm. This wasn't par—"

"No, you listen here. I retained you to do a job dammit, so do it!" Strader's client demanded.

"Listen Ma'am, I don't take to kindly to threats, so ease up, O.K.?"

"No, I won't! My fiancé' recommended your firm, sayin' that your dad was the best in the whole state of Colorado. But nooo, you jumped in and said that you'd run circles around your ol' man, so get to runnin' or I'll slander your firms name so terribly that you'd have to do everything pro-bono just to get another client! Try me if you want to!"

"What is your fiancé's name?"

"Get what I asked for, then we'll go from there. And tell the president that this trackin' shit ain't gonna work. I'm way ahead of the game. I'll call back in an hour. Be near the president, hear?"

She hung up without waiting on a reply.

"He's in the dark sir." Spencer Brown informed the President. "Listen." He said, playing the phone conversation back for the President.

Moore let out a loud sigh and asked, "Where did the call come from?"

"Greenwood, South Carolina, sir."

President Moore walked out on the balcony and lit a Kool. Everyone who knew the president, knew that whenever he smoked that he was either preparing for war, or was actually in one already. Either way, that was a sign that he didn't want to be bothered.

Exactly one hour later, Strader's phone rang. A new area code popped up on the screen. Strader passed the phone to the President.

"President Moore."

"It's good to finally get to talk to you Mr. President."

"Please explain exactly what it is that you are seeking to gain from this Ms...?"

"What I want is that Ms. to turn into *Mrs*. and the only way that that's gonna happen is that you exonerate my fiancé of all his charges and give him a full pardon. Please don't try to play me for a fool Mr. President. I wouldn't play on your intelligence, so please don't insult mine. You get the pardon ready. Once my attorney has looked the paperwork over to make sure it's official, sign it, then put the seal on it. Once it's in my possession, my husband's name will be filled in and you'll get his full confession. Then, you'll have your man, and I'll have *mine*."

"How do I know that this isn't some fraudulent ploy to get someone freed on some prior conviction?"

"Mister President, right now you and the rest of the country are desperate, which calls for desperate decisions and measures. This is a one-shot deal. Although I'm a born Democrat, I will not hesitate to share this information with the opposition. We both know that whichever one of you ends this madness, has basically won the election. I'll call back in two hours. I have a couple runs to make, so have a good day Mr. President. Former…or future, it's your decision that'll mark your fate!"

Spencer looked at the president. "She was in Columbia, South Carolina this time sir. She also switched phones. We're not playing with a rookie sir." President Moore nodded his head and closed his eyes. Another gesture he made when he needed some alone time.

After everyone cleared the office, President Moore pulled out his cigarettes and began chain smoking. *This country damn sho' don't need another Republican in office. The last one ruined this country in 8 years, and they expected me to clean it up in four.* "Ain't that some shit!" the President said taking a deep drag off of his cancer stick.

A full cigarette later, he declared, "Fuck it! I'm going to save this country. I can't please everybody, but I can please the masses. A feat that they think a Black man can't handle. Shit, when dope was coming in heavily, our economy was the strongest in the world. So now all I got to do is propose a bill to eliminate conspiracies, they'll go for it. This shit is hitting too close to home. I'm going to grant this man a pardon. Fuck ya'll Republican bitches! I'm gonna be here 4 more years! And not only will I be marked as the first Black president. I'll be remembered as the best that ever did it! I hate snitches anyway."

***   ***   ***   ***

President Moore had the papers drawn up before Strader's client had called back. He picked up Strader's cell on the second ring. "President Moore."

"Yes, I'm sure you've had ample amount of time to make the biggest decision of your illustrious career."

"Yes I have, and I'm going to grant um… your fiancé' a full pardon."

"Now that was a very wise decision Mr. President. Once we've made copies of the documents, I'll mail you a copy, so that we can make the final preparations to bring my honey home."

"Make sure your end is upheld, or you'll be where your man is now."

"Don't worry about my end. *I guarantee mine*! You'll get your man just as soon as I've gotten mine. Tell Strader that I'll talk to him tomorrow. Good day Mr. President times two." Although flattered, the President hung up without a reply.

CHAPTER 60

"You have a collect call fro—" Strader's client pressed the 5 before her fiancés name was ever said.

"What's up baby?"

"How's my favorite woman and place doin'?"

"Place?"

"Yeah, between those big juicy thighs."

"Well, you'll soon have plenty of time to keep this cat purrin'."

"Girl, you know that shit you got is sho' nuff special."

"Boy, stoooop. You gettin' these panties all wet."

"I'm serious! I'm damn near 60 an' I ain't never thought about lickin' no cunt 'til I met 'cho ass!"

"Well for a rookie, you were damn sho' born with the know-how."

"I used to get on my son about this same shit...now look at me."

"Yeah, I can't wait to look at the top of yo' head again. Let me stop." She said as she slid her hands in her panties.

"Quit playin' with my cat, girl."

"Shudd dup!" she said as she rocked back and forth until she came extremely hard.

"Save it for me baby, I need to taste that."

"Boy, you a mess. I got'cha baby, do you need some money?"

"You know damn well that I don't!"

"Well that's a wife's duty, to make sure her man is all the way straight."

"Well as your husband, I want to say *thank you* for everything you've done, hear?"

"You know I'd walk through fire fo' yo' ass."

"And I'd do the same...but with gasoline boxers on."

"I know you would, that's why I ain't have a problem fulfillin' your instructions."

"Yeah, if I was a pimp, you'd definitely be my bottom bitch!"

"I'd better be your *only* bitch, or you'd be a dead pimp!"

"Girl, you crazy."

"Yeah, about 'cho ass!"

"Baby, I've been thinkin' about al—"

"Too late to think now. What's done is done. Plus, you tryin' to come home to all of this ain't you?"

"Damn right! I'm ready to love yo' thick ass all day and all fuckin' night! For the rest of my days."

"You so damn sweet. Motherfuckas gotta understand the inevitable, so don't go feelin' all bad now."

"Yeah baby...oh shit! There goes the beep."

"That's just the first one." 30 seconds later, the second one sounded.

"Good night baby, I'll talk to you tomorrow. I love you Mister

Gerod Evans."

"I love you to, Mrs. Judy Evans."

After they hung up, Gerod walked over to the CNN T.V. and caught the latest visual of C.J. disguised to the world, but not to the man he called his father.

C.J. was Gerod's chance at freedom.

Didn't God sacrifice his only begotten son? Of course, he did! Now I'll sacrifice mine. Shit, the entire world is snitchin, so why should I suffer being real to a code that's rarely followed now. Fuck that! I'm goin' home to my Big Booty Judy. Damn right, I'm a Judas! Gerod admitted to himself, trying to justify his actions.

Judy Foster's thoughts were the same as Gerod's. To destroy her niece's life would make her a Mrs. Judas. *Fuck it, I can live with that!* she said placing a call to the President.

"President Moore."

"Yes, we spoke yesterday, but to make this even more worth your wild, I have something else for you."

"And that is?"

"Once I have the paperwork, I'll also tell you who your leak is."

"Thank you."

"Don't mention it, just get my baby out!"

The end…for now!
The saga continues…

Made in the USA
Columbia, SC
15 May 2025

57963448R00170